THE TRASH COLLECTOR

POETIC JUSTICE

BY

CHESTER BENNETT

"I HAVE NO DOUBT AT ALL THE DEVIL GRINS,
AS SEAS OF INK I SPATTER.
YE GODS, FORGIVE MY "LITERARY" SINS --
THE OTHER KIND DON'T MATTER."

— ROBERT W. SERVICE, <u>RHYMES OF A ROLLING STONE</u>

TABLE OF CONTENTS

CHAPTER 1

The legendary gunfighter Clay Allison once said he "never killed a man who didn't need killing." Neither have I. No one seems to know exactly how many men Clay Allison killed, but I'd be willing to bet my count's higher. All of mine were also justified—maybe not in the legal sense, but speaking spiritually, I have no qualms about meeting my maker one day and discussing it with him. When all is said and done, that's the only thing that really counts anyway, isn't it?

See, I have this part-time job: I clean up the trash. You may have heard of me. I'm The Trash Collector.

It all started about five years ago on a warm July night in San Luis Obispo. You might say it was a simple matter of being in the right place at the right time.

Reginald Santana—let's just call him Reggie; he won't mind—had been out of prison for about a year by then. Nine years earlier he was convicted of human trafficking of a thirteen-year-old runaway. He hooked her on crack cocaine, then pimped her out. His lawyer got him a plea bargain and he ended up with the minimum: just five to twelve years in the pen. He must have really watched his Ps and Qs while he was in the joint, because he was out on parole after only eight years. He found a job as a surfboard shaper and planned to live forever after in San Luis Obispo.

How do I know all this? Well, I happened to be in SLO and picked up a copy of the local paper. Back in the public interest section, there it was: an article on how parolees from San Luis Obispo's California Men's Colony were doing after their first year of freedom compared to parolees from other prisons.

Evidently Mr. Santana was their shining example of a parolee who had turned his life around and was living on the straight and narrow. I almost puked. Who knows how many young lives he had ruined? And what'd he get? Eight years of room and board on our dime. Obviously someone had dropped the ball somewhere along the line. I knew I could do a better job. Forever after was going to come a lot sooner than Mr. Santana expected.

Later that week I went down to one of the hardware stores and bought a small box of three-and-a-half-inch 16-penny framing nails, an extension cord, a roll of duct tape, gardening gloves and a hammer.

Reggie was pretty easy to find. San Luis Obispo isn't that big and I had the name of the surfboard shop from the article in the paper. I tailed him for a couple of days just to get an idea of his habits and to learn the layout of his neighborhood. He lived in an older part of town full of small, postwar, two-bedroom wood foundation houses with double hung, six-pane windows in the front and a carport instead of a garage.

By and large the lawns were nicely kept and several of the houses boasted well-crafted room additions. Obviously his neighbors took a lot of pride in their digs; him, not so much.

His front lawn was more brown than green, more weeds than grass. It probably hadn't been watered in the entire year since he moved in. The landscaping was, of course complimented by the faded and peeling paint on the exterior of the modest little house he liked to call home.

On his final trip home from work he hit a few of the local bars and slapped a few friends on the back; evidently he was pretty popular with some of the locals. Eventually he headed home. Now it was time for me to go to work.

I grabbed my supplies and hid most of them in the pockets of my military-style field jacket, hoping I wouldn't draw any unneeded attention by wearing such a heavy garment in July. I put the hammer under my belt, behind my back. I also grabbed a lug wrench out of the trunk, taped a rolled-up bath towel around the long end, and concealed it behind my back. I walked up the steps to his front door, planning to say I was having car trouble and had forgotten my cell phone and could I make a call from his phone? I expected him to have a door chain. He didn't. He really should have been more careful.

I knocked and within seconds he opened the door and stuck his head out—nothing more, just his head all of the way out of the door. For whatever reason, he seemed relaxed and actually happy to see me. Maybe it was the alcohol.

Never one to pass up an opportunity, I just went ahead and bashed him over the head with the lug wrench. He immediately slumped to the floor like a struck ox. I pushed through the door, like you see cops do in the movies, hoping I hadn't killed him. That would have ruined all my plans.

The interior of the house was obviously done by the same decorator who had designed the exterior. There was an old, secondhand couch against the wall by the door, a small flat screen television perched on a two-foot-high wire reel against the far wall and a worn leather recliner sitting against a third wall, to the right of the couch, at about a 45-degree angle. God only knew when the floor had last been swept. All-in-all, due to his housekeeping skills, the three or four empty beer cans and the used McDonalds wrappers sitting on the homemade coffee table in front of his couch didn't look at all out of place. Speaking of his coffee table: any hint of pity I might have had for him disintegrated as soon as I got a glimpse of what he had cast in resin into its top. Here was a known sex offender; someone who preyed on young girls. How on earth was he allowed to have a coffee table with a recreation of the old-time Coppertone ad—the one showing a dog pulling a little girl's bathing suit bottoms off—preserved on its top? This was not acceptable.

Fortunately he was still alive—dazed, but still alive, not even bleeding from his head. The rolled-up bath towel had done an admirable job of cushioning the blow. This was going better than I imagined it might. I pulled on the gloves and immediately set about taping his mouth shut, hoping he didn't have asthma or some other breathing problem. It would have been just my luck to have him die before I finished him off.

Once I had his mouth taped shut I rolled him over and taped his wrists and ankles together. He was starting to come around and I thought I might have to bash him again. Fortunately all I had to do was threaten him and he calmed down, probably thinking I was just there to rob him.

As soon as I had his wrists and ankles secured, I realized I had forgotten something very important: I needed to keep his head still and it was doubtful he would be very cooperative once he figured out what I had in mind. I considered beaning him again with the lug wrench, but I wasn't sure how much of that he could take and like I said, I didn't want to kill him...yet. He didn't deserve to go that easy.

After surveying the situation for a moment I came up with an idea. I undid his belt and pulled it off. He seemed to get pretty agitated at this point; Anyway, I pulled the belt as tight as I could over his forehead, then drove a nail through it and into the wood floor on each side of his head. By now he had pretty much recovered and was squirming about. From the neck down he could wiggle as much as he wanted. I really didn't care whether he thrashed about as long as I could keep his head still.

I pulled out the extension cord. He must have thought I was going to strangle him. You should have seen his eyes. In a few more minutes he would probably be praying for me to strangle him. Something else I had forgotten to bring was a pair of wire cutters, so I had to go into the kitchen and root around in his junk drawer. No luck; the best thing I could come up with was a pair of scissors. For the life of me I don't understand why people don't at least keep a basic set of tools on hand. Realizing I would have to make do with what I had, I managed to snip off the female end of the cord and separate its two wires, then with the scissors—forgot my knife, too—I skinned the two wires back about two inches. Once that task was finished I leaned over to him and whispered: "we're almost done, my friend," and brought out the hammer and nails.

Did you know you can live with a nail in your brain? How about two nails? Neither did I until I saw a segment about it on the Discovery Channel. There have been documented cases of people who didn't even know they had a nail in their brain and just went about living their normal lives. There are no nerve endings in the brain, nor in the skull of course. The only painful part of driving a nail into someone's head is getting past the scalp. Of course, if you're the one driving the nail, it doesn't hurt at all.

Here's where I almost screwed up: just as I was centering the nail where I thought it should go, I noticed it was coated with some kind of non-metallic epoxy or something. I wasn't sure what the heck it was for. Maybe it was intended to make it easier to drive the nails. I'm pretty sure epoxy isn't a very good conductor. Good thing I saw that; it might have ruined everything. Anyway, I had to use the scissors again to scrape that stuff off both nails. I then sat down on his chest and pressed my knees tightly alongside each side of his head in case the belt didn't hold.

It would be safe to say Reggie was not thrilled about me hammering nails into his melon, but at least his mouth was taped shut so he couldn't scream. I tried to tell him to hold still because I'm not much of a carpenter and didn't want to accidently hit him in the head, and I damn sure didn't want to hit my thumb, but he didn't want to listen. Anyway, I finally managed to get two nails driven a couple of inches into his head. By then I had decided my next investment would be an electric nail gun.

4

When I stood up to critique my work, I was actually pretty happy about how it looked so far; the nails were driven in at an angle, about three inches forward of the middle of his skull and somewhere around four inches apart. It looked like he had sprouted horns. I went into his bathroom to find a mirror so I could show it to him, but couldn't find one. I tried to describe it to him, but I don't think he was able to fully appreciate my description; guess I'm just not much of a wordsmith. Next, I wrapped the skinned ends of the extension cord around each nail and looked for an outlet. You've probably guessed the rest.

I was actually a bit concerned that we might overload the circuit and blow a fuse, but fortunately it never happened, at least not while I was there. I can say though, his head did smoke a bit and I've never seen a man's eyes bug out as far as his did, as his body writhed and shimmied about like he was breakdancing to music only he could hear. Trying not to disrupt his somewhat rhythmic gyrations, I kicked his coffee table over and onto his lower body. Maybe he could take it along on his trip to hell.

Before long the whole house began to smell like an overcooked pork loin and it was obviously time for me to leave, but then I realized I should leave a note.

I couldn't get beyond the password protection on his computer so I had to write it by hand. I dug up a pen and sheet of printer paper and while still wearing my gloves to avoid fingerprints, wrote:

He won't be trafficking girls anymore;

You'll find his body behind this door;

I drove two probes into his brain;

Now little girls are safe again;

And though electric cooking is a slow process;

At least it doesn't leave a mess.

Love, The Trash Collector

On my way out I tacked the note on his front door with a couple of thumbtacks I found in his kitchen. It wasn't my best work and certainly won't win me a Pulitzer Prize for poetry, but I've gotta say, the penmanship was perfect and no one will ever be able to match it to my handwriting:

```
****  *    *          *        ***  *      * *  *   ** * ** * **    * *
 *   **  *     *       *  ** *  *  *_** ***    *    *   *          _ *
*    *        **   * **  * **    ** * **    *  **    **** ** ***
***        **  *       *** * **** **  *  **       **** ** ***
**            * *  **       ** * *       ***   *       *        *
 * * *        *** * ***    **  *         **** ** ***     *** * *
*  **  *    *        *     * ** **      * ** *     * ** * * * **
***    *  * * *   *** *  ** * *   *     * *  **  *    *   *  **
  ****        **     * ****   * * ** *  * *    * * **   * *
  * *         * **  *   *  ** ***   *   *** * **          *
*  * * *       * * * ***   *    * ** * *  ***     **      **
    * ***  *    * ** * *  ***  * *      * ***   * **
***   *     **** *    * * *  *** ****    * *    * ** * ** *
   * *        * *
```

CHAPTER 2

Deputy Sam Wilson stuck his head into the hallway of Orange County Central Courthouse. "Department Sixty-One is now open for attorneys and law enforcement only." It was 8:15 on the dot. If Wilson was anything, he was punctual, a habit he carried over from his military days.

Six attorneys entered the courtroom through the thick outer door and lined up to sign in at the podium. Others would trickle in all morning. Defendants without attorneys would be allowed in at 8:30. Traffic court was always busy and time-consuming if you didn't have legal representation. It didn't help that in Department Sixty-One traffic cases were only heard in the morning. Afternoons were reserved for other, more serious crimes. Represented cases were called first.

Like all courtrooms, Department Sixty-One was laid out in two distinct sections: the non-attorney section just inside the door, and the section where only attorneys, jurists, and court personnel were allowed. The two sections were divided by a low railing referred to as the "bar." Deputy Wilson's desk sat against the wall just inside the bar and to the left of the podium. Just to the left of the deputy's desk was a small, screened enclosure, often referred to as the "bucket," meant to contain in-custody defendants. Against the opposite wall sat the jury box, with enough seats to accommodate twelve jurors and two alternates.

Looking up from his paperwork and noting the third attorney in line, Deputy Wilson sang out in a mocking voice, "Uh oh, we got problems now. When did a faulty turn signal become a capital offense?"

7

Lee Edwards, the target of the bailiff's good-natured ribbing, turned and matched his sarcasm. "No, Sam, I'm just here to offer my services in case you shoot another carpool lane violator."

Lee and Sam had been friends for a couple of years, ever since they ended up conversing during a court recess and found out how much they had in common. Both men had lived near the San Francisco Bay. Sam had been a military policeman on the grounds of the Army's famed Presidio until the mid-1990s. Lee had attended the University of California at Berkeley as an undergrad and later the Berkeley School of Law—also known as Boalt Hall—just a twenty-five-mile drive from San Francisco.

In high school, Lee was introverted and shy. At the urging of his father, who saw it as a way for his son to build confidence, Lee followed in his father's and grandfather's footsteps and took up boxing under the tutelage of a local trainer. No one could have predicted the success he would achieve.

Lee's timidity outside the ropes was equaled only by his focused ferociousness and natural skills in the ring. As an amateur boxer he began winning local, then state, then national tournaments. At eighteen, with nowhere further for him to go, unless he wanted to wait two years for a shot at the Olympic team, Lee turned pro. His rise through the professional ranks was just as impressive. Within the next five years, encompassing his undergrad schooling and a year he took off to concentrate on boxing before starting law school, he found himself ranked among the top ten light-heavyweights in the world. The fact he was working toward a degree in American History at U.C. Berkeley at the time only increased his popularity and fan base. He hung up his gloves when he realized a title shot probably wasn't on the horizon. There were plenty of fans and supporters who tried to convince him that he was walking away from the sport way too soon, that eventually he would have to be given a title shot. He was now thirty-one, still young enough to make a comeback, but his response was always the same: "Better to retire too soon than too late."

Although his public persona was friendly and charismatic when around friends, or when approached by fans, he privately felt insecure and rarely initiated a conversation with someone he didn't already know. Asking a girl out was far more difficult for him than squaring off against another world-class fighter on national television.

To this day he struggled with his shyness. When he found himself in the presence of strangers he felt awkward and unsure of himself. At social gatherings he would often opt to stand against a wall or sit silently, unable to coax himself into initiating a conversation.

Despite these baseless insecurities, addressing a judge or jury was never a problem. The courtroom was to him just another arena that rekindled a degree of the same controlled aggressive confidence and competitiveness that had taken him so far in boxing.

Sam, an avid sports fan, had seen several of Lee's fights and interviews. It was hard to imagine that the jovial, quick-witted, blond, blue-eyed attorney Sam periodically encountered in the courtroom was the same man who could mercilessly destroy an opponent with no more expression of emotion or compassion than an Old West gunfighter. How could both personalities coexist in the same man?

With his professional boxing career officially behind him, yet still fresh in his mind and reflexes, Lee stayed in shape by visiting local boxing gyms and going through his old pre-fight workout regime or, when the opportunity arose, sparring with a willing up-and-coming fighter. Aside from the physical conditioning, an added bonus was that these sessions were an excellent way to relieve the stress that accompanied the practice of law. The thrill and satisfaction that comes with landing a good, solid punch was something that had never left him and he supposed it never would.

Despite these therapeutic sessions he was afraid he might be starting to feel the residual effects of his pugilistic wars. Other than the fact his hands sometimes hurt, particularly in cold weather, he felt fine physically. However, he was quietly concerned that he may have suffered some neurological damage as a result of thousands of rounds of sparring and competition. He would sometimes find himself at the brink of rage over generally inconsequential issues. If his anger was directed at a specific person, he seemed to find himself holding a grudge for periods of time that were way out of proportion to the severity of the slight or other act that had triggered his anger. Alternatively, he sometimes suffered short-lived bouts of depression. Each of these moods would sometimes be accompanied by headaches that seemed to come and go for no apparent reason. No amount of sparring was ever enough to assuage the anger. The depression would generally run its course in relatively short order, lasting no longer than a day or so. He tried to convince himself this was attributable to the hours and hours of hard work and preparation he put in on each of his cases. However, he could not escape the nagging feeling that there might be more to it. He promised himself he would make an appointment with a neurologist, if for no other reason than to put his fears to rest. However, he never seemed to find the time to make an appointment with his physician for a referral.

After signing in, Lee asked if it was okay if he approached the clerk. This was pretty much an unnecessary request, and most lawyers didn't bother asking for permission. Lee, however, looked on it as a simple courtesy and a way to recognize the bailiff's authority. He had learned long ago that the best move an attorney could make, particularly in a strange courtroom, was to ingratiate himself to the bailiff. Otherwise they could turn what would normally be a quick, routine appearance into a long, drawn-out study in frustration and introspection.

Kathleen Johnson, the court clerk, looked up from behind her nest to the right of the judge's bench and greeted him with a smile. "Good morning, counselor. Do you have a case, or did you just stop by to say hi?"

Smiling back, Lee announced: "actually, I have Retired Marine Corps Lieutenant Colonel Maximillian Sage. He allegedly misunderstood the legislative intent behind designated carpool lanes."

"Allegedly?"

"Well, it is possible he was one person shy of the purely arbitrary number the law says is needed to constitute a carpool for purposes of using the lane."

"Only one person shy? It only takes two to make a carpool."

"That's what I said; it's possible his carpool was just one shy of what the state considers an ideal number. If you ask me, it's all pretty arbitrary. I doubt it would stand up under the scrutiny of the Supreme Court."

The clerk chuckled to herself. "Is your client here?"

"He is, and we are ready."

"Okay, I'll put it up," she said, shaking her head as she turned back to the stack of cases on her desk.

"Thanks, is the hanging judge here?"

"Judge Mackenzie? He's here. Do you need a chambers conference?"

"No, I have a motion before him this afternoon. I just wanted to make sure it was going to go."

"You mean we're going to have the pleasure of seeing you twice in one day?"

"I guess we'll find out how pleasurable it is once the judge takes the bench."

At exactly 8:30, Sam unlocked the door into the hallway and announced, "Department Sixty-One is now open. Turn off your cell phones. If your cell phone goes off while court is in session, it will be confiscated until the end of the court day, which is 5:00 p.m. Additionally, you will have to pay a fifty-dollar fine to get it back. Please, no talking while court is in session; that is to be done outside of my courtroom. If I hear you talking, you will be removed and your case will have to be heard another day. If you have to leave the courtroom for any reason, let me know and I will come out and retrieve you when your case is called. Don't abuse this courtesy; I'm not going to search for you. I'll just stick my head out the door and announce your case. No food or drinks allowed. Don't read your newspapers or books while the court is in session. Please remove your hats and no sunglasses unless they are prescription and you have the prescription with you. Does anybody have any questions?"

The clerk motioned Lee over. "The arresting officer isn't going to show up. Looks like you've won another one."

"That was easy. I'll see you again this afternoon."

Walking past the bailiff's desk he leaned over and whispered to Sam, "The cop's not going to show. If anyone asks, tell them I was brilliant this morning."

"You, brilliant? Sorry, I'm too close to retirement to lose my badge."

"I'll be back for my motion on the Joshua Ward case. See ya this afternoon."

Lee turned to leave and took three steps toward the exit, then snapped his fingers as if he had just remembered something. Turning back to the bailiff, he asked out loud, "Can I still get a parking voucher at the clerk's office? It's been a while since I've been here."

Not bothering to look up from his paperwork, Sam replied: "yeah, same as always, nothing's changed. Go to the attorney window. Your client can get his at window four, if no one's at the window tell him to knock on the glass and keep knocking until someone opens it."

"Are they still good for all the parking lots?"

"Like I told you, nothing's changed."

Their exchange got the attention of the court clerk. Glancing over from her computer screen, she chuckled to herself and shook her head.

Situated on Civic Center Drive in downtown Santa Ana, Central Justice Center is a six-story monolithic structure housing sixty-six courtrooms that are continually packed. Parking is at a premium, something not lost on the various

11

commercial parking lot companies who bought up all the available surrounding properties.

Parking fees vary from lot to lot depending on its distance from the courthouse. There is not, nor has there ever been, any such thing as a parking voucher. The shtick between Lee and Sam was something that had been going on for years. It would be anybody's guess how many eavesdropping attorneys and spectators had fallen for it, much to the chagrin of the overworked men and women in the clerk's office.

Lee continued   up the aisle and motioned to his client who was sitting three rows up in the gallery. Lieutenant Colonel Maximilian Sage, USMC (Ret.) fell in step. At fifty-seven years old the tall and muscular retired Marine with the buzz-cut hair matched Lee's personal statistics, yet displayed the aura of a field grade military officer even in civilian clothes. This was a man that could obviously take care of himself.

Once in the hallway, Lee turned to address his client: "okay, Colonel Sage."

"Call me Max."

"Okay, Max, look, in case you didn't hear what went on in there, the officer didn't show. You win by default. I had to be here anyway because I have a motion on another case later today. I'm going to refund your retainer."

"No you're not. You get paid whether you're marching or fighting."

"I want to; it wouldn't be fair. You didn't need me today. The cop didn't show. You would have gotten the dismissal without me."

"It's fair. Let me ask you something, Mr. Edwards."

"Call me Lee."

"Okay, Lee, You know I was guilty, yet you took the case, why?"

"Everybody is entitled to their day in court."

"Says who?"

"Our constitution."

"Same constitution I served to protect, right?"

"Same one."

"So, you're exercising the same rights I spent most of my life protecting, right?"

"I guess you're right there."

"There's no guessing about it. Good men and women have given their lives so you can do what we have just done in that courtroom. We won today because I had the right to challenge that ticket."

"Okay, I can see exactly where you're headed with this. You win. You ever thought of becoming a lawyer?"

"I hate lawyers."

"Me too, see ya around."

No sooner had Sage disappeared around the corner than Lee's telephone buzzed with a text message: "are you coming back to the office?"

Oh well, it was probably better this way, he thought. *I'll have more time to prepare.*

"I'm on my way," he typed in response.

A little more than half an hour later he pulled into his office parking structure just off Jamboree Road in Newport Beach, conveniently located less than a mile north of the Harbor Justice Center, another of the mix of courthouses in Orange County. Instead of the elevator he opted to take the stairs to his office on the third floor. If he didn't, he would get an earful from Sharona, his office manager, about making healthy choices.

Unlike most attorneys' offices, the waiting room was arranged with Sharona's desk at the far wall, facing the entryway and next to his office door. She insisted on this layout, saying she would be able to immediately see whoever walked in and have plenty of time to greet them as they approached. It seemed out of place without her desk next to the entrance, but she claimed it was more welcoming this way. She was right of course, as always.

Stepping through the door, Lee was greeted with: "hey, Whitey, you're done early. Did you abandon the colonel?"

"'Whitey?'" That's a racial slur, isn't it?"

"Yep."

"You know I can probably file some kind of charges with the Equal Employment Opportunity Commission over that."

"Nope; you're the boss. I'm the subordinate; at least on paper I am. No way would they believe I could harass you."

"Well, there must be something. Research it and then get back to me on that, would ya? Let me know if I have a case against you. And by the way, we won; charges dismissed."

"Cop didn't show, huh?"

"Something like that. Let me know when you go to lunch. Maybe I can get you to bring me back a sandwich or something."

In his office, Lee settled behind his desk and thought briefly how lucky he was to have Sharona working for him, although he was still a bit confused over which one had done the hiring.

One day the strikingly beautiful African-American woman marched into his office and asked to speak with the office administrator. When he explained that he didn't have one, she shook his hand and said: "that's what I thought. You do now. My name's Sharona, Sharona Kane." When he explained that he was sorry, but he didn't have the funds to pay her, she offered to stay on for free for six months before discussing her salary.

The obvious question was "why would you do that?"

"I'm planning on going to law school before long," She replied. "I want to know what I'm getting into; what it's like in the real world, not just what they teach. I've never even set foot inside a courtroom other than to observe. I want to see firsthand what it takes to be a lawyer. No one ever talks about what happens behind the scenes. I'm guessing practicing law is a lot more than what everyone sees; kinda like an iceberg; ninety percent of it is unseen. All anybody ever sees is what happens in the courtroom or some glamorized Hollywood version of what goes on in a law office. I'm not about to plunk down my money and invest my time at some law school just because I was naïve enough to believe what production companies want us to see, and believe me, I know a little about production companies."

"Okay, fair enough," said Lee. "But why me, why not some other, established law firm?"

"Two reasons: first of all, the established law firms have already worked out the kinks, you haven't. Watching how you handled yourself in court yesterday told me *this guy has something going on between his ears*. But watching you scramble through your calendar and pocket notes to come up with available dates for your next appearance told me you're not organized. Maybe you're trying to do too many things at once. Second of all, how many established law firms do you think would be willing to hire someone who hasn't got even one day of law school under their belt?"

"I guess that makes sense," Lee admitted. "So now that you've told me why, tell me how. How are you going to work for me for six months for free? I may sound a bit nosy, but I need to have an idea how you are going to support yourself if and until the day comes when I can start paying you."

"That's simple. I mentioned I know about production companies. There once was a time when I thought I could make it in the movies. I was wrong, dead wrong; let's just say there aren't a lot of production companies looking for a tall, black female lead. Sure, there've been a couple, but how many can you name? Anyway, my agent started sending me on casting calls for commercials. I've landed a few nationally shown commercials and done pretty well. Every time one airs, it's money in the bank for me. I get residual checks from the Screen Actors' Guild every couple of months; pretty good-sized checks. I've got plenty coming in to easily carry me through for the next six months and more. In fact there are a couple of commercials that haven't even been released yet. They're still in the can."

"So why don't you just stick with doing commercials?"

"I get picked for a part, whether a commercial or feature film, based on my look: usually described as 'tall, good-looking black woman.' I'm always going to be tall. I'm always going to be black, but age is going to get me the same way it gets everybody. Before long I won't be getting the callbacks. Also, I want a career where the dress code is something other than a bikini."

Everything she said made sense. The offer was almost too good to be true. Lee stared at her, silently trying to think of a legitimate reason to say no.

"You need me," she said at last.

"What makes you think that?" He responded.

"Do you want me to start with 'look at your office'?" She asked with a sweeping gesture that encompassed both, the reception area and his private office. Like most attorneys, Lee's organizational skills were somewhere between pathetic and nonexistent. He seemed to be constantly looking and scrambling for files and notes, always telling himself that he knew which pile to look under. This was seldom the case. "Or do you want to look into your briefcase for your calendar and show me when you last updated it?" She continued. "I saw you in court yesterday. You're a good lawyer; in fact, you're a very good lawyer. If you didn't have to worry about running the office--which you suck at--and concentrated on lawyering, you could be a great lawyer. You need me." She handed him the manila envelope she carried in her left hand. "Here's my resume. I'll be here at zero seven hundred tomorrow morning. Unless you're in court, you should be here no more than a half hour later."

That was it. She walked out the door without saying another word. The next time he saw her she was standing in the hallway outside his office. It was nearly eight o'clock.

"You're late." She growled, while making a big show of looking at her watch. "And you didn't give me a key."

"I don't even know you. How'd I know I could trust you with my key?"

"What are you afraid of? Do you think I might straighten up your office and then you really won't know where to find anything? And what do you mean you don't know me? I introduced myself yesterday, remember: Sharona? You hired me yesterday, why would you hire someone you can't even trust with the key to the office? I don't know if this is going to work, but I'm going to give you a chance." She said with a wink and a smile. As it turned out, Sharona was the best thing that could have happened to his then-struggling one-man band.

In seemingly no time at all, Lee's office was running like clockwork and actually had the appearance of a well-organized top-notch law office. His appointment calendar was updated daily, footnoted where necessary, and backed up on a password-protected program that he could access from his phone. His files were well organized and he soon found he could actually find what he was looking for. Every morning he received a text message itinerary that even included such items as "1400 hrs. take car to car wash." Because Sharona had convinced him to do personal injury law as well as criminal defense, his clientele—and income—increased dramatically in no small part as a result of her creative marketing ideas. Before long they came to an agreement that Sharona would run all aspects of the office. Lee's job was to know each case he was working inside and out and, as Sharona put it: "be brilliant." When Lee jokingly asked if it would be okay for him to pick out his own suits, Sharona replied that they would have to wait and see how it worked out. Lee thought she could possibly be the most charming, witty and charismatic person he had ever met, yet he sometimes wondered what she might be hiding behind all that wit and charm.

Obviously intelligent and in no way lacking in confidence, she was reluctant to speak much about herself. Over the next few months Lee was able to learn that Sharona grew up in the upscale, guarded gate community of Coto de Caza in southeastern Orange County, California. After graduating from high school, she enrolled at UC Irvine, majoring in political science. As an elective she signed up for the Army National Guard ROTC program. Always out to prove herself, she was the only female in airborne school at Fort Benning, Georgia.

Upon graduation from UCI with her Political Science degree, and four years of ROTC under her belt, she accepted a commission as a second lieutenant in the active duty Army reserves. Immediately after receiving her commission she volunteered for duty in Afghanistan where she was assigned to a military police combat unit providing convoy security. By the time she returned from her second tour she had advanced to the rank of captain. A year later, after four years of service, she opted to serve the remainder of her eight-year commitment in the Individual Ready Reserve, essentially becoming a soldier in name only. She steadfastly refused to discuss her war experiences with anybody, even those closest to her, much to the frustration of her family and boyfriend.

What she left unsaid was that she struggled daily to come to terms with past events in her life and had sought professional help. Her therapist explained to her that eventually she would be able to discuss these issues, but she would first have to reconcile and forgive herself. She often wondered if that day would ever come.

When Sharona was eighteen, her thirteen-year-old sister, Tina, was abducted while walking the two miles from soccer practice to their home. Her body was found three days later. She had been sexually assaulted and brutally murdered. Her killer was never found. What Sharona kept inside was the guilt she felt because, on the day of the abduction, she was late getting to the soccer field to pick Tina up. By the time she got there her sister had already opted to walk home instead of waiting, something she had done on a handful of previous occasions. Sharona immediately drove the route she knew her sister would have taken, but by then Tina had seemingly vanished into thin air. She was ten minutes late to the pickup point, ten minutes she would gladly give her life to get back. From then on Sharona had been virtually obsessed with punctuality.

The residual effects of the murder of her younger sister went well beyond her near obsession with timeliness. During her second tour in Afghanistan, she was involved in a physical altercation that culminated with her killing an Afghani lieutenant colonel whom she perceived as a child molester. The lieutenant colonel had proudly waved a picture of a 13-year-old boy in her face while bragging about his practice of *bacha baz,* a centuries-old tradition of keeping young boys as sex slaves. True to the tradition, the boy was dressed and made up to look like a girl. Sharona slapped the Afghani officer's hand away and snapped that she wasn't interested in his perverted fetishes; the boy was still a child and dressing him up to look like a girl didn't make him a girl and damned sure didn't make him an adult. She then demanded that he tell her how he would feel if that were his son.

The Lieutenant Colonel, not accustomed to being spoken to in such a disrespectful way by a woman--let alone a woman whom he outranked-- demanded an apology. Sharona refused and he backhanded her across the face. He again demanded an apology. This time Sharona's response was to draw her sidearm and put a nine-millimeter round through his forehead.

The shooting nearly touched off a firefight between a company of Afghan National Army soldiers and Sharona's platoon of U.S. Army MPs. She escaped formal charges and court martial only because every member of her squad falsely testified that she had killed the lieutenant colonel in self-defense after he had reached for his own weapon. Within a week of the Judge Advocate General's decision not to levy charges her deployment was terminated and she was rotated home. Other than wishing she had put the bullet in his belly so she could watch him die a slow, agonizing death, she never felt a pang of remorse over the killing of the Afghani, and would not hesitate to do it again if the opportunity arose. She was, however, constantly haunted by the feeling that she abandoned her squad members, each of whom displayed their loyalty by putting themselves on the line to protect her.

At the six-month mark she marched into Lee's office and announced it was time to discuss her salary. By then she had become indispensable and he feared she might leave for greener pastures. She immediately set an amount that was way below what they both knew she was worth. He couldn't believe the words coming out of his own mouth when he told her that wasn't nearly enough and he would find a way to pay more.

"You're worth more," he said.

"Put it back into building the practice." She responded. "Use it to increase our advertising budget. I'm not starving."

This devolved into a negotiating session with each of them on the wrong end of the bargaining table. She finally won out by saying: "that's my final offer. I'm not taking any more yet. Next time, it's going to be a whole different conversation. Accept it or I pack up and leave." Her mind was obviously made up. Lee knew it would be useless to carry the conversation any further. He silently admired her loyalty and dedication.

"You can't just leave without giving two weeks' notice," he said, wanting to at least score some semblance of a point.

"Yes, I can. I'll just file a complaint claiming the racially charged atmosphere around here is so stressful that I can't work. Maybe I'll go on workman's comp; maybe see a therapist, maybe get a real attorney and sue your honky ass."

"You're the one using all the racial slurs."

"Doesn't matter; remember, you told me to research it? Well, I did. Nowhere in the law does it specify who has to make the slurs in order to constitute a hostile environment."

Throwing both hands up in surrender, Lee said: "okay, you win. I'll pay you way less than you're worth, happy now?"

"How could anyone be happy with the meager wages you're paying me? By the way, I'm going to be taking the LSAT next month. Decided it was time for me to start law school. After all, you made it through. How hard could it be?"

"Didn't you just say you weren't leaving?"

"I'm not. I'm going to go to one of the local law schools part-time. Otherwise you're going to forget everything I taught you. If that happens, I might have to turn down the full partnership you'll be offering me someday."

Sharona's 178 on the LSAT eclipsed the score that had gotten Lee into Boalt Hall at Berkeley. She could have easily gotten to any Ivy League law school that struck her fancy, but she stayed true to her word and enrolled part time locally.

As much as he enjoyed reminiscing about Sharona's entry into his world, Lee had more pressing matters to attend to: namely the motion he was scheduled to argue in front of Judge Mackenzie this afternoon. Try as he might, he just didn't feel right defending Joshua Ward. In fact, he wished Ward had never retained him. He had no doubt he would win the motion and Ward would go free. The motion was legally sound. Whether it was morally right was another matter. To top it all off, the case garnered more than its share of media attention. Everybody following it would have an opinion, not only about Lee Edwards the attorney, but also about why Lee Edwards would represent the likes of someone like Joshua Ward.

Just as he began to go over his points and authorities supporting his motion, Sharona stepped in with another excuse to put off his final preparations: "Parkland Rice is here to see you."

"Does he have an appointment?"

"No, he just walked in. He says he wants to talk about the Joshua Ward case."

"Can you tell him I won't have anything to say until the judge hears it?"

"I did. He said he just wants to get a bit of insight."

"Okay, send him in. Would you tell him I don't have a lot of time, though?"

"I already did. I told him this was an important case and you really didn't want to be disturbed. I got him to promise four ringside seats for the fights at the Fairgrounds tomorrow night."

"Well played, who's on the card?"

"Malcolm McAllister is headlining it. It'll be a short night."

"Might be for his opponent."

"I'm betting Malcolm puts him to sleep inside of four rounds."

"Why four tickets?"

"I figured Ricky and me and you and whoever your girlfriend of the month is."

Sighing and slowly shaking his head, overdramatically acting as if he were taken aback by her comment, Lee responded: "I think you just hurt my feelings."

"So, why is it you can't seem to find a girlfriend?" Sharona asked. "It's got nothing to do with your looks, and you're a nice guy. I would go so far as to say a gentleman, even. You get plenty of dates. Why don't they last? Are you that picky, or do you have some kind of torture chamber in your garage and a bunch of bodies buried in your backyard?"

"I wouldn't say I'm picky," said Lee, shaking his head. "It's mostly just a matter of differing interests. I don't have to tell you that Southern California, particularly in the beach cities, has got more than of its share of people of both genders who spend a huge amount of their time looking in the mirror. That's why you rarely see a tanning salon go out of business, even here in sunny SoCal. God bless 'em; whatever turns your prop, but I'm looking for someone who doesn't care about getting the perfect tan.

I guess I want a girlfriend, not a decoration. I want someone who would rather go diving or surfing than sit on the beach with an iPod stuck in her ear; someone who can outscore me if we decide to go to the shooting range.

Also, my interest in professional boxing can be a big turnoff. I'm a third-generation professional fighter. I grew up around it. It's in my blood. I'm not obsessed with the sport; I have plenty of other interests, but it was once part of my life. I would love to find someone who will watch the fights with me and actually be able to argue intelligently over who won. There are plenty of women out there who can do that but I just can't seem to find the one who shares the same interests. Before long I end up getting the 'listen, you're a great guy, but' speech and I'm relegated to the friend zone. And, by the way, I'm not the smooth-talking Casanova you might think I am. I can be pretty awkward, particularly when I'm actually attracted to someone. That can be a turnoff. Some men can relax and adapt in any setting, even among strangers. I know it may sound strange, but I've never had that kind of confidence."

"Yeah, well there probably are a lot of women out there who still think *Rocky* was a documentary. You're a good guy. You're just landing the wrong fish. The right one will be along, probably when you least expect it. In the meantime, don't try to make me believe I've hurt your feelings. You're a lawyer, remember? You don't have feelings."

Shaking his head and trying not to chuckle, Lee just looked up at Sharona and replied: "okay, send Parkland in. In the meantime, why don't you go out to your desk and look up the word 'empathy'?"

Through the door stepped Parkland Rice, owner, editor-in-chief and one of a small but growing staff of reporters for the *Orange County Times*, best described as a localized newspaper. The *Times* was seemingly in a constant struggle for its existence. Rice felt the key was to give as much attention to items of local interest as it did to national news. The sports section often included the results of local surf competitions, bowling and darts leagues and even the various softball league rosters. The Joshua Ward case was more than just a local item, though. It would draw press from all over the state; possibly national press as well. Parkland was anxious to one-up the other news outlets.

Lee and Parkland became acquainted several years back at a surfing competition. Rice was an independent photographer covering a wide range of sporting events throughout California and some of the surrounding states. Lee was little more than a weekend surfer who periodically entered contests as much for the socializing as for the competition.

The seed of friendship sprouted when Lee mentioned he was from Orange County and would be moving there again once he finished law school. Orange County was and is where Parkland called home. By the time Lee moved back down, the *Orange County Times* was a fledgling newspaper desperate for anything newsworthy. Parkland featured Lee in a public interest piece about the hometown boy who went from prizefighting to the often more brutal arena of courtroom battles. The article was well received, and resulted in a very positive effect on Lee's new law practice. He reciprocated by periodically providing insight into the behind-the-scenes workings of courtroom drama. For Parkland there was also the added bonus of having the opportunity now and then to step into the ring for some light sparring with a former contender. The equalizer was usually no more than prime tickets to local events.

Parkland started by asking, "Okay Lee, can you explain to me in words my readers can understand what this motion is all about?"

"Here's the *Reader's Digest* version." Lee responded. "My client was arrested and charged as a suspect in a three-year-old murder case. Because of the special allegations, the District Attorney is going to seek the death penalty if they win the motion we are going to argue today. Our position is that the charges are based on DNA evidence they had no right to collect. If the evidence was obtained in violation of his Fourth Amendment rights, as we are claiming, it has to be discarded and they have to determine whether there is enough legally obtained evidence to support the arrest warrant. If not, they should dismiss the case."

"So, just to get this straight, you're saying the DNA evidence wasn't legally obtained, right?"

"That's right."

"Is there any other evidence linking him to the crime?"

"Nothing really, unless the District Attorney's office is hiding something, the DNA evidence was all they referred to at the preliminary hearing. All they have to do at the prelim is present enough evidence to convince the judge to bind him over for trial. The burden of proof is pretty low at the prelim level, but they are not allowed to hide evidence and bring it out at trial. So far, other than the DNA evidence, all we know of is that the child was abducted during a baseball game at Angel Stadium. My client's cell phone records indicate he was at that game, but so were forty thousand other people. Unless they obtained warrants for everyone else at that game, it would be pretty hard for them to convince the court that my client wasn't singled out because of the DNA evidence. Therefore, the cell phone records are not admissible because they constitute fruit of the poisonous tree."

"The poisonous tree would be the unlawfully gotten DNA sample, right?"

"You got it. It would be one thing if they legally obtained a sample of his DNA, maybe through a warrant, but they would have had to show probable cause for that and he wasn't even on their radar until the DNA results came back a couple of months after his detention for an unrelated disturbing the peace arrest."

"And if you win this motion, a murdering pedophile gets put back on the streets, right?"

"Not necessarily, at least not necessarily forever. The DA should move for dismissal at the conclusion of today's hearing if they lose. Then they can refile at a later date, if and when they get the evidence they think is out there. They won't have to move to dismiss, but without the DNA evidence it would be foolish of them to take it to trial. If they lose at trial, the case is lost forever because double jeopardy would apply. Ward couldn't be retried even if he admitted to the murder after being found not guilty at trial. The case is lost forever."

"What do you think? Did he do it?"

"It doesn't matter what I think. My job is to zealously represent my client, not determine guilt or innocence. Keep in mind, at this point the charges against him are still alleged, not proven. If the prosecution can make a case on admissible evidence, a jury will determine the rest."

"Spoken like a true lawyer. Thanks, Lee. I'll be there this afternoon along with all the other newshounds. This is a huge issue. I appreciate your insight."

"You bet. Just don't forget the tickets to the fight tomorrow night."

"Don't worry about that. I don't want to have to deal with Sharona's boyfriend over it."

"Do you mean Ricky? It's Sharona you should worry about. Ricky's a big ol' teddy bear. He's just there to protect the population from Sharona."

"I'll remember that. See ya in court, counselor."

CHAPTER 3

The hallway outside of Department Sixty-One was packed with news reporters, off-duty police officers and spectators. One spectator in particular was surrounded by reporters. He was holding an eight-by-ten color picture of seven-year-old Cooper Jansen, the murder victim. As Lee wound his way through the small crowd, the tension could be cut with a knife.

Lee could feel the ice-cold stares of the crowd as he approached the door. He had been in the spotlight since the day he announced himself to the court as: "Lee Edwards, attorney for defendant Joshua Ward."

A few reporters and a cameraman approached. Not wanting to distract from the distraught father's display of grief over the loss of his son, Lee waved them off. Just then, the door opened and Deputy Wilson once again stuck his head out and announced the court was open for attorneys and law enforcement only. It was 1:15. All others would be allowed in at 1:30.

Lee nodded to the bailiff and bid him a good afternoon as he passed through the door.

Deputy Wilson just nodded back. As a law enforcement officer, he couldn't suppress the feeling that his friend was doing something that went against all that was right. He was working to get a child-molesting murderer—the bottom of the worst—released. As a bailiff, he understood Lee was just doing his job: he was defending a man's rights in spite of whom or what that man may be. This was blind justice in action. It was nothing personal.

The court clerk stepped through the door leading to the back hallway reserved for court personnel and prisoner movement only. Eyeing Lee, she said, in a slightly less friendly tone than she'd used that morning: "Judge Mackenzie wants to see you in his chambers. David Rogers is already here for the DA's office."

With a courteous nod Lee replied: "thank you, Kathleen," and followed her through the door.

Judge Sylvester Mackenzie had been on the bench for at nearly twenty-five years. Prior to taking the bench he served as a prosecutor for ten years and then as criminal defense attorney in private practice for another five. His full head of silver hair contrasting his black robe gave him the aura of an old west circuit judge, an image that was known to periodically intimidate unsuspecting out of county defense attorneys.

Notwithstanding Lee's penchant for jokingly referring to Judge Mackenzie as "the hanging judge," there was no one else he would rather have on the bench right now. Judge Mackenzie was known as a tough, but by the rules, judge who was never swayed by politics or public opinion. In his entire tenure as a judge not one of his rulings was ever turned over by the appellate courts.

"Hello Mr. Edwards. Find yourself a seat. I assume you know Deputy District Attorney David Rogers," said Judge Mackenzie as Lee entered his chambers.

As soon as the obligatory greetings were made, Judge Mackenzie cleared his throat and addressed the two attorneys. "Gentlemen, based on the written motion and response thereto, my tentative is to grant the motion. Mr. Rogers, unless you can somehow convince me that the DNA evidence was lawfully obtained, I have no choice. I'm not asking either of you to argue your case here in chambers, but I feel it's only fair to inform you both. I'm going to allow you both a lot of leeway in presenting your cases, more than you will have if this thing goes to trial.

We are not here to rule on the validity of the DNA evidence, just whether Mr. Ward's constitutional rights have been violated. I expect the highest degree of decorum from both of you. Be professional; no interrupting or talking over each other. You will each get plenty of time to state your positions. This case has garnered more than its fair share of media attention. There will be newspaper as well as television reporters and cameras in the courtroom. As soon as it gets repetitive, or if I feel either of you are playing to the gallery or the media, I'm going to cut you off; understood?"

Each attorney responded: "yes, Your Honor," more or less simultaneously.

"Are either of you going to be presenting any evidence?"

"Just the Department of Justice RAP sheet, Your Honor," said Rogers.

Looking to Lee, the judge asked: "anything from the defense?"

Lee shook his head and replied: "not at this time, Your Honor."

"Do either of you expect to call any witnesses?"

"No, Your Honor, none from the Defense," said Lee.

"I intend to call the arresting officer who brought Mr. Ward in on the disturbing the peace charge, as well as Sergeant Waters, the shift supervisor who ordered the DNA swabs. We may also call the investigating officer, Trevor Wilkins," replied Rogers.

Trevor Wilkins was a bit of a legend in the department. He was a tenacious and meticulous investigator who rarely missed a clue and seemed to have a special knack for recognizing when a witness or suspect was being less than completely forthcoming. In the field he had a reputation for being a fearless lawman, a trait that had earned him several scars and just as many meritorious citations.

Having grown up on the streets of Oakland, California, best known as the home of the Oakland Raiders as well the Hell's Angels, he could easily have taken another path, but wanting to make a difference, he was drawn to police work. After attending USC on a football scholarship—and picking up the unwanted nickname "Juice" because of his uncanny resemblance to O.J. Simpson—he returned home carrying a brand new a degree in criminal justice and set out to begin his career in law enforcement by applying to nearly every sheriff's department in California.

The San Luis Obispo County Sheriff's Department was first to respond and quickly snapped him up. The rest was history; at least for the next fourteen years, until he struck up a conversation with an Orange County Sheriff's Department SWAT member during a dual training exercise at Camp San Luis Obispo, home of the California Army National Guard. Something the SWAT member said about the OCSD struck a chord with now-Investigator Wilkins. Six months later, his wife was killed by a drunk driver. Trevor was now a single parent and, wanting to escape the constant reminders of what could have been, he applied to the Orange County Sheriff's department and was quickly accepted and working in sunny Southern California.

Within a year the drunk driver's insurance company settled out of court. With part of the settlement he was able to purchase a home on a large plot of land in Cypress Shores, a guarded gate community at the southernmost end of

San Clemente where President Richard Nixon's Western White House was once situated. The rest of the money was invested and put into a trust that would more than pay for his son's college education. Now, sliding into his mid-forties, he looked like he could still start at middle linebacker. Keeping up with a teenaged son can do that to you.

Lee always liked Wilkins. He was a straight-up guy who could be counted on to tell the truth, even when the truth wasn't in the best interest of the prosecution.

"Your Honor, for purposes of this hearing only, we are willing to stipulate to probable cause for the initial arrest." Lee announced.

Turning to face the deputy district attorney, Judge Mackenzie asked: "Mr. Rogers, Is Investigator Wilkins going to be at the counsel table?"

"He will, Your Honor."

"Anything else from either of you?"

Silence.

"Okay, let's get at it then."

As they filed out of the judge's chambers, Lee briefly chuckled to himself.

Judge Mackenzie stopped just short of the door and turned to look at him, then asked: "what's so amusing, Mr. Edwards?"

"Well, Your Honor, it just struck me how much you sounded like a referee giving the pre-fight instructions in the center of the ring," replied Lee.

"How'd I do?"

"You did great. You could have a second career if this judge thing doesn't work out."

As the two attorneys followed the judge into the packed courtroom, Deputy Wilson bellowed: "remain seated and come to order, Department Sixty-One is now in session, Honorable Sylvester Mackenzie presiding."

Each attorney took his seat and the judge ordered the prisoner brought out. Through the back entry two deputies appeared, towering over the diminutive, orange jumpsuit-clad prisoner, Joshua Ward. With no jury present there was no reason for Lee to request that his client be dressed in a suit.

Each attorney then stood and introduced himself to the court. Investigator Wilkins and the Defendant were also introduced.

With this formality out of the way Judge Mackenzie leaned forward and spoke into his microphone: "Very well, gentlemen, for the record, we are here today to make a ruling on a California Penal Code section 1538.5 motion to

27

suppress certain evidence pertinent to this case. Before we get started I want everyone in the courtroom to understand that I will not tolerate any verbal outbursts or displays of emotion. You will be removed. Further, there will be no talking while court is in session. Again, you will be removed. If you want to speak to your neighbor, do it outside of my courtroom."

The judge then turned his attention to Lee and nodded. "Counselor, you may begin."

Stepping to the podium Lee leaned into the microphone and announced: "we'll submit on the moving papers, Your Honor," and returned to his seat. Long ago he was given the sage advice from another judge to "shut up when you're winning." Based on what Judge Mackenzie said in chambers there was every reason to believe he was winning.

"Thank you, Mr. Edwards," said Judge Mackenzie. Then turning to the prosecutor's table: "your turn, Mr. Rogers."

"People call Deputy Mark Wagoner," Rogers replied.

Game on, thought Lee.

What followed was 45 minutes of back and forth questioning and testimony. Nothing that hadn't already been covered in Lee's motion to suppress the DNA evidence, nor in Deputy D.A. Rogers' written response, was presented.

In 2004 the state passed a law that all convicted felons, as well as anyone arrested for a felony, were required to submit to a DNA test, even if that person's conviction predated 2004. If anyone with a felony conviction from prior to 2004 is later arrested or even detained for any reason, they too are subject to unconsented DNA testing. This is referred to as a "qualifying offense." Joshua Ward was arrested on a simple disturbing the peace charge outside of one of the local taverns. Disturbing the peace is not a qualifying offense and Mr. Ward did not consent to DNA testing; in fact Mr. Ward vehemently objected.

What David Rogers was hanging his hat on, however, was a felony cultivation of marijuana conviction that Joshua Ward suffered in 2014. There was no doubt a DNA sample should have been taken from him at that time. However, inexplicably, no sample was taken. If the conviction had not been a marijuana related offense, the state would have been well within its rights to take a sample when he was brought in for disturbing the peace years later.

However, in 2016 the California voters approved Proposition 64, and overnight felony marijuana convictions became misdemeanors simply by filing a petition to the court. Joshua Ward had long been one of the benefactors of Proposition 64 by the time he was arrested for disturbing the peace.

Rogers' position was at least creative: Joshua Ward was once convicted of a felony. The fact his conviction was redesignated and is now a misdemeanor should not change his convicted felon status for purposes of unconsented DNA testing. Alternatively, even if that weren't the rule of law, the watch commander believed it to be the law, thus triggering the "good faith exception" to the rule excluding evidence gained in violation of the defendant's Fourth Amendment rights.

Although the first theory was creative, it was not very persuasive. The order of the court redesignating the conviction as a misdemeanor also carried the statutory wording: "for all purposes." Presumably "all purposes" included DNA testing. The second theory was no stronger. Joshua Ward's rap sheet clearly parroted the statutory wording that the redesignation to misdemeanor was to be "for all purposes." No one was going to believe Sgt. Waters didn't understand that the term 'for all purposes' meant just that. Lee suspected Sgt. Waters simply chose to ignore that fact when he ordered the DNA swab.

At the conclusion of Sgt. Waters' testimony David Rogers announced he had nothing further, there would be no more witnesses. It was time for the attorneys to address the court directly.

Judge Mackenzie focused his attention on Lee: "Mr. Edwards, you may proceed."

At this Lee stood and began his closing argument. "Thank you, Your Honor. The people's own witnesses have established two things: first, that the taking of the DNA swab was not only non-consensual, but that it was actually done over Mr. Ward's objections; second, that in this case there was no good faith exception to the exclusionary rule. Sergeant Waters had in his possession the DOJ rap sheet clearly showing Mr. Ward's year's old marijuana conviction was redesignated a misdemeanor for all purposes by court order. For the people to come now and claim Sergeant Waters misunderstood the law and, therefore, the evidence should be allowed under the good faith exception strains credulity. We are all familiar with the age-old adage: "ignorance of the law is no excuse." People's counsel would have this court believe this only applies to those charged with a crime; those unfortunate enough find themselves seated at the defense table, while those seated at the prosecution table are entitled to a pass. That, of course is not the case, nor has it ever been the case.

Your Honor, The DNA evidence against Mr. Ward was obtained in violation of his constitutional rights. The people have submitted no real evidence to refute this obvious conclusion. Therefore, under Penal Code section 1538.5, the DNA evidence should be suppressed and removed from the database. On that I will once again submit. Thank you, Your Honor."

"Thank you, Mr. Edwards," replied Judge Mackenzie, then, "Mr. Rogers?"

"Your Honor, there is clearly a good faith exception to the exclusionary rule here. Sergeant Waters had every reason to believe a DNA test was in order. The defendant was, in fact a convicted felon. He had been arrested on a felony charge and was convicted of that charge. Sergeant Waters was, in good faith, following long established protocol that required convicted felons to be swabbed for DNA."

Then for good measure and out of apparent desperation, Rogers added: "we have information there could be as many as four more victims, Your Honor. Without the DNA evidence those cases will be at a standstill. We need the sample in the interest of closing those cases, in the interest of justice."

There it was: Rogers was now playing to the audience. This was a sure sign that he knew his case was about to fall apart. Ward's possible connection to any other crimes was not relevant to the issue before the court. They were here today solely to determine whether the evidence was lawfully obtained, nothing more. He was now hoping Judge Makenzie would be swayed by the outcry that would surely come if the evidence was suppressed and an accused mass murdering child killer was let free. Anybody who knew Judge Makenzie also knew he would rule by the law, not public opinion. The words "nice try" passed through Lee's mind.

Judge Mackenzie leaned forward from his comfortable, high-backed leather chair and looked down at both attorneys.

"The court finds there was no good faith exception to the exclusionary rule. The evidence was obtained in violation of the defendant's Fourth Amendment rights. The DNA sample itself is ordered destroyed. The results of the DNA sample are ordered destroyed and removed from the database. Any evidence against Mr. Ward that has been gained as a result of the DNA sample is also ordered destroyed." Staring straight at Deputy DA Rogers, the judge then asked: "is that everything, gentlemen?"

After a long pause, Rogers quietly replied: "people move to dismiss, your honor."

Without being asked to respond, Lee calmly responded: "no objection, Your Honor."

Judge Mackenzie's verbal command was punctuated by the report of his gavel slamming onto its mahogany sound block. "This case is dismissed; defendant will be released forthwith."

The gallery instantly exploded into chaos. Cooper Jansen's father lunged for the counsel table, screaming uncontrollably at Joshua Ward. One of the deputies tasked with escorting Ward pushed the distraught father back, preventing him from crossing the wooden rail, then wrestled him back into the gallery.

Trevor Wilkins remained seated. He had not been called to the witness stand and in fact hadn't expected to be. He was only there because he was the one who wrote the affidavit in support of the request for an arrest warrant for Joshua Ward for murder. He had nothing to do with gathering the DNA evidence and had no idea the collection might have been unlawful until Rogers gave him a copy of the 1538.5 motion. His subsequent interviews with Deputy Wagoner and Sergeant Waters confirmed it. Judge Makenzie's ruling came as no surprise.

While Wilkins gathered his notes and stuffed them back into his briefcase, he glanced at Lee and gave a nearly imperceptible nod. He was clearly not happy without the outcome of the hearing, but understood that the justice system, although flawed, is made of rules that have to be obeyed. Eventually Joshua Ward would come to Jesus.

Judge Mackenzie ordered the court cleared. Deputy Wilson, already standing, set out to do just that.

More than one of the television cameras Judge Mackenzie had allowed into the courtroom zoomed in on Joshua Ward's smiling face as he stood to be escorted back to his holding cell to await his release. Other cameras captured an entirely different emotion on Lee's face as he sat motionless, staring down at the counsel table. There was no smile. If one were to look closely enough, they might have detected a slight grimace, as if he were trying to suppress an oncoming headache.

Back in the office, Sharona watched the proceedings on the television in Lee's inner office. She could understand Lee's reaction. Neither of them wanted Ward back on the streets again, but Lee had a job to do. He was obligated to zealously defend his client no matter who that client might be, or how heinous the charge. Lee was man of the deepest integrity. He had never thrown a fight in his career and had never given less than his all in the legal arena. It was just not in his makeup. *But*, she thought as her mind flashed back to her little sister and how it felt to kill the Iraqi lieutenant colonel, *everyone has a limit*. Lee looked like he was close to his.

Before being led from the courtroom, Joshua Ward leaned over and asked Lee if he would pick him up at the jail and take him home after he was processed out. He was afraid to be seen on the streets. Lee began to shake his head, and then remembered his client's van was impounded for evidence at the time of his arrest. More than likely it would take another day or two before the sheriff's department released it. Reluctantly, he agreed.

The courtroom grew silent. All eyes were on Ward as he was escorted away.

CHAPTER 4

Although the hearing hadn't taken long, it was an emotionally grueling afternoon for Lee. There was little doubt that his client committed one of the most heinous crimes imaginable, probably more than once, but he had to put that aside and do his job as a criminal defense attorney. Although he supposed Lt. Col. Sage would be proud, in his heart he couldn't help but wonder if he had done the right thing. Sometimes what is morally right clashes with what is legally right. In law school he had time and again heard the oft-repeated axiom that it was better to let one guilty man go free than to convict a hundred innocent men. Maybe in this case that wasn't true.

Refusing Deputy Wilson's offer to walk him out through the private hallway, he left the courtroom through the front door. He had never run from confrontation. In the hallway he was not surprised at the finger-pointing and cold stares from those who had been present in the courtroom. Cooper Jansen's father stepped into his path and shoved his son's picture in his face. The boy was wearing the Angels jersey and cap he wore to his last baseball game.

"Look at my son! How could you protect that animal?" he yelled. There was no way to respond other than to let the heartbroken father vent. Eventually the shouts dissipated and the man standing before him lowered his head. The screaming was over.

Lee wanted so badly to reach out to him, to offer some degree of comfort, some degree of solace, but there could be no appropriate response. All he could do was offer a quiet: "I'm sorry, Mr. Jansen," and walk away. Not more than thirty feet in front of him, Investigator Wilkins was worming his way through an obstacle course of television crews and news reporters.

On his way out, he called Sharona to tell her he would not be coming back to the office; he would be taking the rest of the day off. Sharona said she understood, and told him she had watched the proceedings live.

It was an awkward exchange. He had just won a major courtroom battle. His name would be in all the papers and news programs. You couldn't ask for better advertisement. Yet neither of them felt a celebration was in order. True to his competitive nature, he intended to bury David Rogers and he did. It was a hollow victory, however. This time the only winner was the one person who least deserved it: Joshua Ward.

More than four hours after leaving the courthouse, Lee sat in the parking structure across from the Orange County Main Jail waiting for Ward's release. Notwithstanding Judge Mackenzie's order to release "forthwith," the jailers would be in no hurry to process him out. The paperwork normally takes about two to three hours. Hopefully he wouldn't have to come back tomorrow or worse yet, get a late-night call to come get him.

Although he'd anticipated the win, he never expected he would end up taking his client home afterward. If he'd thought it even a remote possibility, he would surely have opted to drive something more fitting like the pickup he inherited from his father. Instead, he had driven the least practical and most expensive of the three vehicles he owned: his brand-new black Porsche 911 GT3.

Sharona was the driving force behind his buying it, saying that to be successful he had to look successful or, in her words, he had to "project an aura of success." He had long before learned not to bother arguing with her. Soon enough he found himself shopping for a high-end sports car. Fortunately, Sharona insisted on accompanying him, saying: "honkies don't know how to dicker." Once again, she was right. When the salesman began explaining the technical aspects of the car he had no idea what was being said. He could have been speaking some ancient, long-lost language as far as Lee knew. Not only was Sharona well-versed in gearhead, she was able to bargain the man down from a ridiculously inflated price to the car's ridiculous MSRP.

After verifying to the salesman that, as Lee's legal administrator and office manager, it would ultimately be her call as to where the car was purchased, Sharona and the salesman left him sitting in the showroom and set out to "dicker." When she emerged a half hour later she informed him that his law firm had just made an investment in a brand-new Porsche to be delivered within two weeks or the deal was off and, oh yeah, an upgraded sound system and optional performance package was included at no extra cost.

On the way back to the office he had to ask her how she had done it.

"Done what?"

"How did you work them down to something less unaffordable."

"It was easy, all I did was tell them they either take my offer or I would have a talk with my homeboys."

"Your homeboys? You grew up in Cota de Casa."

"I call all of my dad's friends 'homeboy.' They get a kick out of it. I took you to that particular dealer because they all buy their cars there. There's no telling how much they've spent on high-end cars over the years, not even counting the ones my family has purchased."

"So you bluffed him into thinking you could convince family friends to go somewhere else, is that what you're telling me?"

"I told the salesman to get the manager on the phone, then I told the manager what we were willing to pay. It wasn't a bluff. My family and friends are loyal. They would have gone elsewhere."

"Damn! I'm sure glad you're on my side."

"That hasn't been decided that yet, Whitey."

CHAPTER 5

Lee was just about to give up and head home when he saw Ward emerge from the shadows and walk toward the corner, cell phone in hand. Lee honked and pulled up to the curb. Ward jumped in.

"Nice ride, man. My cell phone died while I was locked up. I didn't know if I was going to be able to get hold of you."

"Where am I taking you?"

"Take me to my place. I'm sure you know the address; it's all over your client intake form, as well as the arrest records. I'm sure it's been printed in the newspaper too. There's no doubt my neighbors know all about this and have blabbed to all their friends. Before long, everyone on the planet will know my address, if they don't already."

Ignoring Ward's complaint, Lee cut in: "let me give you a bit of advice. I'm not going to ask whether or not you did it. The evidence sure points your way. Right now what matters is the cops are convinced you did it. They are going to be following you whenever you step out of your house, just waiting for a chance to pounce on a discarded cigarette butt or drinking straw; anything they can get another DNA sample from. They'll be going through your trash every time you set it out."

"Is that legal? Isn't that some kind of harassment or something? Can they actually go through my trash?"

"Yes, it's legal, at least the way they'll do it. It won't be harassment because you'll never know they were there. Once you put your trash out, you no longer have a reasonable expectation of privacy over it. It's no longer yours."

"So, what am I supposed to do, burn it, take it to the dump personally, mail it somewhere?"

"That's your problem."

"Maybe I should just move, get out of here; maybe move to another city or state."

"Maybe another country, find one that doesn't have an extradition treaty with the United States."

Lee turned up the sound system and neither man spoke much the rest of the way to Ward's well-maintained two-story house sitting at the end of a cul-de-sac and north of the centuries-old San Juan Capistrano Mission, also known as the Jewel of the Missions.

At their destination, Ward exited the Porsche and circled around to the driver's side, where he motioned for Lee to lower the window. The window came down and Ward stuck his hand out, offering to shake.

"Thank you for everything, counselor, I'll call again if I ever need a lawyer."

Ignoring Ward's outstretched hand, Lee snarled: "don't call me. I won't be there."

Ward took a half step back. After glaring at the attorney for a heartbeat his lips curled into a smirk and he leaned forward as if to share a secret. Resting both hands on the Porsche's roof, he whispered: "you know what, counselor?"

"What?"

"In the end they all screamed for their mommy."

Lee's eyes instantly narrowed and his jaw involuntarily clenched as he jammed his vehicle into gear and hit the accelerator. The engine screamed its rage at the sudden unleashing of its five hundred and twenty horsepower, leaving twin trails of smoldering rubber in its wake as the rear tires boiled the pavement. He had to get as far away as possible and as fast as possible or something very bad was going to happen—right then, right there.

CHAPTER 6

It was after midnight, late by most people's standards, when I rolled around to the back of the standalone building that housed the combined garage/workshop where I parked my pickup. I was dressed all in black. Probably not necessary, but why make it easy for some Nosy Nellie who might have nothing better to do than spy on her neighbors? I unlocked the back door and walked inside, then hit the button on the wall to roll up the garage door and silently pull my pickup out. There was nothing unusual about this. In fact, I could have done it in broad daylight, but I had other things to do the next day—like show up for work, for instance. Tomorrow night was my target date and I certainly wouldn't have time after work to get done what I needed to do before taking care of some more trash. The sooner I was prepared, the more time I would have to make sure I hadn't forgotten something, even something as simple as forgetting a skinning knife like I did way back when I sent Reggie Santana on his journey to hell.

Inside the shop I set about modifying one of the fifty-five-gallon steel drums sitting out back. The drum needed to be thoroughly cleaned and scrubbed inside and out, then cleaned again with solvent. It would not bode well if I were to leave any clues as to where it came from. Once clean, it took me no more than twenty minutes to cut a four-by-twelve-inch horizontal opening about six inches below the upper rim and then paint the entire drum flat black (the better to absorb ambient light. For what I had in mind, light was definitely not going to be my friend). I took special precautions to make sure not to leave aby traces of the paint on the floor. I was particularly proud of my prowess with a cutting torch. The slot looked kind of like a gun port. If you could fit inside, no one would know you were in there.

It was after midnight, late by most people's standards when I rolled around to the back of the standalone building that housed the combined garage/workshop where I parked my pickup. I was dressed all in black. Probably not necessary, but why make it easy for some Nosy Nellie who might have nothing better to do than spy on her neighbors? I unlocked the back door and walked inside, then hit the button on the wall to roll up the garage door. There was nothing unusual about this. In fact I could have done it in broad daylight, but I had other things to do the next day—like show up for work, for instance. Tomorrow night was my target date and I certainly wouldn't have time after work to get done what I needed to do before taking care of some more trash. The sooner I was prepared, the more time I would have to make sure I hadn't forgotten something, even something as simple as forgetting a skinning knife like I had way back when I sent Reggie Santana on his journey to hell.

As soon as the paint dried, I loaded the drum onto my large-wheeled, rough terrain hand truck, and then up the loading ramp and into the pickup it went. It was a crisp winter night, not warm like the night I watched Reggie Santana do the boogie woogie at the business end of an extension cord. San Juan Capistrano can get pretty chilly in the winter, but I would have been open to all bets that Joshua Ward would be sweating before tomorrow night was over. Collecting the trash can be such demanding work.

CHAPTER 7

At eight a.m. Lee phoned the office from his car to ask Sharona if she had scheduled any appointments. As expected, she answered by first pointing out he was supposed to be in the office at seven-thirty: "how do you expect me to run this office if I can't depend on the rest of the team?" She scolded.

"I know; I'm sorry, I should have called. It's just that I didn't get to bed until late last night. I had some trouble sleeping so I went out and tinkered around in my workshop. I guess my mind was still busy thinking about Joshua Ward. I'm on my way in. I sure wish I could tell you what he said to me when I dropped him off, but it's privileged. He had to have known that, otherwise he wouldn't have said it. He said it for no other reason than to taunt me because I told him I would never represent him again. I could have snapped the little twerp's neck and it wouldn't have bothered me a bit."

"I can just imagine what he said."

"No. I don't think you can. My blood is still boiling."

"Well, what he's done is bound to come back to bite him at some point. You can bet on it. He's not smart enough to stay out of trouble. Parkland Rice is going to be here in two hours. He'll be bringing the tickets to the fights tonight. Did you find a date?"

"No, I haven't really had time to ask anyone."

"You want me to fix you up?"

"It would never work out anyway. I'll just tag along with you guys. I'll be there in twenty minutes," said Lee.

"That'll be plenty of time for me to find you a date. In fact, I might know just the right girl."

Fifteen minutes later, Lee entered his office and Sharona informed him that she'd moved Parkland Rice's appointment up. He would be there in no more than twenty minutes. Other news outlets wanted an interview as well.

"You just earned yourself a lot of free publicity. You're kind of a celebrity," she said cheerfully.

"I just wish he'd been a more deserving client."

"Look at it this way: your client was the United States Constitution, not Joshua Ward. You know that as well as anybody. You did the right thing." She replied.

"But the problem is Joshua Ward got the benefit."

CHAPTER 8

Parkland showed up ten minutes late and Sharona was all over him. He knew better. She did not suffer late arrivals lightly, no matter who they might be. He once witnessed her deliver a level five tongue-lashing to a city councilman who had the temerity to show up five minutes after his scheduled appointment time. She was the gatekeeper, and woe be to the poor sap who failed to learn that right out.

She ended the dressing down with: "I'll see if he still has time for you. You can't imagine how busy he is. You really need to be on time. You might have to come back. You're not the only newshound trying to get an audience with him."

Finally satisfied that Parkland was sufficiently chastened, Sharona lifted the receiver on her desk phone and punched the button for Lee's extension, then in her most professional voice simply said: "Mr. Rice is here."

"Go ahead and send him in," Lee responded.

Parkland Rice appeared in the doorway wearing a flowered Hawaiian shirt, board shorts and sandals and what looked like a very expensive camera strapped around his neck.

Lee stood for the obligatory handshake.

"Nice outfit, Parkland. Is this casual Thursday or something?"

"I own the newspaper. It's casual day whenever I say it is. You should try it."

"Sharona won't let me."

"Huh?"

"Never mind. What's up? What can I do for you?"

"I'm looking for a quote from you about yesterday's motion to suppress the DNA evidence against Joshua Ward. What do you think, did the cop really know he was violating Ward's Fourth Amendment rights when he took the DNA swab?"

"Sure, I do. I thought I made that petty clear. He knew the law. He just ignored it."

"David Rogers did a pretty good job of trying to convince the judge otherwise."

"There is no way he could have thought he would win."

"Then why did he contest your motion? Why the big show yesterday?"

"Think about it: Cooper Jansen's murder was sensational news, and rightly so. All the major news outlets carried the story. It went unsolved for more than two years. Then all of a sudden there's an arrest and it's back in the news. The evidence appears to be overwhelming. The public wants blood and they want it now. The District Attorney is an elected official. How do you think it would look next election if the D.A.'s office was to dismiss the charge without a fight? This way the public won't blame the D.A.'s office, or even the Sheriff's Department for that matter. They are going to see it as some slick defense attorney using a technicality to get his client freed. They are not going to acknowledge that what they call a "technicality" is also called the Constitution."

"Can I quote you on that?"

"I don't care, go ahead. That's up to you. But I want you add this: Joshua Ward was going to walk anyway, regardless of whichever attorney was at the counsel table on either side. Our judicial system is based on facts. The fact was his constitutional rights were violated. You can't change the facts. You just have to find them."

"That's a pretty modest statement."

"It's true."

"What about Ward? I didn't see any hugs or handshakes after the judge made his ruling."

"You never will, either. We all know he's guilty of at least one, if not more, of the most heinous crimes imaginable. I did my job, that's all. Personally, I couldn't care less if he gets hit by a train. He doesn't belong on the street."

"You don't really want me to put that in the paper, do you?"

"No, don't. I guess I just needed to vent a little. Just say my job isn't to determine guilt or innocence. I'm here to ensure that anyone who is accused of a crime, no matter how heinous, is treated fairly. It's what our constitution demands."

"Okay, that's all I need. Can I get a picture?"

"Fire away. Just don't spend too much effort looking for my good side."

By noon a local television news program and a newspaper reporter from the *Orange County Register* also requested interviews. Sharona told the television crew to be there no later than one-thirty or they would find the door locked. The reporter from the *Register* was put through for a telephone interview.

By three o'clock the camera crew made their exit and Sharona stepped into Lee's office with a smile on her face.

"I got you a date for the fights."

"Really, you didn't bribe your cousin, did you?" Lee had met Sharona's cousin Tamara on a couple of occasions. She was a knockout and never lacking for prospective dates. Apparently, the Kane genes ran deep.

"I tried, but she said she doesn't date lawyers."

"What if I promised to change professions?"

"Not a chance."

"Okay, so fill me in on the particulars."

"Her name is Krystal, with a K. She's a graphic artist. She's my age. I met her in my Constitutional Law class, so she probably doesn't hate lawyers yet. Trust me, you're gonna like her. She's a boxing fan; might even know more boxing trivia than you do."

"Do you think she'll like me?"

"Probably not. Anyway, we're all meeting for coffee at five o'clock at Vitaly Café in Costa Mesa same as always. After the fights we can have a late dinner somewhere. I just closed the office and forwarded the phones to the answering service. You should have plenty of time to go home and practice being nice."

"How about I go home and practice being charming?"

"Let's just shoot for nice. See you at five. Dress like you're going to the fights with a pretty lady."

CHAPTER 9

Lee, dressed in tan slacks and a light blue long sleeved dress shirt under a brown leather bomber jacket, walked through the front door of Vitaly Café at four-fifty. Quickly glancing left and right, he spotted Sharona and her boyfriend sitting at the far end of the room. Despite his imposing size Ricky was just a big softy, particularly around Sharona. Lee couldn't remember ever meeting a more genuinely nice person.

Ricky and Sharona had been in an exclusive relationship for nearly three years. The two seemed perfect for each other. For the last several months, Ricky had been after Sharona to move in with him, but each time he suggested it she balked at the idea, saying only that there were some personal issues she needed to straighten out first. She steadfastly refused to further discuss the nature of those issues. Ricky, afraid he might lose her if he pushed too hard, only brought it up occasionally, mostly to let Sharona know that his feelings about her hadn't changed and that he saw a future with her.

Spotting Lee, Ricky motioned him over. Two empty seats remained at the table. The men shook hands and exchanged greetings before Lee took a seat with his back to the door, directly across from Sharona and to the left of Ricky.

"He can't make it to work on time, but he can show up early to meet a lady. By the way, you look nice," said Sharona.

"Have you ever met Krystal?" Ricky asked.

"No, I haven't, I'm kind of flying blind on this."

"You owe Sharona big time."

"Why's that?"

"You're about to find out."

Just then a perky female voice asked: "excuse me. Is this seat taken?"

Lee turned around and looked up into the prettiest ice-blue eyes he had ever seen. Krystal's honey-blond hair cascaded past her shoulders and formed a perfect backdrop to her beach-tanned complexion. When she smiled, Lee could have sworn the entire café got just a little bit brighter.

As he stumbled to his feet, Sharona greeted Krystal: "hey girlfriend, you found us. You know Ricky. The klutz trying to find his feet is Lee. Lee, meet Krystal Svenson, that's Krystal with a K."

Krystal looked Lee in the eye and stuck out her hand. Tall and athletic, she was dressed in a loose-fitting long-sleeve turquoise sweater, skinny jeans and knee-high black boots. "Nice to meet you Lee, I'm Krystal." Turning to Sharona, she said, "I hope I'm dressed appropriately."

Lee couldn't imagine anywhere she wouldn't look appropriate. "You look great. It's nice to meet you too, Krystal with a K. I'm Lee, Lee Edwards."

Taking her seat, Krystal smiled and said, "Sharona tells me you were once Leroy Edwards, the professional boxer."

"I still am."

"Really, still a professional boxer?"

"No, still Lee Edwards."

"Why is it you never had a ring name?"

"We just couldn't agree on one. My manager wanted to call me the 'Berkeley Bomber,' but I thought it sounded too corny, also too much like a name you might find on the FBI's Ten Most Wanted list. No one wants to go to an arena that might blow up."

"I promised Krystal you'd tell her all about the time you got your brains beat out, that is if you can remember," said Sharona.

Not about to take the bait, Lee replied: "which time, you mean the first time?"

Krystal stepped in: "my dad and I used to watch him on TV. He was really good. I never would have thought our paths would cross, though."

"Don't encourage him," Sharona replied.

The get-acquainted part of the evening went well. The conversation was fun and lively and the four of them enjoyed the coffee and blueberry muffins Sharona had ordered. Before long, Krystal excused herself to go to the ladies' room.

Lee leaned toward Sharona. "Where did you say you found her?" He asked incredulously.

"What do you mean?"

"C'mon, she's an actress, isn't she? You met her on movie set somewhere, or she's in one of your commercials, isn't she? You probably coached her. Tell me you didn't coach her. Tell me she's for real; look me in the eye and tell me she's for real."

"Don't you like her?"

"Are you kidding? What's not to like? She's smart, quick-witted and gorgeous, and she likes boxing. What more could a man ask for?"

"So why don't you think she's real? When she comes back, ask her something about boxing. By the way, she likes you. I can tell. There's no accounting for taste, I guess."

"I'll bet you ten bucks when she comes back, she's going to say she just got a phone call. Something's come up. We'll have to take a rain check."

"You're on. Wanna put another ten on whether you can stump her on boxing trivia?"

"Deal."

Krystal returned. "What'd I miss?" She asked.

Turning his entire chair toward her, Lee, slowly and as if lost in thought, leaned his head back and looked at the ceiling for a couple of seconds while rubbing his chin with his right forefinger. Finally turning his attention back to Krystal, he said: "Sharona says you know boxing trivia."

"I know a little. What's the question?"

"Who took the title from John L. Sullivan?"

Without hesitation, Krystal smiled and answered: "That would be 'Gentleman' Jim Corbett. He stopped Sullivan in the 21st round in New Orleans on, I believe, September seventh, 1892. Corbett lost the title in Carson, Nevada on March 13, 1897 when 'Ruby' Bob Fitzsimmons put him down for keeps in the 14th round with a punch to the solar plexus."

Lee and Ricky exchanged glances, disbelief obvious on each of their faces.

"Thank you, Krystal." Sharona piped in. "You just won me ten bucks."

Pretending to be hurt, Krystal stuck out her lower lip in an exaggerated pout. "You didn't think I would know that? I thought everyone did. Now it's my turn. Who was the only heavyweight world champion to win the title lying on the canvas and lose it standing on his feet?"

"That would be Max Schmeling." Lee answered. "He won the vacant title when he dropped to the floor from a low blow. He didn't get up until his

47

opponent was disqualified. He later lost his title by decision," Lee said with a slight smirk. No one was going to beat him at boxing trivia.

"Who did he win it from and who did he lose it to?" Krystal asked.

"I don't know. I just know he won it on the canvas and lost it on his feet. I give up."

"He won the title when Jack Sharkey fouled him and lost it two years later when Sharkey beat him by split decision." Krystal replied.

With a look of awe on his face, Lee shook his head and asked: "how do you know this?"

"My dad and I used to quiz each other on boxing trivia to see who would have to clear the table."

Lee turned to Ricky and asked: "did you know about this?"

Ricky raised his hands in surrender and said: "I'm as dumbfounded as you are, buddy."

Turning back to Krystal, Lee said: "I'm impressed. I don't know what to say."

Laughing, Sharona looked at Krystal, "Do you realize what you've just done, girlfriend? You've just made a lawyer admit that he doesn't know everything. That never happens, particularly not with this one."

As they rose to leave, Sharona tapped Lee on the shoulder and whispered, "That's another ten you owe me, Blondie."

In the parking lot of the Vitaly the decision was made that everyone would ride to the fights in Sharona's Ford Explorer. Ricky had to catch a plane to Dallas later that night and she was going to drop him off at John Wayne Airport on her way home after dinner. Vitaly Café would be on their way back. Although Krystal and Lee could have gone together in either of their cars, Lee felt this arrangement would be less awkward, after all, he and Krystal had just met. Ricky went back inside and secured permission from the manager for them to leave the two cars.

CHAPTER 10

The fights, held in a World War II-era Army Air Corps hangar on the Orange County Fairgrounds, went as expected. Under the auspices of Fight Club O.C., the promoter could be counted on to debut local talent and showcase established fighters who were well on their way to a title shot. Parkland came through as promised with ringside seats midway between the corners. He usually joined them but was absent tonight, leaving an empty seat next to theirs. This was a rarity, especially when Malcolm McAllister was on the card. Lee scanned the arena and while he did see one of the sports reporters from the *Times*, he didn't see Parkland.

Each of the six preliminary fights was hard fought and competitive. The excitement served to prime the crowd for the main event: the battle featuring middleweights Malcolm McAllister and Armando Ruiz.

Before long, it was time. Malcolm "The Punisher" McAllister, fighting out of the Jackrabbit Gym in Long Beach, California, was putting his record of twelve wins—eleven by knockout—and a single loss on the line against the more experienced Armando Ruiz out of Guadalajara, Mexico, whose own record was eighteen wins—twelve by knockout—and six losses.

The fight more than lived up to everyone's expectations with each fighter landing heavy punches. Malcolm stalked his opponent relentlessly, throwing an even mixture of head and body shots. Every time it seemed he might get caught on the ropes, Ruiz countered with left hooks and straight rights to Malcolm's head.

Finally, in the fourth round, McAllister's body punching began to take its toll. Ruiz noticeably slowed down and slightly lowered his guard in order to better protect his rib cage.   Immediately pouncing on the opportunity, Malcolm feinted with a right to the body and followed with a four-punch combination of left hooks and short rights to Ruiz's head. Ruiz slid to the canvas. He wasn't going to beat the referee's count.

As Malcolm was making his way back to his dressing room, amid the thundering cheers echoing through the packed arena, he glanced in Lee's direction and paused to offer a wave of acknowledgment. Krystal instantly swiveled her head to look directly at Lee and in a surprised tone asked: "do you know him?"

"Yeah, I've worked out at Jackrabbit a few times. I'm surprised Sharona didn't mention it. Nicest kid you'll ever meet."

"I'm not sure Ruiz thinks he's so nice."

"Actually, they both made a new friend tonight. That's how it works with warriors. I'll introduce you sometime."

Dinner was at Maestro's Ocean Club in Newport Beach. Billed as a high-end chophouse, it more than lived up to its name. Over everyone's objections, Lee paid the bill. It could not have been a better evening.

Back at Vitaly's parking lot, Krystal and Lee exited the Explorer. Sharona piled out as well, openly curious how this evening would end for them. Standing just a couple of feet apart Krystal flashed a blinding smile and leaned forward to kiss Lee lightly on the cheek, then stepped back and told him she really enjoyed herself and thank you for the great evening. She then fell silent and stood there in front of him.

Breaking the silence, Sharona called out: "hey, dummy, she's still standing there. Aren't you going to ask her out again?"

Quickly glancing in Sharona's direction Lee replied: "hey, I've got this." Then, turning back to Krystal: "I'm glad you enjoyed yourself. I had a great evening too and I'm really glad we've met. Would you like to go out again?"

"I would love to go out again." She replied.

"That's great. Can I call you this week?"

"Of course."

Turning to Sharona, with an exaggerated swagger in his voice, Lee said: "See? I told you I've got this. Your offer of assistance is appreciated, but unnecessary. You may leave now."

Sharona smiled and responded with: "good night guys" and reached for the door handle. She backed the Expedition alongside Krystal and Lee then stopped and lowered her window. "Hey, I've got an idea." She said." We have horses in San Juan, out on the Ortega Highway. Why don't we all go for a ride this Sunday? You do know how to ride, right?"

Krystal nodded enthusiastically. "I do. I've been around horses since I was a little girl."

Sharona turned to Lee and raised her eyebrows: "how about you, cowboy?"

"Do broomstick horses count?"

"You ever get thrown?"

"Couple of times; he was a mean ol' cuss. My mom finally put him back in the broom closet till he changed his attitude."

"Okay, maybe we'll have to bubble wrap you. What do you say, are you up for it?"

"I'd love to." Krystal smiled and nodded.

"Count me in." Lee added.

The night was coming to an end too quickly. Lee couldn't remember a better first date. As Sharona's car pulled out of the parking lot Krystal and Lee turned to walk back to their own vehicles. Krystal's Lexus was parked about four spaces beyond Lee's Porsche. As they passed by, Krystal admired the car, then asked: "that's not yours, is it?"

"Part of it is. Most of it belongs to the finance company."

"It's beautiful."

Lee fought a furious internal battle to keep from saying something corny like: "nowhere near as beautiful as you." Finally, he came up with a simple: "thank you."

When they reached Krystal's car, she put out her hand again and said: "I really did have a wonderful time. I hope you're looking forward to going riding this weekend."

Lee took her hand, chuckled and drew in a breath. "I'm going to be making a fool out of myself, but I can't think of better company to be in when I do."

"Trust me, it'll be fun. If worse comes to worst, I know first aid, so you have nothing to worry about."

The two of them looked at one another silently, hand in hand in the darkness for an instant that seemed to last forever. Finally breaking the silence, Lee said: "I really had a great time too," then hugged her before turning to walk back to his car.

CHAPTER 11

Alone in his house, Joshua Ward couldn't get the warning from his lawyer out of his mind. He probably shouldn't have said what he'd said. He was sure his attorney couldn't go to the police with it. There was such a thing as attorney/client privilege. He knew that much. His biggest and most pressing problem was keeping his DNA from the cops. One slip-up could cost him his freedom, maybe even his life. *They could be outside right now watching my house, hoping I leave something somewhere with my DNA on it. How did things get to where they were now? No doubt I'll have to move away, but how would I accomplish that? How could I sell the place without holding an open house? Wouldn't that just invite undercover officers to inspect the place and find a way to recover a DNA sample? How did I get into this mess? I've always been so careful.*

The antique grandfather clock in the living room chimed two times. Two a.m.; *where had the time gone?* He trudged upstairs. He needed to sleep. He was no longer thinking clearly. He needed to figure this out. He was beyond exhausted from the stress of jail and even more so with this latest development. Sleeping in his own bed again would be a luxury after all the nights on a jailhouse bunk, yet he had a nagging feeling that the comfort of a good night's rest would be elusive tonight. He couldn't shake the mental image of the cops rummaging through his trash.

In all the years since he inherited the house from his parents, he never worried about locking the doors. He lived in a good neighborhood. People in bad neighborhoods locked their doors to keep out the bad guys. He had never encountered any bad guys in this neighborhood. *Now I have to lock my doors to keep the cops out.* For the first time ever, he shut and locked his bedroom door. He then flopped onto his bed and, despite his worries, instantly fell into a deep slumber. He never thought to lock his front door. Old habits die hard.

Sitting behind the wheel of the pickup a figure wearing all black from ski cap to the bottom of the rubber-soled shoes silently wiped a handful of coins, erasing any fingerprints. A pen light with the batteries purposely run down enough to cast only a dull glow was added to tonight's inventory and secured with the rest of the items in one or another pocket of the cargo pants. These would come in handy, particularly in a big old house at night.

The garage door rolled open and the truck silently idled forward. It was very late. The target should be asleep by now. If not, the nine-millimeter Ruger would have to be employed to deal with him in a more expedient manner than was intended. That was not the plan, however. The ability to adapt is often the difference between success and failure. It was time for The Trash Collector to go to work.

CHAPTER 12

The pickup silently idled to the end of the cul-de-sac and swung around, coming to a stop in front of Joshua Ward's spacious front yard. Its headlights had been shut off since before making the turn at the corner of Camino Capistrano a block away. The driver emerged and quietly closed the door, then walked briskly to the front of the house; best not to skulk in the darkness. That would look suspicious; much better to just walk directly up the front porch steps. This was an old house. It should be easy to jimmy the lock if necessary. Best of all, the house was dark.

Tightly grasping the front door handle, The Trash Collector gently tested the thumb lever. There was little resistance as the latch quietly receded.

Slowly, The Trash Collector pushed the door ajar and slipped into the darkened house. There was no reason to move quickly and spoil the surprise.

Once inside, the door was dead bolted in case the prey somehow managed to get loose and try to escape. *You can't be too careful.*

With the yellowish illumination of the pen light bulb drawing its power from the final gasps of the dying batteries, the intruder surveyed the interior of the house. All the drapes and blinds were shut tight. Joshua Ward evidently didn't want anyone to know he was home. He wouldn't be home much longer.

Of most interest was the stairway to the left of the entryway; fourteen steps to the top. The bedrooms would be upstairs. Joshua Ward would be in one of them. Fittingly, the house was as quiet as a mausoleum.

The Trash Collector slowly ascended the stairway, stepping only on the outer edges of the stairs, making as little noise as possible. The time to break the silence would come soon enough.

The eighth step emitted a high-pitched creaking moan that seemed to echo through the darkness. Freezing in place, The Trash Collector pulled the Ruger. *You can't be too careful.* After waiting an eternity for a figure to appear above the stairwell, the pistol was replaced in its holster and the climb resumed.

In the pitch-black master bedroom Joshua Ward's eyes flew open. Something pulled him from his sleep. It sounded like someone, or something, on the stairwell. *Could someone have broken in, or was it just the sound of the old house settling in for the night?* He lay on his bed trying not to hyperventilate, listening intently for another sound, hoping he wouldn't hear one. What could he do if someone had broken in? Calling the police was out of the question. He reached for his nightstand and retrieved the snub-nosed .38 caliber revolver and placed it under his pillow. *If someone was breaking in, they were going to end up as dead as Cooper Jansen, the little brat who brought this all on.* Hearing nothing more, he drifted off to sleep again.

The Trash Collector finally reached the top of the stairs. Across the landing and slightly to the right stood the open door to a bathroom. Three feet to the left was a closed door to what would certainly be the master bedroom. With a better picture of the house's layout and satisfied the door to the master bedroom was closed, The Trash Collector went back downstairs, carefully avoiding the eighth step, then retrieved a dinner plate from a kitchen cabinet and re-ascended.

At the top of the stairs the Trash Collector silently backed into the bathroom and placed the dinner plate on the vanity. The penlight was extinguished and secured in a pocket. A few of the coins were carefully withdrawn and one of them was tossed onto the hardwood floor outside of the master bedroom.

Joshua Ward shot up in bed. *What was that? It sounded like something fell. Had there been a small earthquake? Maybe it shook something off one of the tables.*

He heard it again: a flat chirping sound as something either bounced or skittered down the stairs to the living room below. *What could it be? Did some animal—possibly the neighbor's cat—get in? Didn't I properly secure all the doors and windows? Maybe it wasn't a cat. Maybe it was a mouse, or a rat.* The exterminator hadn't been out in quite a while.

Once again, the sound pierced the stillness of the darkened house, this time accompanied by the distinctive rattle of a coin spinning to a stop. The hair on the back of Ward's neck rose and a chill ran down his spine. He could feel goosebumps rise on his forearms.

Joshua Ward silently whispered: "please God, let it be a mouse." He heard the sound again, then again. The darkness grew silent again, save for the jackhammer pounding in his ears as his heart raced, pushing his blood pressure skyward. His body flushed with adrenaline.

He fumbled for his bedside lamp, instantly bathing the room in harsh bright light.

Smiling at the sight of light escaping from under the bedroom door, the Trash Collector retreated into the darkness of the bathroom and picked up the dinner plate.

Standing at his bedroom door with the revolver in his right hand and the doorknob in the other, Ward considered his options. *Should I stay barricaded in my bedroom and pray that whatever is invading my home will just leave? Should I confront it? Maybe I should quietly open the door and sneak down the stairs and maybe surprise the intruder? Should I make as much noise as possible and maybe scare whomever or whatever was down there*? He was out of his element. *It always seems so easy on television, why can't it be the same now?*

Standing in the darkened bathroom, The Trash Collector reviewed all potential scenarios. Joshua Ward was a coward; that much was obvious from what he had done to little Cooper Jansen. Cowards could be unpredictable. *Will he come through the door carrying a weapon? If so, what kind of weapon will he have: a knife; a club; a gun, or maybe even a sword? Will he be swinging or shooting wildly? Anything is possible. Be ready. You can't be too careful.*

The dinner plate flew through the air and crashed on the floor in an explosion of shattered china.

This was too much. Ward tore the door open and raced into the hallway, stopping at the top of the stairs. Then, with the gun pointed down into the darkened house, he stepped back to the bedroom door and quickly slammed it shut. The sudden shift from the bright light of his bedroom to total darkness temporarily destroyed his night vision. Standing at the top of the stairs, he yelled as loud as he could that he was armed and anyone in the house had better get out immediately. Blindly staring down the open chasm of the stairwell, struggling to control his fear, he was unaware of the dark figure suddenly behind him.

The Trash Collector's foot pistoned into Ward's back flush between the shoulder blades, launching him headfirst down the stairwell. Instinctively he dropped the revolver and put his arms out to brace himself. His right arm crumpled on impact, snapping the humerus and sending a jagged end ripping though his triceps before spearing itself the rest of the way through his upper arm. His body tumbled and somersaulted to the floor below, coming to rest with his right arm bent at a grotesque angle halfway between the elbow and armpit.

The first thing Joshua Ward noticed as he slowly came back to consciousness was the dull glow cast by the stairwell lights, spreading enough illumination that he could recognize he was lying face down on the floor of his living room. An excruciating pain radiating from his right arm shot through his entire body. He was unable to move any of his extremities. His left arm was somehow restrained behind his back and his knees were bent and also restrained. He turned his head only to see a puddle of blood seeping onto the floor beneath his shoulder.

"Hey there, Sunshine," came a cheerful voice from behind. "I wasn't sure you were going to make it. You took an awful tumble. You need to be more careful. You could have broken your neck. I wouldn't be surprised if you have a concussion. Lucky for you I was here. You could have died. Your arm's in pretty bad shape, too, it was bleeding a lot all over your nice hardwood floor so I cinched it off with a tie strap. It's not bleeding nearly as much now, although you'll probably lose the arm. You know what they say: 'use a tourniquet to save the life, not the limb.' All in all, though, you owe me big time for saving your life."

"Who are you?" cried Joshua Ward. "What are you doing here?"

"To answer your first question: I'm your worst nightmare. I'm sort of a trash collector. I clean up garbage the system won't or can't. And as for your second question: I'm here to do just that. Don't bother struggling. You can't get loose. I don't think Houdini could get loose from the predicament you've gotten yourself into. You might notice your left hand and both of your feet are bound together. Your right arm is useless, so there was no reason to bind it. Don't try to break loose; it'll just be a waste of time and energy. Anyway, the strap binding your left hand is connected to the ones holding your feet. The police department calls it a hog tie. Now you just sit tight. Don't go anywhere. I'll be right back."

After the intruder disappeared through the front door, Joshua struggled with all his might to free himself. The bindings refused to loosen and all he accomplished was to induce even more pain throughout his body.

57

Outside, the intruder opened the pickup's tailgate and unfolded the loading ramp, then walked the fifty-five-gallon drum down the ramp on the hand truck and through the front door.

"Your chariot awaits, kind sir. Did you miss me?" The intruder parked the hand truck next to Ward's helpless form on the bloodied floor. "Now, here's what's going to happen next: I'm going to duct tape your mouth shut and put you in this barrel. Why the duct tape? I'm glad you asked. We need it because putting you in this barrel is going to hurt, a lot. We don't want your screaming to wake the neighbors and, believe me, you're going to scream. Once we get you into the barrel, I'll pull the tape off. Then we're going for a ride. You'll sit in back in your little barrel. Pretend we're on an airplane and you're riding in coach."

It took about three minutes to load Ward into the barrel, making sure he was facing the rectangular port cut into the side. He had to be lifted under the armpits and placed inside knees first, putting enormous strain on his broken arm. As predicted, he cried out for all he was worth. However, the duct tape muffled his screams to no more than a series of faint, plaintive cries and whimpers. His attempts to resist were useless. He was destined to spend the rest of his miserable life in a thirty-three-inch high, twenty-two-and-a-half-inch diameter steel barrel.

Once the wounded prey was planted in the barrel, the Trash Collector unceremoniously ripped the duct tape from his lips. The ensuing panicked screams were now muffled by the surrounding steel.

"Shush now," whispered the dark figure. "We mustn't wake the neighbors. Good thing you're a runt. Otherwise I'd have to saw your legs off to get you in there and I'll be damned if I didn't forget my SkilSaw. That means I would have had to use a hacksaw or a steak knife or something. It might have taken all night."

Looking up at his captor, the little man sobbed: "why are you doing this?"

The reply came in a mocking tone: "oh, I think you know: Cooper wasn't the only one, was he?"

"I don't know what you're talking about. I'm innocent. I swear."

"Well then, maybe I've got the wrong person. That makes you an innocent bystander. Have you ever noticed all the horrible things that happen to innocent bystanders? They get killed all the time. In fact, I'm pretty sure, if you look it up, you'll find that innocent bystander is one of the most dangerous jobs out there; probably right up there with professional Russian roulette player. I sure wouldn't want to be one. It seems like we always hear about something terrible happening to innocent bystanders. You never hear about an innocent bystander hitting the lottery or anything like that, do you?"

Sobbing now, Joshua Ward pleaded: "please don't do this. I didn't do it, please."

Feigning compassion, the intruder replied: "well, if you really didn't do it, I guess I owe you an apology...Sorry."

The interior of the drum grew even blacker as the cover was laid in place and the bolt ring was fitted around the upper rim, then tightened with a crescent wrench. It was time to take out the trash.

From outside of the drum came a command whispered through the port cut into the side. "Don't make any noise. Don't thrash around. I'm going to take you to a place I've picked out, a place you probably know. Someone is bound to come along sooner or later and find you. I promise you someone will come along and let you out. You won't be in there all night"

"Why are you doing this?" Ward whimpered.

"I'd be willing to bet Cooper Jansen wanted to know the same thing," was the only answer he got.

Before wheeling the barrel out to the waiting pickup truck, the Trash Collector went back up to the master bedroom. The light was still on. It didn't take but a moment to locate Ward's trousers and extract his wallet before turning off the light off and exiting the room. Once back downstairs and in the living room the wallet was pushed through the slot in the side of the drum.

"Here, you're going to need this."

"For what, is it money you want? I can get you money, just let me out."

"I don't want your money. You need your wallet because if the police find you without your identification, they're likely to mistake you for a vagrant or something. Let's go."

As soon as the barrel was pulled up the loading ramp into the pickup's bed, it was laid on its back, still secured to the hand truck and with the slot facing up into the night sky. The Trash Collector climbed into the driver's seat and silently idled toward the intersection a block away before turning on the headlights. It would be only a ten- or twelve-minute ride to their destination. At this hour it should be deserted. If not, there were other options.

CHAPTER 13

When I got to the intersection with Camino Capistrano, I made a right and drove another three miles to Avenida Junipero Sierra, named after a Catholic Priest who was a driving force behind the Spanish conquest and colonization of California and who founded a total of nine missions in the state. Joshua Ward could definitely use a priest at this point. At the intersection I turned right and right again when I got to the southbound Interstate 5 on-ramp. Nine miles later I turned off the freeway and onto Avenida Califia in the beachside city of San Clemente. I continued down Califia to the deserted parking lot at the end. We were now at San Clemente State Beach.

As soon as I stopped, I could hear my prisoner whining to be let out. You'd think that by now he would have caught on to the idea that releasing him wasn't in my plans. Although I guess I really can't blame him; hogtied and alone as he was would have to be horribly uncomfortable. In fact, I guess it would be downright painful with his leg and arm muscles cramping up and all. Add to that he was stuffed in a freshly painted fifty-five-gallon drum with the top sealed shut and I it would have to be awfully claustrophobic. I probably should have thought to ask him if he had claustrophobia before I stuffed him in there, but no one can think of everything. At least the tourniquet was working. He hadn't bled to death and, mercifully, he probably couldn't feel the muscles in that arm cramping up on him.

I had to laugh at the first thing I saw when I got out of the truck: I was parked right under a street sign that cited both state and city ordinances prohibiting the dumping of trash, which was kind of counter to what I was about to do. As much as I hated to violate the law, those ordinances would be ignored tonight.

The whole damn time I was unloading the drum, he kept whining. I don't know about you, but I personally don't have a lot of patience. I finally picked up a rock and beat it against the side until he shut up. Once he quieted down, I told him how annoying his pleading and whimpering was getting to be, and how rude it would be if he were to wake up anyone living nearby. Truth be told, there were no homes within earshot and we were the only vehicle in sight. He could have screamed and cried all he wanted. No one was going to hear him. I just said that because he was starting to give me a headache.

When it became obvious he wasn't going to listen to me, I told him to shut the hell up or I would pull him out of his drum and rip his arm the rest of the way off and beat him to death with his own fist, possibly making him the first person ever to bare handedly beat himself to death, on top of that, it would probably be ruled a suicide. He seemed to quiet down for a few seconds; maybe he was trying to figure out if that could be true.

Next, he wanted to know where we were, as if it mattered. I told him we were at the beach and if he would quiet down he could hear the ocean. Evidently he didn't want to listen to the ocean, because he started pleading with me not to put him in the water. That was something II hadn't thought of. I thanked him for the suggestion, but told him that wasn't going to happen. Dragging him across the sand would be too much work and I really didn't want to get my socks wet.

I reminded him of my promise to put him somewhere that he would be seen and let out of the drum, probably sooner than he expected. I wasn't about to go back on my word. I also pointed out that it was a beautiful, clear night and while he waited to be let out, he could sit—or kneel, or whatever he wanted to call it—and gaze at the stars through the observation port that I personally cut into the drum just for his viewing pleasure. How cool was that?

As I trucked him to what I thought would be the best place for him to see someone coming, the barrel jostled and lurched across the uneven dirt path leading from the metered parking to a set of train tracks, then to the beach. He kept up his annoying begging the whole time, finally resorting to calling me "sir." That was nearly the last straw. I told him to knock it off. He finally quit when I told him that if I heard one more "sir," I would take him up on his earlier suggestion and set him adrift in the ocean.

Getting him over the first rail of the tracks was pretty easy thanks to the large, all terrain wheels on the hand truck. As soon as I got him between the tracks, I made a sharp turn to the south and continued on with the load bouncing behind in a rhythm set by the spaces between the railroad ties.

After towing him about a hundred yards down the tracks I decided this was as good a place as any to offload my cargo. He had hardly shut up since we'd arrived and my headache was getting worse as a result.

I released the strap securing the barrel to the hand truck and explained the plan: the slot in the drum was facing north, which was a good thing because in about an hour a train would be coming from that direction. From where we were, the tracks were pretty straight and since it was a clear night, he should be able to make out its lights from about three and a half miles away. I told him to figure on it pulling about a half dozen cars, which meant the total weight would add up to somewhere around five hundred tons, or just over a million pounds, give or take.

On the drive to the beach I calculated in my head the total weight of the barrel and its soon-to-be-late inhabitant and came up with about 170 pounds, providing my guess that he weighed about a buck-thirty was correct. Giving away that much of a weight advantage made it doubtful that would be able to stop a train dead in its tracks, no matter how much he leaned into it, but of course he was free to try. After all, in the end it would be his call. The alternative was to come up with a way to signal it to stop. A million pounds of steel rolling down the tracks at fifty miles per hour is not going to stop on a dime. Even with brand new disk brakes it takes about a mile to stop. That meant he would have to get the engineer's attention as soon as possible. Imagine our mutual disappointment when I found out he had forgotten his Berry pistol and was out of road flares. Obviously, he was never a Boy Scout or he would have come more prepared.

He started screaming and whining again when I told him I had things to do and needed to get going. I bid him goodbye and good luck and headed back to my truck. The closer I got to my truck the more my headache went away. By the time I got behind the wheel, I was feeling pretty good. There would soon be one less piece of trash to clean up and, as I promised, in about an hour someone would come by and open the barrel.

I started the engine and backed out of my parking space, scrolled through iTunes and drove away listening to Johnny Cash singing "Folsom Prison Blues."

CHAPTER 14

Muted screams erupted from within the barrel as the figure outside removed the strap holding it to the hand truck, then receded into the darkness. The screams were answered by nothing more than the crashing of waves less than a hundred yards away. Ignoring his severely fractured arm, Joshua Ward slammed his shoulders back and forth, trying desperately to tip the tiny steel tomb onto its side, hoping to upend it over one of the rails where it might roll free of the tracks.

Somewhere in the darkness a steel monster was rapidly approaching, racing to deliver its passengers to their destinations and oblivious to the fact that it was also about to deliver Joshua Ward to eternity.

Inside the drum a tiny, distant flash of light drew Ward's attention. "Oh God, please, not already, it can't be the train, not yet, please God," he begged out loud.

Maybe it was just my imagination. Yeah, that was it: just my imagination. My hour couldn't possibly be up yet. I had to have imagined it. The light flashed again, still too far away to tell whether it was any closer than the one before. *Maybe it was stopped on the tracks.* He slammed his body harder into the walls of the drum. *Did I just feel it move, rock just a tiny bit?* The light flashed again. It was still far away. *I still have time.* He tried again with all his might to upend the steel coffin. *If only my arms and legs weren't bound; if only I had more room; if only I had more time; if only.*

Three and a half miles to the north, the southbound Amtrak raced past the North Beach Rail Station at 49 miles per hour. Just four minutes and seventeen seconds down the track Joshua Ward was fighting for his life.

The light was now noticeably brighter. On the verge of panic, Joshua put all of his strength into his only chance of survival. *He had to upend the barrel.* Still disregarding the pain, he slammed his head into the underside of the lid. It refused to budge. He rocked furiously back and forth and side to side while every muscle in his body screamed its defiance. He put his mouth to the viewing slot and screamed for all he was worth. *Someone has to hear me. Someone has to come and help.*

No one heard. No one came to help.

The light grew brighter.

Two minutes, twenty-nine seconds.

Sitting at his post in the locomotive, the engineer peered into the blackness ahead. There were no vehicle intersections on this portion of the route. It was too late for pedestrians to be on or around the tracks. They were right on schedule. It would be another good run.

One minute, eight seconds.

But for his fear-driven heightened senses, Joshua Ward would not have felt the nearly imperceptible shudder rising from the wooden ties between the tracks and invading his steel prison.

Twenty-four seconds.

Soaked in sweat and shaking uncontrollably, Joshua Ward violently twisted his body as he continued to fight furiously against his restraints, hoping against hope that at least one of the plastic straps would fail, that he might somehow free himself. His breathing was now mixed with violent fits of coughing. Between his ever-weakening screams he sucked in air until it felt as if his lungs might explode. He was nearly exhausted, losing strength he couldn't afford to lose. With all of his might he threw his head back and forth, side to side, slamming it into the sides of the drum.

The entire inside of the drum was now bathed in blinding light.

The shuddering grew stronger, a volcano preparing to erupt, anticipating its own inevitable doom.

Eighteen seconds.

Now completely overtaken by panic, Joshua Ward continued to slam himself back and forth, hoping against hope for a miracle.

The drum danced between the tracks, its rhythm set by the oncoming train, ritualistically building in intensity, celebrating the sacrifice soon to come.

Eleven seconds.

Now in a mindless panic, Ward intensified his thrashing even more: forward and back, side to side, slamming his head into the solid steel above, oblivious to the pain radiating through his body.

The sound of the train whistle drove him even further over the edge. He answered with his own mindless screams.

Seemingly controlled by some demonic, invisible hand, the drum bounced and shook furiously.

Five seconds.

With the train's shrill whistle piercing the tattered remnants of his sanity and its burning lights invading even the darkest crevices of his being, Joshua Ward put his face to the narrow opening. He had to look.

Joshua Ward died screaming.

CHAPTER 15

Lee Edwards awoke to the relentless, shrill siren of an emergency vehicle at exactly 6:00 a.m. His bedroom windows were shut tight. It couldn't be coming from outside. He knew exactly where it was coming from. Several months ago Sharona gave him the alarm clock, saying: "all lawyers should awaken to the sound of money." He put it across the room so that he would have to get out of bed to shut it off.

As had by now become a morning ritual, he threw his pillow at it without rising from his bed, hoping to knock the loud, obnoxious thing off his dresser. He missed.

Lee was never was much for getting up early. To make it easier he imposed his own strict 10:00 p.m. weeknight bedtime and had been remarkably obedient to it. The only exceptions were occasions when he had a good reason to stay out later. Last night was definitely one of those exceptions.

Finally facing the fact that he was out of options for dealing with the damned thing, he pulled himself out of bed and hit the "off" button, then headed to the shower. This morning he would forgo making himself breakfast and instead settle for coffee and a pastry from the neighborhood donut shop. Maybe if he didn't tell Sharona about it the pastry he could get her to run out and get each of them a breakfast bagel or something.

Sharona was surprised to see Lee walk through the door at 7:25: "Good morning, sir."

"Sir, what's that about? Is it already time for you to tell me what your next raise is going to be?"

"No, I just thought you deserved it after last night. You were actually borderline charming. With a little training you might get there."

"Well, I had a great time and I do owe you."

"That's right, you owe me twenty bucks. What'd you think of Krystal?"

"Wasn't it obvious?"

"Evidently not, she called me this morning to tell me she had a really great time, but wondered why you didn't kiss her goodnight."

"Are you kidding? You don't know how much I wanted to, but I was afraid of coming on too strong; you don't know how hard it was not to. What'd you tell her?"

"I told her you mentioned something about her breath."

"Seriously? No! You didn't, you didn't say that...did you? That would be just like you to say something like that. What if she doesn't know you were kidding?"

"Come on, are you that gullible? I told her exactly what you just said: you really liked her and didn't want to come on too strong."

"Good; thank you for that."

"And that you thought her breath smelled bad."

"I'm going to kill you. You know that, don't you?"

Sharona stared back and chuckled, then shook her head. "Relax Romeo. I'm the one who set you up; remember? She's not some shrinking violet who can't tell when I'm pulling her leg.

"Do you think I should go out and buy some cowboy boots? I want to at least look like I have a clue as to what I'm doing."

It was all Sharona could do to keep from laughing; he was trying so hard to impress Krystal without looking like it. "You won't need them. If you have work boots or hiking boots that'll be fine, but if you want to get a pair I can go with you.

On the ride tomorrow I'm not going to take you anywhere I don't think you can handle. It might be a bit chilly, at least when we start out and we'll be going through a lot of sage and other plants that can snag a nylon jacket. If you don't have a durable light jacket get one made by Levi or Carhartt. If you decide you want some boots, we can get you a jacket at the same place."

"That would be good. Maybe we can go after work or sometime tomorrow if you have time."

"Either way is fine. My dance card is empty until Ricky gets back."

67

The phone rang and Sharona picked it up, assuming a businesslike demeanor. "Law office of Lee Edwards, how may we help you?"

She listened for a minute and laughed before lowering the phone, and told Lee, "It's Parkland Rice. I'll transfer it to you."

Lee picked up the phone at his desk. "Hey Parkland, before we get started, I want to thank you for the tickets. The fights were great and I had one of the best evenings I can remember. Where were you? We had an empty seat in our row; I figured it was yours. I wanted you to meet someone."

"Yeah, I'm sorry I missed it. That was my seat. I would have been there, but at the last minute I decided to load up my truck and head up the coast for some spearfishing. Kind of a short vacation; let my assistant editor take care of the paper for a couple of days."

This was not like Parkland. He rarely took time off from the paper and never without planning well in advance; he wasn't a spur-of-the-moment type.

"So, did you just call me to brag? Where are you?"

"I never got out of town. Have you seen the news this morning?

"No, what's going on?"

"A guy you might know got splattered by a train in San Clemente late last night, or more accurately, early this morning. My guy got the tip about 5:00 a.m. The train conductor called it in."

"That's horrible. Is it someone I should be concerned about? What makes you think I might know him?"

"Sounds like they're pretty sure that once he's positively identified it's gonna turn out to be someone you knew. Apparently he was stuffed in a barrel and set on the tracks at the state beach."

"Are you serious? Who would do something like that? Who was it?"

"You have to keep this confidential. No one is supposed to know yet, but one of my sources told me they found a wallet. If he's the guy who owns the wallet, it's going to be big."

"Damnit, who is it?"

"Joshua Ward."

"No way! Are you kidding me?"

"Not one bit. He's scattered all over the tracks. They didn't even know if they were going to be able to get fingerprints. Someone did a hell of a job on him."

"You gotta be kidding me."

"Remember after you got his charges dropped you told me you didn't care if he got hit by a train? Looks like you got your wish."

"That's kind of suspicious, isn't it," said Lee with a smirk on his face.

"Just sayin'."

Lee hung up and asked Sharona to come in. She would be interested in seeing this. He quickly flipped through the channels of the television in his office until he found a Los Angeles news program. With Joshua Ward's notoriety something this spectacular would be news all over the country.

The picture came on and sure enough there was a reporter on scene, standing next to a yellow strip of crime scene tape. The camera panned over the reporter's shoulder and focused on a mix of Orange County sheriff's deputies and criminologists combing the area around the train track. At the bottom of the screen a banner read: "Grisly find in San Clemente." He thought about Trevor Wilkins' somewhat odd reaction to Joshua Ward's dismissal, and wondered if he would be on the case.

CHAPTER 16

Thirty miles south of Lee Edward's office Trevor Wilkins felt like he had slept in. He sat up in bed and contemplated, then decided against, watching the news on the television mounted over the dresser directly across from his king-sized bed. *Why spoil a day off by seeing more examples of man's inhumanity to man?* After all, he saw plenty of it at work. He rolled out of bed and stretched before heading to the shower.

Trevor was seldom home during the week; at least not during the day. Today he was going to stretch his weekend by taking a vacation day to spend with his son, Charles, who was also home in recognition of one or another of the school holidays. There were plans to meet for breakfast with their favorite neighbors, Jim and Becky Kovac. They first met the Kovacs strolling by one morning on what Jim called their morning walk and Becky called "the death march." The Kovacs were not only great neighbors, but also excellent role models for Charles. Becky was a hard-working workers' compensation attorney who had simultaneously worked for two competing firms while putting herself through law school. It was no small testament to her work ethic that she was eventually promoted to partner at the firm she eventually picked. She was genuinely friendly, but something about her told Trevor to count his blessings that she practiced workers' comp instead of criminal defense. He would never want to cross swords with her in a courtroom.

Jim was an airline pilot and retired Air Force colonel. Unassuming and modest, he was the epitome of a man who knows his accomplishments speak for themselves. Much to Trevor's delight, Charles soon developed an interest in both the law and in flying. After all, what teenager hasn't at one time or another dreamed about being the next Atticus Finch, delivering a spellbinding argument before a dozen jurors, or an airline pilot, expertly navigating a passenger jet filled with 300 or more trusting souls through the skies?

One day Trevor jokingly mentioned to him that someday in the future he would have to pick one profession or the other. Charles countered with: "who says? There's no law against me doing both." Trevor had to admit he didn't know of any such law and wondered if Charles had gotten that bit of legal advice from Becky. Every time they met, Charles had a seemingly endless string of questions about becoming an airline pilot and about becoming an attorney. Jim and Becky always took the time to answer his questions and never seemed bothered.

To top things off, like any sixteen-year-old, Charles was interested in fast cars. Jim owned two immaculate, show-quality GM muscle cars: a Viper Blue 1967 Firebird 400 convertible and an equally pristine red 1968 Chevy SS/RS Camaro. Before long Charles's interest shifted from Ford products, which Trevor favored, to GM muscle cars. Trevor often said he would someday have a talk with Jim about brainwashing his son; maybe he could get him to clean up his room.

It was a little after 10:00 a.m. and the four of them were enjoying each other's company at a favorite breakfast café in Oceanside, twenty miles south of San Clemente, when Trevor got a call from Scott Donaldson, Trevor's sometime partner. Donaldson knew Trevor was off that day and would have never called if it weren't important. Excusing himself from the table with a promise to be right back, he rose and walked out into the brisk morning air.

Answering the call on what would have surely been the last ring before going to voicemail, he growled into the phone: "it's my day off. Don't tell me I need to come in."

"Not yet, but I wanted to be the first to break the news to you. We think Joshua Ward was murdered sometime last night or this morning," said Donaldson.

"Why do you think that?"

"Well, we've got a body and we've got his ID."

"Okay, go on."

"We can't positively match the body to the ID yet."

"Look, just tell me what's going on. My omelet's getting cold."

"Okay, the body we have was run over by a train. Whoever was inside is mushed up so badly we don't have a face to match with the ID."

"So, assuming it was Ward, what makes you think he was murdered? Maybe he committed suicide. He had to know we were closing in on him."

"No, it was murder, no doubt about that. He was stuffed inside a steel barrel and then put on the tracks. There are tie straps locked around what's left of his wrist and ankles. We're pretty sure he was still alive before the train hit him."

"Why's that?"

"A couple of hundred feet down the tracks we found a lid that appears to go with the steel drum. If he was dead when he was put into the can, why put a lid on it and why restrain him? Also, the can is pretty much destroyed, but it looks like there was some kind of an air hole cut into it."

"Gee, what a shame, couldn't have happened to a nicer guy, I'm going to miss him. Can I get back to my breakfast now?" Trevor deadpanned.

"One last thing: we did a welfare check of his home. There was blood and a broken plate on the floor and a gun on the stairway, and a bunch of loose change lying around. There might have been some kind of scuffle. Maybe the blood belongs to whoever took Ward out."

"Yeah, maybe it does. I'm betting it's going to turn out to be Ward's."

"Why do you think that?"

"Just a hunch, now can I get back to something more important than Joshua Ward, like my breakfast?"

"I'll need to look at your files."

"I'm hanging up now. My omelet is getting cold." With that Trevor terminated the call and shut his phone off. This was father-son weekend. He didn't need any more interruptions.

Back in the café, Becky asked if everything was okay and offered to let Charles hang out with them if he needed to go. Trevor smiled and shook his head. "Everything's fine."

Jim was explaining aerodynamics to Charles; specifically how power could equal lift while attitude could equal speed. Charles was listening so intently that he hadn't even noticed his dad's reappearance. Trevor was once again struck by how patient Jim could be. It was his day off. He shouldn't have to be thinking about flying.

Finally aware that his dad was once again seated at the table, Charles asked: "hey Dad, is everything okay, do you have to go back to work?"

Shaking his head, Trevor answered: "everything's okay. We're good for the weekend."

People like Joshua Ward needed killing. Onetime, back when Trevor worked for the San Luis Obispo Sheriff's Department, he made a decision that went against everything he'd been taught about bringing criminals to justice. It was a decision that could jeopardize everything he had worked for. It was a decision that would label him a criminal himself. It was the right decision then and it was still the right decision, regardless of what the law said. Although the murder scene was less than two miles from his home in Cypress Shores, he would not allow himself to be pulled into the investigation. It was his day off.

CHAPTER 17

It was still dark outside on what would turn out to be a beautiful Saturday morning when that damned siren went off again. Saturday was Lee's day to sleep in. Last night, for some reason, he decided to stay up late and watch a Netflix movie featuring Steve McQueen as Tom Horn, the ruthless vigilante/range detective from the late 1800's. Much to his surprise he learned bright and early the next morning that he forgot to turn off the alarm clock before going to bed. His forgetfulness probably cost him at least three hours' sleep.

For just a moment in his mind's eye he saw himself retrieving the nine-millimeter from his nightstand and killing that cursed clock. However, his good sense prevailed and he followed his traditional wakeup routine by grabbing a pillow and hurling it toward the ear-piercing sound. Also following tradition, he missed. The clock continued to mock him. Good thing he hadn't tried to shoot it. Why would he ever think he could take it out with a pistol if he couldn't even hit it with his pillow? It still hadn't learned to shut itself off, so he climbed out of bed and while fumbling for the off button, muttered to the clock that it had been granted a stay of execution, "at least until I can get some target practice in."

By nine o'clock he was puttering around in his workshop, looking for something to do just to kill time. His plan was to call Krystal this morning at ten; not too early and not so late that she might already be gone for the day. He swept the floor and waxed his surfboard, then decided to go out to his shed and do some welding on the roll bar he was building for his pickup just in case he ever decided to take it four-wheeling.

By nine-thirty he decided to put off finishing the roll bar and instead walk down to the beach to check out the waves. He wasn't all that interested in the surf. What he really wanted to do was break in the brand-new cowboy boots Sharona helped him pick out.

At 10:00 a.m. on the button, Lee picked up his cell phone and punched in the number Krystal gave him just a couple of nights ago. She picked up on the third ring.

Lee stammered into the phone: "hi Krystal, it's Lee, Lee Edwards."

"Hi Lee, Lee Edwards. Would it be okay if I just call you Lee?" she laughed.

"You might have to check with Sharona first." He replied.

The conversation got better and better as they talked. She lived in Huntington Beach, just a little more than a thirty-minute drive up the coast from Lee's residence in South Laguna and yes, she would love to ride with him to the stables tomorrow. In fact, she suggested, since South Laguna was closer to San Juan Capistrano, maybe she should drive down and meet him at his house. "That way I can snoop around for any clues that you might be an axe murderer or serial killer." She said with another laugh.

"You won't find anything. I'm a very meticulous axe murderer. Some of my clients are experts at it. I've learned from the best."

"Then how do I know I can trust you?"

"Of course you can trust me. I'm a lawyer."

Before long, Krystal said she had to get going. She was going to spend the rest of the morning and probably part of the afternoon going over her torts assignment for law school. However, before they hung up, she said there was something she wanted to ask: "did you really buy a pair of cowboy boots just to impress me?"

"Where did you hear that? It had to have come from Sharona. She told you, didn't she?"

"I would never divulge my sources. Just answer the question, counselor."

"Uh, well I did buy a pair of boots, and, yeah, I guess they are cowboy boots."

Krystal was thoroughly enjoying his unease. "Answer the whole question, counselor." She demanded.

"Okay, yes, I did buy a pair of cowboy boots so you wouldn't think I looked like some kind of dork."

"That's sweet. I'm flattered." She said with a lilt in her voice, then added: "I'll see you tomorrow, and I'll make sure to bring a breath mint."

Lee was flabbergasted. "Hey, wait a minute! I never said any such thing. Sharona made it up. Oh my God, I'm going to kill Sharona. Did she really say I said that?"

"See you tomorrow Lee, Lee Edwards." Krystal responded with an undeniably playful tone in her voice.

CHAPTER 18

Sunday couldn't have gone better. Krystal looked stunning, yet natural in her cowboy boots and jeans and Levi's jacket and with her hair in a ponytail that stuck out of the rear of her baseball cap. Lee, on the other hand, couldn't quite pull off the ranch hand look. About the only things he was wearing that didn't look brand new were his Levis and his Dodgers baseball cap. His boots still needed breaking in and his canvas Carhartt jacket was stiff and not yet sun-faded. He couldn't have cared less, though. No one would be looking at him, or Ricky for that matter, when they could be looking at Krystal and Sharona.

The stables were about two miles out of downtown San Juan Capistrano and just off California Highway 74, also known as the Ortega Highway, best known for its dangerous curves and traffic collisions as well as the notoriety it had gained in the early 1980s as a dumping ground for William Bonin, also known as the "Freeway Killer."

Lee and Krystal arrived in his Porsche and pulled in right on time at 10:00 a.m. Sharona and Ricky were guiding a couple of horses into a four-horse, fifth-wheel trailer nestled into the bed of a dark red crew cab pickup that Lee assumed was the ranch truck. These were the last two horses to be loaded, and Sharona explained that they would be transporting them about five miles up the highway to Ronald W. Caspers Wilderness State Park, an 8,000-acre park with plenty of trails to follow and no traffic to worry about. She told them there were mountain lions and rattlesnakes living in the park, but they probably wouldn't encounter any at this time of year.

Lee thoroughly enjoyed being on horseback. Sharona had picked out the perfect horse for him: one that was a little spirited, but responsive to his commands. About two hours into the ride they came on a trough and Sharona said it would be a good place to water the horses. They dismounted and walked their horses to the trough.

Standing next to her horse, Krystal held the reins and patted its shoulder as it drank. Sharona reached over and took the reins from Lee, then nodded her head toward Krystal. Taking the hint, Lee walked directly over to Krystal and stepped between her and the water trough, then leaned forward and kissed her. Krystal seemed mildly surprised, but quickly recovered and returned his kiss.

"Hey, knock it off you guys, you're scaring the horses." Sharona laughingly called out. "I'm sure glad that's finally over."

"Me too," said Krystal, smiling up at Lee.

The ride ended too soon. Sharona proved to be an excellent guide: taking them on a route that accommodated each rider's skill level without making it too easy for the most experienced. It was obvious Krystal hadn't exaggerated when she said she'd grown up around horses. She was every bit Sharona's equal as a horsewoman.

Back at the stables they unloaded the horse trailer and Krystal showed Lee how to curry a horse. Sharona handed him a curry comb and gestured toward his mount. "Have at it, cowboy," she said. "Just make sure to give him a wide berth when you walk behind him. Horses love to kick lawyers."

Once the horses were groomed, they were led back to their stalls and given hay and pellets scooped from a fifty-five-gallon steel drum near the barn door. Lee thanked Sharona for the incredible day, and just like that it was time to leave. It had been one of those magical days that there are too few of.

CHAPTER 19

Trevor Wilkins sat at his desk. It was just 7:30 and he was on his second cup of coffee. Breakfast had been a first cup and an apple fritter that he consumed on his way to work. Monday mornings were always hard. Today would not be any easier. He and Scott Donaldson were planning to meet and go over the file on Joshua Ward. The remains found on the railroad tracks in San Clemente were still not yet positively identified, although the results from what fingerprints the medical examiner was able to get were expected to come back at any time. It was, of course, sensational news and all of the newspapers splashed the story across their front page, complete with whatever pictures of the crime scene they were able to get. Despite the constant stream of questions from the various reporters Donaldson was careful not to divulge the discovery of Ward's wallet, nor the evidence found during the welfare check of Ward's home. Despite these precautions, one newspaper, *The Orange County Times,* was somehow able to obtain that information and in an effort to one-up the competition included it in its front-page article. This information was going to be released at some point anyway, but it was always preferable to do that at a time when the Investigators felt was right. The *Times* apparently had a source within the sheriff's department. They didn't need that.

At a little after 8:00 Donaldson walked into Trevor's office and sat down. Picking up a few pages of the file that Trevor had already reviewed and set aside, he asked, "Who did it?"

"Who did what? Kill Ward or leak the story to *The Orange County Times*?"

"Who killed Ward, of course. Right now, I couldn't care less who the leaker is."

"Whoever killed Ward did us all a favor. We know he killed the Jansen boy. There is no doubt, and I had enough evidence to show he was good for at least four others. We found their DNA in Ward's van when it was in impound. He kept locks of hair taped to the pages of a picture album that was in there. We sent them off to be analyzed. Wanna bet who they almost certainly belonged to? The evidence would have been overwhelming on at least five child abduction murders. If his 1538.5 motion hadn't been granted, we would have him well on his way to San Quentin and their magic needle.

I know the law says Ward's death was a murder and it's our job to find the killer and bring him or her to justice, whichever is in this case. I'll do my job, but Ward needed to die. If there was one iota of evidence to show Ward may not have committed those crimes it would be different, but it's not there."

"Sounds like you're rooting for his killer."

"I'm rooting for justice."

"So what happens to the DNA evidence if it turns out that it's Ward on those tracks? Can we tell the parents of those four other boys we think we found their killer?"

"As far as I know we won't ever be able to tell them their son's DNA was found in his vehicle."

"If Ward is gone, you'd think there would a motion of some kind to set aside Judge Mackenzie's order." Said Donaldson.

That's something you would have to ask the D.A.'s office.

"How do you think his lawyer sleeps at night?"

"Pretty well, I bet. It's all a big game. We bring him the clients, and he gets the big money to do what he does."

"So, who killed Ward?"

"Good question. By my estimate there are an endless number of potential suspects. The 1538.5 hearing was televised and from what I heard some of the feeds were broadcast—or at least reported—nationally. So, out of 300-plus million people who could potentially have watched or had knowledge of the outcome, how many are out there who want to be vigilantes? Closer to home, Conner Jansen's father would have plenty of motive; so would the parents of at least four other little boys who met the same fate. Let's start with the vigilantes. You start in New York and I'll start in Los Angeles, and we'll meet in the middle and go over our notes."

"Very funny, how about we start with you," Donaldson interjected with a grin. "You had him dead to rights and he got away. That had to hurt. If you confess right now, we can clear this up in record time and we'll probably both get medals."

"Okay," Trevor responded. "I'll confess if you promise to testify that you beat it out of me."

"Who you gonna hire for a lawyer?"

"Lee Edwards."

"Screw him. He's a suspect too. Maybe Ward didn't pay him."

Just then Trevor's desk phone buzzed. Trevor lifted the receiver and the receptionist said: "Parkland Rice from the *Orange County Times* is on the line. Should I transfer him?"

Frowning, Trevor responded: "tell him I'm busy. He'll get a statement from the department when we have something to say," then hung up.

Less than two minutes later the receptionist buzzed again. "He says it could be about Joshua Ward. He doesn't want a statement. He said it's very important that he speak with you. He said he might have some evidence."

Wondering if one of the reporters from the *Times* had picked something up at the crime scene, he said: "okay, put him through," then activated the speakerphone. "This is Investigator Wilkins. You are on speakerphone with me and Investigator Donaldson. What can I do for you?"

"Investigator Wilkins, hi, this is Parkland Rice from the *Orange County Times.* I have something I think you need to see."

"Go on, what is it?"

"I'm not sure," came the response. "It might be nothing or it might be important, but I think you need to see it."

"If you don't know what it is how do you know I need to see it? Describe it to me."

"Well, I think it's a letter of some sort. It came in an envelope addressed to me in care of the newspaper. Inside is some kind of note with both our names on the top."

"I don't have a lot of time. What's it say?"

"That's the thing: I can't read it. I'm pretty sure it's written in Morse code. It's all dots and dashes."

Trevor looked at Donaldson. "We'll be right there. Don't touch it."

Twenty minutes later the investigators walked into Parkland Rice's office. Parkland greeted each man with a handshake. Aside from suspecting that

81

he might be getting information from someone inside the department, both investigators had a favorable impression of him. He always reported the news in a fair, unbiased manner.

Parkland closed the door, then pointed at an unfolded sheet of paper on his desk. "There it is," he said. "It may be nothing. It may be something. I can't read it, but the salutation is to both of us, so I didn't want to toss it."

Both investigators examined the paper. The salutation was clearly printed by a word processor and read: "To Investigator Trevor Wilkins, OCSD and Parkland Rice of the *Orange County Times.*" The rest was a series of dots and dashes, just as Parkland said. The code was short and handwritten:

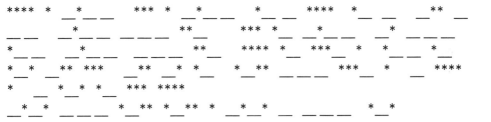

"Is that Morse code? Anybody know what it says?" Parkland asked.

"It looks like it. We need to figure out what, if anything, it all means," said Trevor. "Look, I know you have to report the news and the message or whatever it is came addressed to you, but we don't even know if it's connected to any active or cold cases. It might even be something some crank dreamed up. We just don't know. Until we find out, I would appreciate it if you don't put anything about it in your paper. In return, we'll promise not to flush out whoever is leaking information to you, deal?"

Parkland thought it over for a few seconds. The note could be some kind of a hoax and he certainly didn't want to jeopardize his paper's credibility. "You have a deal. Just promise me that if it turns out to be newsworthy, you'll give me the first crack at it."

"You've got it," said Trevor. "By the way, we are going to need you to come down to the Sheriff's station and get fingerprinted."

"Why?"

"Because I doubt you wore gloves when you opened the envelope, or when you handled the note. If the note turns out to be relevant to any of our cases, we need to be able to eliminate your fingerprints."

Nodding, Parkland replied: "okay that makes sense. I'll come in this afternoon if it's okay."

"This afternoon would be fine. Thank you for contacting us about this."

Donaldson walked to their vehicle and retrieved a plastic baggie and a pair of surgical gloves while Wilkins stayed behind and took pictures of the note with his smart phone. When Donaldson returned, he put the note and envelope in the baggie and secured it with a seal and initialed the seal. The two investigators then thanked Parkland Rice again and left.

Once in the car, Trevor turned to Donaldson and said: "I didn't want to say it in front of him, but it is Morse code and I can read it."

"So, what does it say?"

"I'll need a pen and paper."

Back in his office with Donaldson staring over his shoulder as if the characters on the note might suddenly reappear in cursive, Wilkins downloaded the picture he took from his iPhone onto his computer and stared at it briefly before he started printing one letter at a time on his scratch pad. Sensing he was in the way, Donaldson took a seat in front of Wilkins' desk. When Wilkins finally finished deciphering the note he looked up and said: "I haven't done this in a long time. Anyway, it says:

'Hey hey,

What do you say,

Now you have Ward's DNA.'"

"Well, I guess that pretty much confirms that it's Ward. How do you happen to know Morse Code?"

"When I was a kid I had a ham radio operator's license. You had to know Morse code to get a license back then. I'm pretty sure that requirement has since been eliminated."

"Is it like riding a bike, you just instinctively know it once you've learned it?"

"No, it's more like reciting a poem you knew a long time ago: it comes back to you."

"So, is that it, just a short little poem?"

"No, there's more."

"What more?"

"The last line says: "Love, The Trash Collector." That makes this case a hell of a lot bigger."

"How so?"

"When I was with San Luis Obispo County Sheriff's Department, a parolee was murdered. Whoever did it drove a couple of nails into his head, then hooked an extension cord to the nails and plugged it in."

"Whoa, really?"

"Yeah, really, but there's more. The killer left a note; a poem, actually. It was handwritten in Morse code and signed 'The Trash Collector.' The case was never solved."

"So why handwritten in Morse code?"

"C'mon, don't you see? We're being taunted. How do you analyze or compare a series of hand-written dots and dashes? Whoever did this is saying: 'here you go, I've handwritten my messages and all the writing samples in the world won't help you catch me.' The salutation and address were done on a printer because the note had to get to its destination, but they couldn't be handwritten. I'd bet a year's pay we aren't going to get any prints off the letter or envelope. I'd bet another year's pay the stamp is one of those you peel and stick and so is the envelope flap. We're dealing with someone too smart to screw up and leave that kind of evidence."

"So why was it addressed to you?" asked Donaldson. "Why not send it directly here instead of going through a newspaper?"

"It was probably sent to me because I was the investigating officer on both cases. My picture was all over the papers in San Luis and I was on national television at the Ward hearing. As for why he sent it by way of the newspaper, I have no idea."

"Publicity maybe?"

"I don't think so. We never heard from the Trash Collector again after the murder in San Luis Obispo and we never disclosed there was a note. If this person—or persons, plural, for that matter—wanted publicity, they could have sent it through the newspaper up there just like they've done down here. It's got to be more personal than that. It's a note to say: 'I'm still here,' or maybe 'I'm back'."

"That can't be a good thing."

Trevor responded in a somewhat more cheerful voice: "well, we've already narrowed down our list of possible suspects. There's only what: about three hundred thousand or so people living in San Luis Obispo County? And there can't be any more than three million in Orange County, give or take. That's way better than the three hundred million we started with."

"Let's start with Ward's attorney," said Trevor. "Before I left the courtroom I heard Ward ask for something. I think he asked for a ride home. Edwards might have been the last to see him alive. Or he might know if there were any death threats."

CHAPTER 20

Monday morning started off with a routine DUI case. Melania Sanchez was stopped by a Newport Beach Police Department motorcycle officer and subsequently failed a field sobriety test. The officer put her under arrest and took her to the station where she blew a .13 on the breathalyzer; way above the legal limit. The only real issue was whether the officer was justified in making the initial stop. Not surprisingly, Ms. Sanchez denied any bad driving. The case sounded interesting to Lee until he saw the dash cam video. Something about the way she was driving caught the officer's attention and he dutifully activated his dash-cam from about two car lengths behind her. The video included the part where she came to a traffic light at an intersection and made a complete stop without encroaching into the pedestrian crosswalk. Unfortunately, the tape also showed the light was green at the time.

After a thorough review of her case Ms. Sanchez finally agreed to plead guilty and accept her punishment. With the help of the official court interpreter the arraignment was over in less than five minutes. Fifteen minutes later the paperwork appeared and Lee was free to return to his office. This was his only scheduled courtroom appearance of the day.

On his way out of the courthouse Lee remembered he had missed a call while tending to Melania's hearing. As he suspected, the display indicated the call was from Sharona. The voicemail was short and direct: "call me." Lee hesitated for a few seconds. The office was only a short distance from Harbor Court and he would be there in a couple of minutes anyway. On the other hand, Sharona knew where he was and also knew he would be coming back petty early. If she felt it was necessary to leave a voicemail it had to be important.

Lee called her back. Sharona answered with: "are you on your way in?"

"Yeah, I am. What's up?"

"I just wanted to make sure you weren't going somewhere I didn't know about. You have an appointment with Investigators Trevor Wilkins and Scott Donaldson from the sheriff's department."

"What time and why am I just learning about this?"

"They just called this morning. I told them you should be back by 1:00. I wanted to put them off until tomorrow or Wednesday, but you're booked solid with court appearances and client appointments. It sounded pretty important."

"It must be. Why else would they want to personally meet with a defense attorney?"

"Maybe they finally discovered that you manufactured your own bar card. I've been sending them anonymous tips since I started here. Do you want me to get you a lawyer, one with a real bar card?"

Sharona's good-natured insolence never failed to brighten his day. "You know that if I get arrested you will be out of a job, don't you?"

"What job? If this were a job, I'd be getting paid what I'm worth."

"I'm on my way in. How about I stop off at the deli and pick us up some lunch?"

"Sounds good; see ya in a bit."

At one o'clock, Wilkins and Donaldson walked into the waiting room and handed Sharona their cards, then introduced themselves. Sharona took a cursory look at their cards and buzzed Lee in his office. "Sheriff's Department Investigators Wilkins and Donaldson are here to see you."

Lee told her to send them in, and stood up to greet the two investigators. He didn't know Donaldson and, as men do when meeting for the first time, instinctively sized him up: late thirties to early forties, five foot nine or ten, at least thirty pounds overweight with a sizable paunch, thinning brown hair laced with silver strands, and a ruddy complexion. Unlike Wilkins, Donaldson did not present himself with the grace and coordination of an athlete. Lee handed each investigator a business card then took a seat behind his desk and gestured to the leather chairs in front. "What can I do for you?"

Noticing a framed picture of Lee casually stepping over a fallen opponent, Donaldson asked: "is that you?"

"Well, it used to be." Lee replied.

"So, you really are the same Leroy Edwards? Some of the guys at the station were speculating on that."

"I guess their suspicions are correct; can't get anything past you guys." Lee responded.

"Anyway, I'm pretty sure you didn't come in to rehash my boxing career. What can I do for you?" Lee asked.

"We're here to get some information on Joshua Ward." said Trevor.

Lee nodded. "That's what I suspected. I don't know how much I can help you, but I'll be willing to discuss anything that isn't covered by attorney-client privilege."

"You know he's been murdered, right?"

"Yeah, I heard. A real shame. Guess that one wasn't back on the streets very long, huh?"

"The problem is that we now have another murderer out there. Whatever Ward was, he's now a homicide victim and we have to catch his killer. We can't have vigilantism or retribution or whatever the motive might have been. So, excuse my ignorance, but doesn't attorney-client privilege expire at the death of the client?" asked Donaldson.

"Unfortunately, no, it continues indefinitely. You'd be surprised to learn that the law firm of the lead attorney in the Lizzy Borden case still keeps the files confidential. Attorney-client privilege still applies. That case dates back to 1892. All the players are long dead and if they released those files it could possibly clear up one of the all-time American cold cases, yet they are bound by privilege."

"No kidding? I didn't know that."

"It's true. Personally I think the rule is a bit over-broad, but that's the way it works."

"Okay, unfortunately I suppose that's going to drastically reduce what you can tell us."

"Well, I'll tell you what I can," said Lee.

"Do have any idea who would want to kill Joshua Ward?" asked Trevor.

Lee's eyebrows shot up as if he thought Trevor was putting him on.

"Let me rephrase that and narrow it down. Do you know of anyone who is capable of killing Joshua Ward and would have a reason to do so?"

"Let's narrow it down even further: anyone who would be capable of stuffing him in a fifty-five-gallon drum in order to kill him?" asked Donaldson.

"Was he dead or alive when he was put in the barrel?"

"We think he was alive," said Trevor.

"Okay," responded Lee. "That probably narrows it down. I'm assuming you have already considered Cooper Jansen's family members."

"We haven't spoken with them yet. In fact, you're our first interview."

"Well, we did get a few death threats here at the office. Some directed at him, some at us."

Donaldson looked surprised: "directed at you?"

"And Sharona," Lee replied. "Defense attorneys get them all the time. We get more of them than prosecutors do. And I'm pretty sure we get fewer Christmas cards."

"Did any of these threats seem more serious than the others?"

"We don't ignore any of them. We take appropriate precautions, but we're not about to put a steel door out front, or put Sharona behind bulletproof glass or anything like that. Would you like to see them?"

"You mean you keep them?"

"We do." He said, then reached for his phone. "Sharona, would you copy the threats from the Ward case and bring them in, please?"

"Did Ward ever mention anyone he was afraid of?" asked Trevor.

"Sorry, that gets into privileged conversation. I can't talk about that."

"Understood, let's narrow down our earlier question a bit further. Is there anyone you personally suspect in this killing?"

"No one jumps out at me, but I promise to contact you if anyone comes to mind."

Sharona stuck her head in and looked at Lee, putting on her most professional demeanor. "I've got those copies, Mr. Edwards."

"Thank you Sharona, come on in."

Sharona put the manila envelope on the desk then returned to the reception room. Both Investigators looked surprised by the thickness of the envelope. There were probably thirty or more pages inside.

"All of those are from the Ward case?"

"They are." Lee responded. "It was a highly publicized case. In my world the more publicity a case gets, the more threats I get."

Lee handed Trevor the envelope and the two investigators rose to leave. Just as they reached the door, Lee said: "if you find this guy, tell him I'll represent him pro bono if I can get past the conflict of interest issue. Despite you're positions on it I'm not going to lose any sleep over the loss of Joshua Ward. He needed killing."

CHAPTER 21

There he was again: that damned cat, skulking across the floor of the storage room. Anthony Mesa, the part-time bouncer/bartender at his Uncle Manuel's Hasta la Vista Cantina, was busy mopping. It was a slow night and it was getting late. Anthony hoped he could convince *Tio* Manuel to close a little early. Getting rid of the cat was just one more chore that needed finishing before he could go home.

"*Tio,* that cat's back." Anthony called.

"You must have left the back door open again when you went out to the dumpster." Manuel replied from behind the bar, where he was re-stocking bottled beer.

"I was just out there for a minute."

"I told you that's all it takes."

"Open the door. I'll try to chase him out."

Manuel walked through the storage room at the back of the small building and opened the door leading to the alley. He instantly noticed an older model white car to his right idling by the dumpsters. Two men with shaved heads were spray-painting his wall. Stepping quickly through the rear door, Manuel shouted: "hey, get out of here! What do you think you're doing?"

Maybe because of Manuel's short stature, or maybe because they had him outnumbered two-to-one, neither man seemed concerned. Ronald Carpenter, by far the larger of the two, often used his size for intimidation. He stepped into Manuel's comfort zone. "Who's gonna make us?" He growled.

"I'm going to" said Anthony as he stepped through the door and Manuel stepped aside. Standing just shy of arm's length from Carpenter, Anthony, at six foot four and two hundred and sixty pounds, was an equal match. Jesse Cardinal, the second skinhead, froze in his tracks, unsure what to do.

"Get outta my face, beaner," yelled Carpenter.

Manuel smiled inside. This punk was yelling to hide his fear. It's the quiet ones you have to be careful around.

Eye-to-eye with Carpenter, Anthony placed his hands behind his neck and leaned slightly back as if relaxing in an easy chair and apparently exposing his midsection. He looked relaxed and unconcerned. By all appearances, he had dropped his guard. "Make me." He replied.

Manuel had seen Anthony assume this deceptive pose before; his posture looked non-menacing and could go a long way toward defusing the situation. However, he was actually now prepared to do battle if necessary. Troublemakers who took the bait seldom left under their own power. Anthony's fingers were not interlocked behind his head.

The skinhead took the bait. Thinking he had Anthony at a disadvantage, he quickly brought the spray can up, intending to spray Anthony's eyes before going to work on him with his white-laced Dr. Martens boots.

He wasn't near quick enough. Anthony reacted with rattlesnake-like speed. His right hand shot toward the skinhead's face, index and middle fingers locked straight out and slightly spread.

There was no time for Carpenter to react. Anthony's fingers dug deeply into the skinhead's open eyes, temporarily blinding him. He cried out in pain and his hands flew up to cover his eyes. He folded forward and dropped to his knees, the spray can falling from his grasp.

Anthony wasn't done yet. As if going for a field goal, he stepped in and fired his foot into the skinhead's face, the force lifting the punk's head and dropping him onto his back. He wasn't going to be getting up any time soon.

Now trying to rein in the adrenaline coursing through his veins, Anthony took a step toward the second skinhead. In the calmest voice he could muster and without taking his eyes off his next potential adversary, he pointed at Jesse Cardinal and stage-whispered: "you're next *puto.*"

Jesse didn't want any part of it. He raised his hands in surrender and slowly shook his head.

Anthony glared at him. "You're not as stupid as you look. Now get your Nazi ass in the car and get the hell out of here." Pointing down at Ronald Carpenter, still writhing in pain, he said: "take that piece of trash with you. If you ever come around again you're not gonna like what happens. You got that, *pendejo?*"

Nodding slowly, Cardinal answered in a subdued voice: "yeah, I got it." He slowly bent forward, keeping his head up so as not to lose sight of Anthony as his hand reached for the spray paint.

Anthony took another step forward. "You hungry?" He growled. "Cause if you touch that can I'm gonna feed it to you."

"I was just going to throw it in the car."

"Leave it there. You punks are done for the night."

Miguel and Anthony watched as the two skinheads drove away.

"Do you think we should call the cops?" Anthony asked.

"No, the cops aren't going to do anything except make a report. Those guys aren't coming back. I don't want to deal with the Alcohol Beverage Control Board. Too many incidents, and they could shut me down. It'd be more trouble than it's worth. I'll get someone out here tomorrow to clean up my wall."

"I should have made them do it."

Miguel chuckled at the thought, then said: "throw those spray cans away, we still have to catch that cat before the health department takes away my 'A' rating."

"You worry too much, *Tio*. Just tell them we have a cat because we can't control the rats without him."

Anthony always had a way to make Miguel laugh. The big man tossed the spray cans into the dumpster and the two returned to the task of herding a feral cat out of the cantina.

An hour later and three blocks west, a white 1971 Oldsmobile 442 pulled up to the curb. Inside were Ronald Carpenter and Jesse Cardinal, staring at the dim glow cast on the sidewalk by the Hasta la Vista's large marbled window. It was Ronald's car, but Jesse was behind the wheel. Ronald sat directly behind him in the back seat nursing his broken and bloodied nose. A civilian version of a Kalashnikov AK-47 that they had just retrieved from one of the gang's rented garages lay beside him. The curved banana clip held thirty rounds of 7.62 x 39-millimeter ammunition, each bullet casing carefully wiped clean and coated with WD-40. It was getting late. Although the cantina would be closing soon, they were prepared to wait all night if necessary. Somebody had to pay for the beat down.

Four blocks east of the Hasta la Vista and on the same side of the street sat the Fourth Street Grocery and Deli, a small, all-night convenience store. Twenty-four-year-old Stephanie Alarcon was working the graveyard shift with a little over half an hour to go. Trying to stay busy, she walked into the storage room to retrieve items to replenish what had been sold throughout the day. Time passed faster when she kept busy and this close to midnight it was always slow.

Worn out from working two jobs, she kept telling herself it would soon be worth it. She and her husband, Richard, a hardworking city employee, were saving for a house of their own. She would then be able to quit her night job and cut back on her hours at the beauty parlor to spend more time watching her daughter, Janine, grow. It was a warm summer night and Richard would be getting some much-needed sleep. There was no need to wake him to come pick her up. She would walk the four blocks home.

Her replacement finally arrived at eleven-fifty, like always. They exchanged pleasantries and Stephanie told him the cash register was about out of receipt paper and she had been unable to find any to reload it with. Saying he knew where it was, he bid her goodnight. Stephanie grabbed her purse and a plastic bag containing a tube of teething gel and a box of tropical fruit mix. Janine loved tropical fruit mix. She accounted for the items on the ledger, put them in her canvas shopping bag and walked out the door.

Even at this late hour Stephanie felt safe walking home. It was a short walk and there were plenty of streetlights. The only times she ever felt uncomfortable was when she walked past the Hasta la Vista. During the week it closed at midnight, the same time she got off work. Once in a while as she passed by she would hear catcalls and whistles from one or more of the patrons who had a bit too much to drink.

That all came to an end a couple of months ago when Manuel and Anthony got wind of it and stationed themselves outside at closing time to make sure everyone was on their best behavior. She eventually struck up a friendship with both men and on more than one occasion—usually Cinco de Mayo or some other traditionally rowdy holiday—one or the other had escorted her to her door just to ensure her safety.

As Stephanie was leaving the convenience store, Miguel and Anthony were giving up the notion that they would find the cat. They'd thoroughly searched the stock room, the main room, behind the bar and both bathrooms, and even looked into the heating ducts. The cat was nowhere to be found.

"He must have gotten away while we were outside," said Anthony.

"Maybe he did. Let's go home. I'll look again tomorrow. Are you coming in tomorrow?" "I can be here about six." Anthony replied. His hours were planned around his studies at Santa Ana College.

Stephanie turned right and began her stroll. She was less than twenty feet from the Hasta la Vista when Miguel and his nephew exited through the front door, still hoping to spot the cat.

By the time the two men stepped onto the sidewalk, Stephanie was five feet closer. In the semi-darkness, with the streetlight behind her, she smiled and thought: *my protectors*.

On the other side of the street, three blocks away, Jesse Cardinal and Ronald Carpenter alerted.

Anthony glanced to his left and saw Stephanie. He offered his usual greeting: "*buenos dios, chica bonita.*"

"*Que pasa, mis amigos?*" She replied with a smile.

Inside the Oldsmobile, Ronald rolled the windows down and growled: "let's do it."

"There's three of them. Let's wait." said Jesse.

"I don't care how many there are, just drive."

Jesse put the Oldsmobile into gear and did as he was instructed.

Stephanie and her friends were now standing no more than four feet apart and facing each other in the wash of light escaping through the frosted front window of the Hasta la Vista. She was the only one facing west and the only one who saw the white car approach. Its lights were off.

Miguel and Anthony heard the speeding vehicle approach, but paid it little mind. Fourth Street wasn't a particularly busy street, but it was not uncommon for the occasional carload of kids to speed by.

The Oldsmobile slid to a stop in front of the cantina. Ronald Carpenter emerged from the back seat and leaned out the window yelling "white America," then quickly brought the AK-47 up and began pulling the trigger, spraying bullets in all directions.

The attack was deadly effective. Bullet holes pockmarked the doorway. The large opaque marbled glass window disintegrated under the hail of gunfire. Ronald Carpenter continued firing until the AK had nothing left, then ducked back through the window, burning his hand on the smoking barrel in the process, and screamed at Jesse to: "go, go, go!"

Jesse floored the accelerator. The muscle car peeled rubber as they made their escape while both occupants screamed "white America, white America" through their open windows. The assault took less than twenty seconds.

Little more than a block away, Richard Alarcon awoke to the crackle of gunfire. Still half asleep, he glanced at the bedside clock. It was midnight.

Thinking it nothing more than a prank, probably a band of delinquents setting off fireworks, he waited silently to hear if the noise had wakened the baby. Hearing nothing but soft, contented snoring from Janine's crib, he drifted back to sleep. Stephanie should be home soon.

CHAPTER 22

Investigator Donaldson was already on the scene by the time Trevor arrived. It was just a little before 2:00 a.m. but a crowd of spectators were gathered behind the yellow crime scene tape. The street was cordoned off at the corner of Fourth Street and Avenida Santa Ynez, no more than seventy-five feet to the west of the Hasta la Vista. The Hasta la Vista's small parking lot filled the space between the cantina and the street corner. About six hundred feet to the east, access was blocked at the corner of Fourth Street and Avenida Verdugo. The alley to the rear of the cantina was likewise cordoned off.

Trevor worked his way through the crowd and began to step through the barrier when a young deputy called out: "please stay behind the barrier, sir." Trevor flashed the badge hanging from a chain around his neck. It had been under his windbreaker and he apologized for not keeping it visible. "No problem, sir," the deputy responded. Wilkins just nodded in acknowledgement. He hated being called "sir," but this was not the time to say anything.

Spotting Trevor, Donaldson immediately approached and greeted him: "looks like we've got a drive-by. Three victims, we don't know the connection to each other yet. Two are DOA, one was transported before I got here. It looks like they might have been gunned down as they were leaving the Mexican restaurant over there. There are twenty-four shell casings in the middle of the street. Eight of them are smashed, probably run over. I'm pretty sure we are going to find out they are 7.62 millimeter, I'm betting they used an AK."

Both Trevor and Donaldson were well acquainted with AK-47 rounds. If Donaldson said they were probably AK-47 rounds, you could take it to the bank.

"Any witnesses?" asked Trevor.

"Don't know yet. The 911 calls started coming in about shots fired just after midnight. I've got deputies canvassing the area. First on scene was a Deputy Sullivan, James Sullivan. I've got him sitting in my car waiting to speak with us. I wanted to wait until you got here. The second responder was Deputy Arthur Samuelson. He got here about a minute or so behind Sullivan. Samuelson's the one who called for medical assistance. He's waiting for us in his patrol car."

"Show me the shell casings," said Wilkins. Donaldson led him to a point short of the white dividing line in the middle of the street and directly across from the front entrance of the Hasta la Vista. Just as he had said, twenty-four expended cartridges lay on the ground.

"Okay," said Wilkins. "The expended rounds are in the middle of the street, so, assuming it was a drive-by and assuming it was from a car and not a bicycle or motorcycle, and assuming the car stayed in its lane, the car must have been heading east, otherwise the casings would be closer to the victims, either on the sidewalk, or in the gutter, or both."

"That's what I'm seeing," said Donaldson.

"So, the question is, was the shooter in a vehicle when the shots were fired, or was he or she on foot, or did he or she drive up in a vehicle and stop and get out? I'd say they were in a vehicle. A standard AK magazine holds 30 rounds, assuming a full clip. If a killer is going to fire twenty-four rounds, they're going to fire all thirty; after all, why stop? My bet is the missing casings were ejected back into the vehicle as he or she swung the weapon to the right. An AK ejects its shells to the right; that could put them back into the vehicle when the weapon is swept to the right. The shooter had to be stopped at the time the shots were fired because otherwise we wouldn't have casings confined to this area, they would have been spread down the street. Agree?"

"Absolutely," said Donaldson. I'm also thinking we're looking for some kind of muscle car."

'How'd you come up with that?"

"Look here." Donaldson raised his flashlight and illuminated two patches of burned rubber in the eastbound lane extending from just behind the litter of shell casings. Wilkins' gaze followed the beam and he instantly understood what Donaldson was getting at.

"Two burn marks, equal length," said Wilkins. "You're probably right: those definitely came from a Posi traction rear end. You won't find that on grandma's Prius. Good call."

97

"There's more, follow me," replied Donaldson. Another hundred feet or so east of the first set of burn marks, the investigators came on shorter but otherwise identical, parallel tracks of burned rubber. "I'm thinking this is where they hit second gear. I know grandma's Prius won't do that either. I'm going to go out on a limb and say our killer's getaway car has a standard transmission, most likely four on the floor. You ready to take a look at the victims?"

"Nothing more here?"

"Not that I could find."

Although Donaldson was already wearing white paper booties over his shoes, he pulled a small plastic bag from his back pocket containing two more pairs. After replacing his with a fresh pair and handing a set to Wilkins, the two walked to the front of the Hasta la Vista, where two bodies lay still in the predawn darkness.

The front door lay open and loose on its hinges where SWAT officers had forced their way in. In front of the door Anthony Mesa lay on his side, facing east with his legs on the sidewalk and the upper part of his body in the recess of the doorway. His right arm lay across his chest and his hand rested on the concrete. The entry skirt to the front door was built on a slight incline and a massive amount of blood streamed onto the sidewalk and trailed to the curb. His wounds were concealed beneath his shredded lightweight brown jacket and tan khakis.

On the sidewalk, no more than three feet away and below the shattered remnants of the front window, Stephanie Alarcon lay on her back, covered in broken glass and staring through sightless eyes at the heavens above. Blood was slowly leaking from a bullet wound under her left armpit and a pool of blood and brain matter congealing on the concrete below her head. Her purse and what appeared to be a plastic shopping bag lay next to her body. The contents of the bag were spilled across the sidewalk. From the contents of the bag it appeared that she either had, or was caring for, a baby.

It was obvious that Stephanie had taken at least two rounds. The medical examiner would confirm this on the autopsy table. From the location of the wounds, it probably didn't matter in what sequence she was hit. Either wound would have been fatal. A soft-point projectile entered her head just above the left eye and expanded on impact, then exited through the right rear, taking a baseball-sized portion of her skull with it. The wound to her body would no doubt have been equally devastating.

Stepping back, Trevor asked: "how badly wounded was the other victim?"

"According to Deputy Sullivan he was conscious but in a lot of pain. Sullivan said he appeared to be bleeding from wounds in the upper thigh and hip. He said the best he could do was put direct pressure on the wounds until the paramedics got here."

"Let's go talk to Sullivan."

Deputy James Sullivan exited Donaldson's official dark brown sedan as the two investigators approached. Trevor immediately noticed the dark blood stains on Sullivan's spruce green uniform and black athletic shoes.

Trevor extended his hand and introduced himself. "Good morning Deputy Sullivan, I'm Investigator Wilkins, you've already met Investigator Donaldson. What happened when you got here?"

"I got here at about 12:05, and reported in to the dispatcher right away. I pulled into the parking lot; that's my patrol car right there." He said as he pointed to a marked patrol vehicle that was pulled halfway into the parking lot on the west side of the Hasta la Vista. "My headlights flashed over the female on the sidewalk as I pulled in." He continued. "There was what appeared to be broken glass all over the sidewalk and all over her. I started to get out of my car when I saw those two cars sitting side by side at the rear of the lot." He pointed to a newish, dark-colored Chevy Impala and an older white Ford Taurus. "I didn't know whether there was somebody in them, it could have been a trap for all I knew. I started to call for backup when Deputy Samuelson pulled in alongside me. We shined our spotlights on the cars and couldn't see anyone inside, so we approached from as far apart as we could get. I was alongside the wall to the restaurant and Samuelson was on the passenger side. Except for the training we do at the range, that's the first time I've actually drawn my gun.

When we determined there was no one in either car, I went to the front to check on the victims while Samuelson called for the paramedics and SWAT and more deputies. We still didn't know if there might be someone in the restaurant, but we had both seen all the blood on the sidewalk and knew that if they were still alive we would have to do something right away."

"Okay, so what'd you do next?" Trevor asked.

"Two males were lying in the doorway. One was a smaller, older guy. The other is the big guy still lying there. He was on top of the older guy. I could hear moaning. The door was closed so I knew if there was anybody inside he couldn't see me if I went to them. It turned out the moaning was coming from the smaller guy. We checked the area around them for weapons. We didn't find anything. The female was lying right under the picture window in the front. We couldn't get to her without possibly exposing ourselves. We could tell she had a head wound. There was a lot of blood and what I assumed was brain matter. I was sure she was dead, so we concentrated on the two guys in the doorway. It may sound horrible, but I hope she was dead when we got here. I wouldn't be able to live with the thought that I might have been able to do something for her, but didn't."

"You did the right thing," said Trevor. "She was almost certainly dead before the shooting stopped. You couldn't have done anything for her."

"The big guy was not responsive." Sullivan continued. "But like I said, the other guy was moaning like he was in a lot of pain. I had to move the big guy off of him. I didn't want to move him at all in case he was still alive, but we didn't know. We knew the other guy was alive, though. There was a lot of blood and we didn't know if both of them were bleeding or just the guy on top, so we pulled him off the other guy.

"The smaller guy had at least four bullet wounds: two in his upper right thigh and two more in his right buttocks. They looked to me to be through-and-through. I'm guessing he was hit twice. He was bleeding pretty good, but not spurting like if he had been hit in an artery. Samuelson got the first aid kit and I applied field dressings to his wounds and then applied direct pressure where it looked to be bleeding the worst.

"The paramedics got here right after we got the field dressings on the older guy. They loaded him up and took him away. They checked the other guy and said he was dead. They wanted to tend to the female, but we wouldn't let them because she was lying right in front of that window and the building wasn't yet secured.

"The SWAT guys and three or four more patrol deputies and another ambulance showed up just as the paramedics were leaving. The SWAT team breached the door and cleared the building. All they found was a cat."

"There are some expended shell casings in the middle of the street, right in front of the cantina. We think they might have come from the perpetrators. Some of them are smashed. Do you have any idea how they got smashed?" asked Wilkins.

Deputy Sullivan shook his head: "I didn't even know about them, didn't see them. At one point the SWAT guys were pulled up in front, so were the paramedics. If I knew they were out there I would have been sure to protect them. Sorry."

"Don't worry about it," replied Donaldson. "You did a good job out here tonight. You possibly saved a life."

"Thank you sir. By the way, between Samuelson and I and the SWAT guys tromping around and us pulling the big guy off the other guy, I guess we pretty much contaminated the crime scene."

"That's okay," said Donaldson. "You did the right thing. You did a good job."

"Thank you, can I get back to work now?"

"Yeah, go ahead," said Donaldson.

While waiting to be interviewed, Deputy Samuelson radioed in the license numbers of the two vehicles in the parking lot. They came back registered to Manuel Trejo and Anthony Mesa. Both had addresses in Santa Ana. The investigators thanked him and told him to go ahead and get back to work, then walked to the front of the Hasta la Vista.

While surveying the scene, Fred Duval, the medical examiner, approached with a slip of paper in his hand and handed it to Donaldson. The paper had two names on it: Anthony Mesa and Stephanie Alarcon. Each name had a Santa Ana address next to it.

"This is what we got from the drivers' licenses." He explained. "Both were DOA. The female took two rounds: one went through her head. It entered just above her left eye and exited behind her right ear. I'm sure I don't have to tell you what the exit wound looks like. The other round entered the left side of the chest cavity and exited just under her right armpit. It appears the male took at least four rounds; I'll be able to confirm that when we do the autopsy. Some of those rounds were possibly through and through. The third victim, the one they took to the hospital, could have been hit by the same rounds that hit the DOA in the doorway."

Glancing at the slip of paper and then at Donaldson, Trevor asked, "You wanna go check on the third victim or make the notifications?"

With a deep sigh, Donaldson replied, "You're senior. I'll make the notifications. I'll get a couple of deputies to start canvassing. I'll also have the criminalists measure the tire marks in the street. It might help narrow down the type of vehicle we need to look for."

"Don't put Samuelson or Sullivan on the canvassing detail. I don't want some slick defense attorney to claim their testimony was tainted by after-acquired information," replied Wilkins.

Stephanie Alarcon lived nearby, at 402 Avenida Santa Ynez. It was at the end of the block on the right-hand side. Donaldson parked in front of the small, well-kept 1950s-era single story. As he approached the porch he was impressed by the well-trimmed front lawn and small flower garden bordering the fence on the far side. Stephanie and her husband had obviously taken great pride in their home and worked hard at keeping it nice. At the thought of Stephanie working in her garden he looked down at the cement walkway, and his mind briefly flashed back to her lifeless body lying in a pool of blood no more than a block away.

He stepped up onto the porch and rang the doorbell, waited a few seconds and rang again. He heard a stirring behind the door and a voice called out: "who is it?"

"Orange County Sheriff's Department."

"Just a second." The door opened a crack and a young man looked through the gap. "Can I help you?"

Predictably, Richard Alarcon alternated between despair and red-hot rage, trying valiantly to remain stoic and not display the emotions swelling just below the surface. He at first insisted on going to the scene; he had to see his Stephanie, but Donaldson told him it would be best for him to stay home and tend to their daughter. The coroner would call later today for him to come to the morgue and identify the body. At the mention of their daughter, Richard lost all control of the anguish he was trying so hard to hide. Donaldson quietly expressed his condolences, and then walked to the door. As he reached for the handle he heard a baby cry from a darkened bedroom. Janine had just awakened to a world vastly different from the one her parents had planned for her.

It was now after 5:00 a.m. Night was slowly retreating to make way for another summer day. In no hurry to bring the devastating news to the Mesa home, Donaldson was tempted to stop for coffee, but in his heart he understood it would be unfair to the family. They had a right to know and the sooner they were told the sooner the healing process could begin. He began the short drive to Anthony Mesa's home on Mission Avenue.

1621 Mission Avenue was a somewhat newer and larger version of the Alarcon's rented home. It too had a well-trimmed lawn and cement walkway leading to the front door. All that was missing was the flowerbed along the fence. Less than a half hour after ringing the doorbell, Donaldson let himself out. Just like Stephanie Alarcon, it appeared Anthony had no enemies. Although he had periodically been threatened by one or another rowdy drunk he had eighty-sixed from the Hasta la Vista, none of the threats were ever taken seriously. Manuel's style was to just laugh them off.

As Donaldson turned his car around to head back to the crime scene, his cell phone began to buzz. He pushed a button on his steering wheel and Trevor's voice came through the speaker. "Where are you?"

"I'm just leaving Mesa's home." He replied.

"Okay, I'm just leaving Orange County Global Medical Center. The other victim is Manuel Trejo, the owner of one of the cars in the parking lot at the Hasta la Vista. He's Anthony Mesa's uncle. He owns the Hasta la Vista. He was hit in the right thigh and again in the right buttocks, both through and through. He might have bled to death if Sullivan and Samuelson hadn't been there. Otherwise, none of the wounds is life-threatening and there was no other damage, no arteries were hit. He's going to be okay. Anyway, I've ordered that nobody be allowed inside the cordoned-off area behind the Cantina. I guess there was a fight involving Anthony and a couple of skinheads. Trejo called them Nazis. They were tagging the back of the building. They left their spray cans behind and Anthony threw them in the dumpster. Trejo said they were driving an older white car, full sized, not a compact. Traffic is starting to build. I should be there in a few minutes."

When Trevor arrived back at the scene, Donaldson was standing at the front of the Hasta la Vista with one of the criminalists. Trevor asked if he was finished gathering evidence from in front of the Cantina.

The criminalist replied: "yeah, I've got everything I could see."

"Then you got the shell casings in the middle of the street?"

"Marked, photographed and bagged. I also took measurements of the tire marks. Our crime scene photographer took pictures as well."

Trevor nodded, then replied: "Good job. Just out of curiosity, what did you come up with on the tire marks?"

"Well, the ones in front of the bar are 36 feet long. The ones down the street are 13 feet. Had to have been a pretty powerful car to leave that much rubber," he replied.

"What about the width and the track?"

"I measured that in four places on the long set of marks and again in three places on the marks down the street. The most consistent measurement I got was 57.7 inches. Couldn't get much as far as tread width and gaps—the street isn't in the best shape. I took pictures of what I could."

"Good job, thanks," said Trevor. "Now I've got another location I need you on."

"I know, behind the bar, in the alley. Investigator Donaldson already filled me in."

"Okay, let me tell you what we are looking for," replied Trevor. "There was a fight back there that might have involved the perpetrators. It happened between the back door and the dumpster and no more than ten feet out from the wall. I need you to look for blood evidence. Also, there should be some fresh graffiti on the wall. I need pictures and paint samples. Then, in the dumpster, there should be a couple of spray cans. The paint on the wall should have come from the spray cans. I need them bagged and dusted. Take the photographer with you. Oh, and I almost forgot, look for any tire marks back there also, okay?"

"Yes sir, I'm on it," responded the criminalist.

Trevor pursed his lips and said: "you know you don't have to call me sir, right?"

"I know. I just do it to bug you." The criminalist responded with a smile.

Behind the building the two investigators surveyed the area from across the alleyway.

"'WAW,' White Aryan Warriors," said Donaldson, reading the graffiti.

"Punks," was Trevor's only response.

CHAPTER 23

An incessant buzzing slowly pierced sleep's dark veil as Ronald Carpenter began to realize his cell phone was announcing a call. It had been a long night. After bagging the two mud people he and Jesse wiped down and dismantled the AK and sawed it into several pieces. After destroying the gun, they sprayed the pieces with WD-40 in the misguided belief that it would defeat fingerprint analysis should any of the parts be found. After wrapping the pieces in newspaper they disposed of the parcels in several dumpsters within a fifteen-mile radius around Santa Ana, Orange and Anaheim. It was nearly 5:00 a.m. before they were finished. They were lucky they didn't get pulled over by some curious pig.

Ronald Carpenter forgot to turn off his phone when he finally flopped down onto his bed for some much-needed sleep. As exhausted as he was it took some time before he drifted off. His mind kept replaying the events of last night and sleep proved to be evasive. Now that damned cell phone was summoning his attention, drawing him from his slumber. His eyes were almost swollen shut from the broken nose and his head ached tremendously. As he sat up he felt an even sharper pain in the back of his head. Reaching back, he felt a good-sized knot and withdrew his hand to look at the tips of his fingers. Sure enough they were covered by a thin smear of semi-dry blood. *Where did that come from?* He wondered. *Maybe I hit my head on the pavement after that beaner attacked me.* Squinting at the clock he saw that it was a little after 7:00 a.m. He couldn't have gotten more than an hour's sleep. He slid his thumb across the phone's screen to accept the call.

"Ron, turn on Channel Two. The news is on. They're at the Hasta la Vista right now." Jesse sounded like he was hyperventilating.

Carpenter turned on the TV, and anxiously waited while it progressed through its warm-up routine. By the time he flipped to Channel Two, the segment was over and they were going to a commercial break.

"I missed it. What'd they say?" He asked.

"They said there was a drive-by shooting last night in Santa Ana. There were three victims, two were killed. They said the victims who were killed were a man and woman."

"What?"

"The third person was taken to the hospital with non-life-threatening injuries. The police are following up leads and are looking for two persons of interest. That's us. They've got a description of us. Mid to late twenties, one about six foot three to six foot five, two hundred thirty to two hundred fifty pounds, the other six foot to six foot two, two hundred pounds, shaved heads, driving a white, older model car. Damn it! We shoulda just left."

"You said 'persons of interest.' Are you sure that's what they said, not suspects?"

"No, they said 'persons of interest, driving a white car.' That's us, man."

"Calm down. There's a million white cars and a million guys with shaved heads."

"But they didn't just kill somebody."

"I said calm down. First of all, it was self-defense. They attacked us in the alley. We defended ourselves."

"If you think anybody is going to buy that it was self-defense you're delusional. It was a good hour or so after the fight when we snuffed them. You started it with the old guy. The woman wasn't even there."

"We did the right thing for the cause, man. I told you, there are millions of people that fit that description and that many white cars. If that's all they got there's nothing to worry about."

"Maybe they have more that they're not telling. The guy who got away can identify us."

"He might not live that long."

CHAPTER 24

Wednesday morning came too quickly for Manuel Trejo. The attack that took his nephew and Stephanie Alarcon happened less than a week ago. He was released from the hospital just two days later. The doctor instructed him to take it easy for a couple of weeks as the healing progressed. The same doctor also wrote a prescription for Percocet, to be taken as needed. Manuel steadfastly refused to fill the prescription, claiming he got a bad reaction from opioids. The truth was the immense guilt he felt would not allow him to do anything to ease his own suffering. *Why am I still alive when two young people, full of dreams and opportunities, are not?* A baby girl will never know her mother. His nephew will never reap the rewards of his hard work and ambition. *Why couldn't I have taken at least one of their places?*

Today would be Anthony's mass, and there would be a graveside service at the cemetery afterward. Tomorrow would be Stephanie's turn to be laid to rest; same church, same cemetery. He would attend that one also. The notice had been printed in the local newspaper. Anthony was well liked and had been involved in many youth programs. There would certainly be a large turnout. There was some solace in that. He hoped Stephanie's services would be as well attended.

He sat up in bed and fumbled for his crutches. He could walk a few paces unaided, but not far and it was very tiring. The crutches would shorten the time it took to get ready before his sister, Anthony's mother, came to pick him up. On the way home from the hospital they had stopped at a medical equipment rental and picked up a wheelchair and the crutches. He hated the idea of being in a wheelchair, even temporarily, but promised his sister he would use it for at least a week before going to the crutches. That promise was broken as soon as she left his home, but today would be spent in the wheelchair under her watchful eye.

It was no surprise, in fact it was expected, that no more than half the mourners accompanied the hearse from the church to the cemetery. After all, the mass took more than three hours. During the mass Manuel sat in his wheelchair at the front of the congregation with the rest of the family. He felt as if everyone's eyes were on him the whole time. Ignoring his sister's admonitions, he rose for every hymn and kneeled—in pain—for every prayer. It was the least he could do for Anthony. It was now time for the procession to the cemetery. Food would be served at Anthony's home after the graveside services.

The procession followed the hearse through the narrow cemetery road until it stopped near a sheet of Astroturf covering what would be Anthony's final resting place. The mourners were walking to the gravesite when the quiet was broken by the cackle of a Harley-Davidson motorcycle that pulled in and stopped behind the line of parked cars. The rider and passenger sat and watched without removing their helmets or raising their darkened visors, as if deciding whether to wait for the mourners to clear the road before riding past.

The driver of the black limousine parked directly behind the hearse. He retrieved Manuel's wheelchair from the trunk, and pushed it to the open rear door.

As Manuel limped to his wheelchair, the motorcycle slowly rolled forward. Manuel looked up, expecting an expression of sympathy. The passenger calmly pulled a sawed-off twelve-gauge shotgun from under his black leather vest and pulled the trigger. A deafening boom echoed through the cemetery. Manuel pitched backward against the limousine and slumped to the ground as the assassins sped away, leaving behind only the echo of the shotgun blast and the roar of the fleeing motorcycle.

The biker's aim proved deadly. Every one of the lead pellets penetrated Manuel's body, shredding every vital organ in their way. He was dead before he hit the ground. As expected, none of the witnesses could provide much in the way of identification: black Harley-Davidson motorcycle with two riders, both clad in black, height and weight undeterminable, nothing more.

Within twenty minutes, Ronald Carpenter's burner phone chimed. Displayed on the screen was the number of the other burner he had purchased at the same time. The message was short and to the point: *It's done. Make sure you pay up.*

Carpenter turned the phone off without responding. The only remaining witness to the drive by at the Hasta la Vista was no longer a factor. He would certainly be sure to pay up—maybe include a bonus. These guys were nothing to mess with. He sighed with relief and set out to find somewhere to dispose of the phone.

CHAPTER 25

Four a.m. and Steve McMillan's rear view mirror lit up like a Christmas tree, except the lights on this tree were all red. McMillan had plenty to fear from the cops. He had been out all-night delivering product for Ronald Carpenter. In this case, the product was crystal meth, and it more than helped pay the expenses of the White Aryan Warriors. As a soldier in the WAW, McMillan's duty was to do the bidding of President Carpenter and Vice-President Jesse Cardinal.

Like most every Thursday night into Friday morning, he had been busy. It seemed like every retailer was out of product and needed it for what McMillan liked to call "the weekend sales event." Because of this he had been constantly on the go for at least twelve hours. Fortunately, at nearly every delivery he was offered a taste. If not for that, he would never have been able to keep up the pace. The immediate problem was that he still had more than three ounces stashed under the seat, and he was on felony probation for an assault with a deadly weapon conviction dating back two years ago to when he pulled a gun on a bouncer. With no lawyer on retainer at the time, WAW randomly landed on Lee Edwards for representation.

Thanks to a McMillan's clean record to that point, Lee was able to negotiate a plea agreement that did not include a gun allegation and called for only six months of local jail time and three years of supervised probation. However, because of the nature of the assault, the prosecutor was insistent that among the terms of his probation was a waiver of his Fourth Amendment right against unwarranted searches and seizures. Any cop could lawfully search his vehicle for any reason, or no reason.

McMillan pondered his options. *Should I pull over, or try to run?* Driving around at 4:00 a.m. would be suspicious enough. Add the Fourth Amendment waiver to that and you were guaranteed a search of the vehicle. No doubt the cop would find the product. Possession for sale could get him two, maybe three years. Add the probation violation and he could be facing what: maybe another three or four? Pulling over did not seem like a good option.

On the other hand, he'd seen plenty of pursuits live on television. They seldom ended well for the runner. An added charge of felony evading had to carry an additional sentence; how long was anyone's guess. He pulled the car to the side of the road.

It took less than ten minutes for the officer to determine McMillan's probation status, find the drugs, and place him under arrest. As he sat in the patrol car he noticed the reason for the initial stop: he had a busted taillight. He was going to go to prison because of a lousy taillight; *or maybe not.* He suddenly realized he might be able to help himself. His attorney would have to carry the torch, but he just might be able to get himself out of this jam. All he would have to do is keep his mouth shut until he spoke with his lawyer, *just like the mobsters did in the movies.*

CHAPTER 26

The shrill scream of that damned siren pierced the air again, jolting Lee from sleep. He wondered how it could possibly be 6:00 a.m. already. He and Krystal had gone to a Hollywood play, then a late-night dinner at Tao Los Angeles, an exclusive Chinese restaurant that, despite its name, was located in Hollywood. It was after 2:00 a.m. by the time he dropped her off and made it home, replaying the whole evening in his mind and thinking about how much he enjoyed being with her made the late-night drive more enjoyable. In the three months since they began dating, their relationship just kept getting better and better.

He should have known better than to get tickets for a Thursday night play. He should have gotten the tickets for tonight instead. Now, here it was, time to get up and pay the piper.

At the office Sharona greeted him with a fresh bagel and cup of coffee: "good morning, how was the play?"

 "How did you know we went to a play?"

"How do you think? Krystal told me. She's wanted to see that play for a long time. She was excited. You're scoring a lot of points, lover boy."

"Did she say anything about being excited to be going with me?"

"Yeah, but she might have been lying about that part."

Lee shook his head and headed for his office. "What's on the agenda today, anything pressing?"

"Yeah, actually there is. Don't spill anything on your shirt. You need to get over to Central Jail. You have a new case with an old client. We start getting any more of these and I'm going to consider offering a frequent felon discount."

"Fill me in."

"Do you remember Steve McMillan? You got him the deal of the century on a P.C. 245?"

"Yeah, the white supremacist; what'd he do now?"

"A connection I have at the police department told me possession for sale of methamphetamine. It makes sense that that would be the drug of choice for those knuckle-draggers. Anyway, he left a voicemail at 6:00 a.m., said he wants to see you ASAP. He sounded pretty desperate."

"Desperation breeds dollars."

"You're learning, Whitey."

Orange County Central Jail is another monolithic structure built in the late 1960s and located just a short walk from the Central Courthouse. Unlike regular visits, which are done through a thick glass window with a telephone on each side—the better to record conversations—attorney visits are conducted in a large room with several long tables. Because attorneys often bring documents that need signatures, there are no barriers between an inmate and his lawyer. And due to attorney/client confidentiality concerns, the conversations are not recorded.

Even sitting across the table from McMillan, Lee could clearly smell the strong meth-induced chemical odor on his breath. White supremacists were his least favorite clients. Most of them wanted to act like tough guys and at some point during the conversation you could expect to hear a reference to the superior white race and how the bloodline needs to be protected from the "mud people."

Pulling out a pad and pen, Lee said: "looks like you've gotten yourself into a pretty big jam this time, Steve. You're going to need a lot of help. You're looking at some hard time. Judges take it personally when you violate probation."

"I know. I screwed up. I shoulda checked to make sure all my lights were working."

"A better idea would have been to not get into that kind of activity in the first place."

"You tell me how to get a good-paying job when the beaners are flooding across the border and working for peanuts under the table."

There it is, thought Lee. "Okay," he said. "That's not what I came to discuss with you. You know the drill. You got popped this morning. They have seventy-two hours to arraign you, not counting weekends. My guess is that you will be arraigned next Tuesday. I'll have my legal administrator check to confirm that. We'll discuss bail at the arraignment. It's going to cost you fifteen thousand up front, short of trial. If we go to trial you can add another twenty grand, payable before trial."

Shocked at the price, McMillan responded: "fifteen thousand are you serious?"

"You're looking at a pretty long stretch in state prison. Unless one of us pulls a rabbit out of a hat you're going down on two felonies: the new one and the one I got you probation on. You can be sentenced to double the statutory sentence on the new one because you picked up a strike on the first one. That's six years on the meth charge alone, maybe another three on the assault charge. I wouldn't be shocked if the judge sentences you consecutively. Hell, I wouldn't be surprised if he adds a fine for the broken taillight on top of that. You don't like it, find another magician."

"I just might have a rabbit." McMillan whispered.

"I'll knock off five grand if you do. Let's talk."

CHAPTER 27

As expected, McMillan's arraignment was held on Tuesday morning in Department C-42, Judge Richard Folsom's court. The entire process took less than three minutes. Lee often joked that one day he would teach a parrot to recite "acknowledge receipt of discovery, waive formal reading of the complaint, enter a plea of not guilty, deny all special allegations, priors and enhancements and waive time for preliminary hearing and trial, Your Honor," and send it to handle his arraignments. Judge Folsom accepted the plea and, after a bit of discussion over attorney availability, set a felony settlement conference in three weeks and the preliminary hearing in forty-five days in Department Sixty-One, Judge Mackenzie's court. The trial date would be sixty days after that.

As per the Orange County Superior Court Felony Bail Schedule, the standard bail for each charge was $25,000, although the judges were quick to point out that the schedule was not the rule; it was merely a very persuasive suggestion. After commenting on the violation of probation charge, Judge Folsom levied a $30,000 bond. Thanks to the White Arian Warriors McMillan would be out before noon. These skinhead gangs took care of their own, or at least they liked to appear that they did. At some point they would expect McMillan to pay them back one way or another.

As McMillan was led out of the court's holding cell, Lee pointed at him, then at himself while gesturing to call, and then tapped his watch. McMillan understood: he should call as soon as he was released.

Once out of the courtroom, Lee called his office. "Hi Sharona, were you able to get me an appointment?" He asked.

"I did," she responded. "Don't know who it's with yet. They said to just give your name to the receptionist and someone will come out to meet you. You need to be at their main office at two."

"That's great, anything else?"

"Krystal called. She was taking a break and said it was nothing important, just wanted to say hi. She said you guys are going to the desert for some four-wheeling in your truck this weekend. I told her that wouldn't be a good idea."

"Why wouldn't that be a good idea?"

"Because that's where you bury the bodies."

"How 'bout if you and Ricky come along?"

"We can't. Ricky's got another conference, Seattle this time. Our flight leaves this afternoon, so I'll be knocking off early today. You guys have fun and tell Krystal to call me if she survives. "

At 1:45, Lee presented himself to the receptionist sitting behind the thick safety glass at the Orange County District Attorney's office. When asked if he had an appointment, he replied: "I do, I just don't know who with."

The receptionist gave him a skeptical look and said: "okay, go ahead and have a seat. I'll check to see if anybody is expecting you."

It was at least another five minutes before a well-dressed man in his late fifties or early sixties emerged and introduced himself as Senior Deputy District Attorney Richard Stokes. They exchanged business cards and Stokes asked: "what can I do for you?"

"Can we discuss this in private, Mr. Stokes?"

"Call me Richard," Stokes replied, and gestured to the receptionist who buzzed them in.

Stokes' office was standard for a county official: a bookcase against the wall mostly filled with family pictures and sports memorabilia. A large mahogany desk and a comfortable leather chair that told Lee that other than high-profile cases this man's courtroom battles were mostly behind him. This was an office that screamed authority.

"Sit anywhere you like," said Stokes. "What can I do for you?"

"Well, I'm pretty sure I have access to information that can solve a couple of homicides: three victims, two incidents. My presumption is that they are still being investigated."

Stokes' eyebrows shot up. "Really, what do you have?"

"About three months ago there was a drive-by shooting in front of a little cantina called the Hasta la Vista. Two killed, one wounded."

"Yes, there was. One of the victims was a young mother just walking home from work."

"The other two were the owner of the bar and his nephew." Lee responded. "The nephew was DOA at the scene. The uncle survived for about another week, then he was gunned down in the cemetery after his nephew's funeral. I have a client who claims to know who did the drive-by and who hired the hitmen."

"What about the hit in the cemetery?"

"He says that was hired out to a couple of bikers by one of the guys who did the drive-by. He doesn't have the names of the hitters and isn't sure he can get them, but he knows without a doubt who pulled the drive-by."

"Tell me the rest. There has to be a reason he has a lawyer, and there has to be a reason you're sitting in my office instead telling this to the investigator."

"Yeah, my guy has a felony strike on his record. In fact, he's still on probation. Last week he was picked up on possession for sale of meth. I did his arraignment this morning. Anyway, surprise, surprise, he doesn't want to go to prison. You drop the charges; he gives you the bad guys."

"We can probably work with that," Stokes replied, leaning back with his arms crossed. "But it's gonna have to go like this: he gives us the bad guys first, and testifies if necessary, then and only then do we drop the charges. Is he still locked up?"

"No, I'm pretty sure the bad guys bailed him out this afternoon."

"How did that happen?"

"They're all part of a Nazi Skinhead gang."

"He's taking a hell of a chance. His life will be worth zip by the time this is over."

"You don't really care, do you?"

"Not a bit. I'll find out who the investigating officer is and set up a meeting with you and your client."

"Name the time and place. I'll have him there."

The time and place turned out to be the following Tuesday at 10:00 a.m. in Stokes' office. Lee and his client arrived five minutes early and Trevor and Donaldson were already present, seated at opposite ends of the desk, leaving

117

Lee and his client the seats between them. Lee had a feeling the seating arrangement was an interrogation method meant to intimidate his client.

Stokes opened the conversation: "okay, first of all, I want everyone to know I'm recording this conversation. I'm not going to share it with anyone except for trial prep if this thing gets that far, or for impeachment if Mr. McMillian's testimony suddenly changes. Other than that, I will retain the option of sharing it with Investigator Wilkins and Investigator Donaldson should a valid need arise. Mr. Edwards, you will be notified if the need to share it with either of our two deputies arises and you will be offered the opportunity to be in attendance. Is that understood?" The two cops and Lee nodded and said: "yes." McMillan said nothing. Stokes asked: "is there a problem Mr. McMillan?"

"No, no problem, I understand." He finally replied.

"Good," said Stokes. "Let's get started. Mr. McMillan, I guess the first question is who killed Anthony Mesa and Stephanie Alarcon?"

"Ronald Carpenter and Jesse Cardinal," McMillan responded in a near-whisper.

"And how do you know this?"

"I heard 'em bragging about it."

"When and where?" asked Stokes.

"The first time would have been about two weeks after it happened. It was all over the news, so we all knew about it. We were sitting around Carpenter's house drinking beer and doing crank and pretty soon Ronald and Jesse started talking and laughing back and forth like they had some kind of secret and were kind of talking in code."

"Hold up a second," said Trevor. "When you say 'we,' who are you referring to?"

"White Aryan Warriors. Ronald is the president, Jesse is the vice president."

Trevor nodded as if he had expected that answer. "How many members are in your White Aryan Warriors?"

"Fifty or so, maybe more," McMillan lied. Both Investigators knew that in truth the fledging gang had no more than ten members, give or take.

"Go on," Stokes said.

"After a while someone asked what was going on. Ron looks at Jesse and says: 'we snuffed a couple of beaners,' just like that, like it was no big deal. He was pretty proud of it, actually. He even went out and got a teardrop tattoo under his left eye. It means he's killed someone."

118

"We know what it means," growled Donaldson.

McMillan continued. "At first we didn't believe them, at least I didn't, but the more they talked about it the more I realized they were telling the truth."

"How do you know they were talking about the murders of Anthony Mesa and Stephanie Alarcon?" asked Donaldson.

"They said it happened in front of a Mexican bar on Fourth Street in Santa Ana. They said they had a beef with a couple of guys from the bar, that they got jumped. They waited for the bar to close, then drove up and opened up on them."

"Did they say what the weapon was?" asked Donaldson.

"It was an AK-47. Ronald said he was pulling the trigger so fast his finger started to cramp up before he ran out of ammo. They said they cut the gun into pieces and threw the pieces in dumpsters all over the city."

Wilkins and Donaldson exchanged glances. Their suspicion that the shell casings came from an AK-47 was confirmed.

Looking up from his notepad, Wilkins asked: "what kind of car were they in?"

"Well, they said that after dumping the AK they spent the rest of the morning wiping down the 442, so I'm assuming it was Ronald's Oldsmobile. He also has a Toyota Camry that he drives when he's moving product. It doesn't attract as much attention as his 442. Since the shooting, he's kept the Oldsmobile in his garage most of the time."

"What color is the Olds?"

"It's white, of course. Why would it be any other color?"

Ignoring the wisecrack, Wilkins asked: "stick or automatic?"

"It's a stick shift, four on the floor."

Wilkens nodded. So far everything matched his notes. The fingerprints on the discarded paint cans were a match for Carpenter and Cardinal, and DMV records showed Ronald Carpenter owning a 1971 Oldsmobile 442. Manuel Trejo told him from his hospital bed the shooters were driving a white car, and research into which vehicles showed a rear track width of 57.7 inches conformed several GM products including muscle cars like the Pontiac GTO and the Oldsmobile 442.

Up to this point though, the only thing the evidence from the crime scene proved was that Carpenter and Cardinal likely the ones who tagged the rear wall of the Hasta la Vista, and that possibly a late '60s/early '70s muscle car had burned rubber in front of the cantina. There were no fingerprints on the spent shell casings, and nothing to tie it all together until now.

Donaldson glanced at Trevor. Anticipating the next question, the other man nodded. "Tell us about the hit on Manuel Trejo," said Donaldson.

"They were afraid Trejo could identify them. They sell crank to a lot of bikers. Somewhere along the line they found two guys who would do it. I don't know who they were. All I know is they used a shotgun so there would be no bullets to trace."

"Any idea where the bikers are from?"

"Not really, they sell a lot of product around Orange and L.A. counties. Sometimes they go out to San Bernardino. I know the Hells Angels have a chapter out there, but I don't know if they had anything to do with it. They've just never said and I know better than to pry. We were all wired and had been drinking. They just kinda got to talking about it, like bragging about it."

"How much did they pay for the hit?" asked Wilkins.

"They didn't say, and no one came out and asked. It was more like somebody was joking and asked: 'how much to bag a beaner nowadays?' Either Ronald or Jesse, I can't remember which, said something like, 'Not as much as you think, not when they take it out in trade.' I assumed that meant they paid them in product. I didn't ask. It was something that just came out while we were sitting around. It's not like I was trying to get information or anything."

The room went quiet, with each man apparently lost in thought. Stokes glanced at the two investigators and asked: "anything else?"

"Nothing from me right now, unless Investigator Donaldson has something," replied Trevor.

"Yeah, one thing," said Donaldson. "Why'd they shoot the girl, Stephanie Alarcon, what did she do?"

"She was a bonus: wrong place, wrong time. We call it 'collateral improvement.'"

The room fell silent again as Trevor and Donaldson tried to digest this last statement without displaying any visible signs of anger. Finally Trevor broke the silence. "I don't have anything else."

Donaldson shook his head and quietly responded: "neither do I."

"Okay, here's what I'll offer," said Stokes, looking from Lee to his client. "McMillan here testifies to exactly what he said here today and he will be available in case any more information is needed. He won't be asked to wear a wire or get any closer to Ronald Carpenter or Jesse Cardinal than he already is," then, looking at the two investigators: "I expect those two won't be on the streets very much longer anyway."

With determined expressions, the investigators nodded silently.

Stokes said: "he'll continue to face the charges he's currently facing until after the murder case is resolved, whether or not he is called on to testify. After that, we dismiss the charges. We can make arrangements for witness protection if necessary. If he runs or changes his testimony, I will personally pursue the charges against him and I will ask for the maximum sentence possible. Is that agreeable, gentlemen?"

Lee exchanged another glance with his client. McMillan looked at Stokes, nodded almost imperceptibly and said: "I'll do it."

Stokes pursed his lips and rocked back in his chair. "Good, we're set then," he said. "Don't forget what I said about making yourself available if any more information is needed."

"I can still have my attorney with me though, right?" asked McMillan.

"Absolutely."

At that, all five men rose and exited the office.

CHAPTER 28

It was four o'clock Sunday morning and Ronald Carpenter was caught completely off guard. One moment he was sound asleep on his living room couch, having been unable to navigate his way to the bedroom after a night of heavy drinking with his fellow warriors, and the next thing he knew his front door was bashed in and the room was filled with black-clad men shining lights in his eyes and yelling at him to lay on the floor and put his hands behind his back. It didn't help his comprehension that he had been up for more than twenty-four hours straight doing meth.

Two deputies wearing bulletproof vests stood over him as he was cuffed. At least four more cleared each room with military precision, guns drawn. The entire process took less than a minute.

"What is this shit?" Carpenter screamed.

"Shut up," one of the deputies standing over him barked.

A tall African-American man, also wearing a bulletproof vest, stepped into Carpenter's view and waved a document in his face, then said: "Ronald Carpenter, I'm Investigator Trevor Wilkins from the Orange County Sheriff's Department and you are under arrest for murder." Then, following official protocol despite the fact he could recite the Miranda warning in his sleep, he pulled a card and read: "you have the right to remain silent. Anything you say can and will be used against you in a court of law. You have the right talk to a lawyer and have one present while you are being questioned. If you cannot afford an attorney one will be appointed before any questioning if you wish. You can decide at any time to exercise these rights and not answer any questions or make any statements. Do you understand these rights, Mr. Carpenter?" He then glanced at the Nazi flag draped above the couch and the WAW tattoo on Carpenter's neck, and added: "or should I call you Mr. President?"

"I don't know what you're talking about. I want a lawyer." Carpenter replied.

"That's probably a good idea, son," Trevor responded, waiting for what would surely come out of Carpenter's mouth.

"I'm not your son, boy," said the Nazi, spitting out the final word.

Trevor looked straight into Carpenter's eyes, then winked and softly said: "are you sure about that, son?"

Trevor motioned toward the front door. It was time for the ride downtown. As he exited the house, behind the two deputies and Carpenter, his cell phone vibrated. At this hour it had to be Donaldson reporting on the simultaneous raid on Jesse Cardinal's residence. Cardinal lived in Silverado, a small, tight-knit rural community in the Santa Ana Mountains of eastern Orange County.

Trevor answered without a greeting. "How'd it go?"

"Well," replied Donaldson, "I know why you picked Carpenter's house in Fountain Valley and gave me Silverado Canyon."

"Why's that?"

"Because everywhere you look there's poison oak. You can't help but to walk into it in the dark. I'll bet everyone we had posted outside has got it. I'm pretty sure I walked into a bunch of it alongside his driveway."

"It's all just luck of the draw, my friend," Trevor chuckled. "Other than that, how'd it go?"

"Like clockwork, he didn't know what hit him. He had what looked like about a gram of meth sitting on his dresser plain as day. Misdemeanor quantity, not enough to worry about, no scales or packaging material. I guess he never figured the cops would come knocking."

"Has he said anything?"

"Oh, you know: we planted the dope, he doesn't know anything about any murder, and he's going to call the DEA, DOJ, FBI, Men in Black, and whoever else he can think of to rain misery down on us. After that, he lawyered up. How about you? Did you get anything?"

"Same here, he lawyered up, although we did discuss the possibility that we could be related."

"Find any weapons?"

123

"A couple of handguns, nothing very interesting. The boys are still searching, though. Maybe something will come up, how 'bout you?"

"Nah; I'm guessing one of the lower ranking members has a whole cache stuffed somewhere. We're on our way in. I'll see you there."

CHAPTER 29

The Sunday brunch Lee and Krystal enjoyed together at the modest little restaurant just off Coast Highway in Huntington Beach had become a regular routine. Afterwards he would drop her off at her apartment. She would then head to the law library to study and he would either go to the office or take the rest of the day off to kick back. This afternoon would be dedicated to washing his pickup. Four-wheeling in the desert and picnicking next to a huge saguaro cactus with Krystal the previous weekend proved to be exceptionally fun. By the time they got back he was too tired and worn out to even think about washing the truck. Today, though, he couldn't think of any excuses.

Just as they were backing out of their parking space, Lee's phone came to life with the guitar riff from the song *Bad to the Bone*. Lee looked over at Krystal and counted to three with his fingers. On three, he activated the hands-free control on his steering wheel and in cheerful unison they called out: "hi, Sharona."

"Hey guys," answered Sharona. "I hate to take you away from whatever you're up to, but we just got a forwarded call about what appears to be a co-defendant murder case. Whoever called didn't leave his name, but said there were two guys: Ronald Carpenter and Jesse Cardinal, who needed to talk with you at Orange County Main Jail right away. He said you were their attorney. I looked them up online on the inmate locater and they were arrested this morning. They're in Central Jail. My contact is off today, so I couldn't verify the charges."

"I know exactly who they are," Lee replied. His tone changed from cheerful to dead serious. "Look, I need to talk to you first. Can you meet me at the office in about an hour?"

Noting the change in his demeanor, Sharona asked: "is everything okay?"

"I'll explain when I get there,"

With a worried look on her face, Krystal asked: "what's wrong, babe?"

"Hopefully nothing, it's a long story. I'll tell you about it later."

Back at his office with Sharona, Lee laid out the facts of the McMillan case and how he would be testifying against his two fellow gang members. He explained that although he was never Carpenter's or Cardinal's attorney, they must have mistakenly assumed that, because the gang once paid for him to represent McMillan, he worked for all of them.

"So here's the deal," said Lee. "I can't represent them, but I can't tell them why. They are going to know soon enough there's a snitch. It won't take long after that to figure out who it is. They also know I'm McMillan's attorney, and they are going to see it as a huge betrayal by both of us. They're gonna want to distribute some payback. These guys are extremely violent. I wouldn't put anything past them. They killed a witness in a cemetery in front of his family. Just being associated with me could put you and everybody around me in danger. The last thing I want to do is put you in jeopardy; so as much as I don't want to say this: maybe it's best if you went somewhere else. You should be working in an office where you can really show off your talents anyway, not in some small-time show like this one. I would, of course, give you the most glowing reference the world has ever seen."

"So you're telling me I'm fired?" asked Sharona. "Because that's the only way I'm leaving. Since the day I hired on we've worked as a team and I'm pretty sure you will agree that things have gotten better, but we're still building and have a long way to go. I'm not going to turn tail and leave my teammate out to dry just because a bunch of worthless slime balls want to start something. I don't run and I don't abandon my team. If they want to come, let them come. They will pay a heavy price; one they can't afford. If you think differently, you have no idea who I am. You don't know what I'm capable of." This was a side of Sharona that Lee had never seen before, but he had no doubt she could back up everything she said.

"Of course you're not fired. I could never do that." Lee replied. "I just don't want anything to happen to you because of me."

126

"Good," she replied, her voice suddenly bright and cheerful again. "Cause I wasn't going to clean out my desk anyway and Ricky is just waiting for the chance to pretzelize anyone who tries to fire me, even if it turns out to be you."

"Pretzelize, is that even a word?" he asked with a smile.

"Of course," she deadpanned. "Look it up: the act of twisting someone into a pretzel."

Serious again, Lee asked: "would you at least keep a gun handy? I know you know how to use one."

"You mean like the nine-millimeter in my desk drawer?"

"Are you serious?" He asked, surprised.

"It's been there since I started working here. I was planning to bring it out next time we negotiated my salary."

Lee could only shake his head. He should have known. Sharona was no one to mess with.

CHAPTER 30

Lee was back in the Orange County Central Jail's attorney visit room, when the jailers brought in Ronald Carpenter. Swaggering to his chair, he sat down and fixed Lee with a blank stare. It was nearly 8:00 p.m. and the skinhead looked exhausted.

Returning Carpenter's stare, Lee finally broke the silence. "Ronald, I'm Lee Edwards. We got a call that you want me to represent you. Is that correct?"

"Yeah, you're our attorney. We need you to do your job," said Carpenter.

Leaning forward on the table as if to share a whispered secret, Lee replied in an admonishing tone: "let's get something straight: I'm not your attorney. I represented one of your gang members once. I didn't represent anyone else, just him."

"But the brotherhood paid for it." Carpenter responded.

"That doesn't make me your lawyer. Anyway, I already told your co-defendant I can't take the case." Lee had purposely spoken with Jesse Cardinal first. He hoped the fact he had ignored their arbitrary ranks and spoken with the vice president before speaking with the president would not be lost on Carpenter.

"Why not?"

"I have a conflict. I once represented one of the guys you are accused of killing in a civil case. It was a big case with a huge payoff from an insurance company." Lee was able to tell this lie without breaking the stare-down. He had played the stare-down game with men a lot tougher than Ronald Carpenter.

"You're representing Steve McMillan, and he's a Warrior." Carpenter observed.

"He's not charged with killing my former client, although I may have to get off his case if the DA adds a gang enhancement to the charges. Anyway, I can refer you to a couple of attorneys."

"Are they any good?"

"They're the best. If I were facing the charges you are, these guys would be the first ones I would call. Look, I've had two cases from you guys and I have never had to haggle over my fee and you always pay upfront with no hassles. Why would I want to ruin a relationship like that by referring you to anyone other than the best? The state is without a doubt going to seek the death penalty, and these guys have a lot of experience with capital cases. Their names are Jim Wessel and Tom Connolly. They're from San Diego. Either you or one of your guys needs to look them up and call them as soon as you can. Tell your guy to drop my name on them."

"Any reason you can't call them for us?" asked Carpenter.

"Plenty of reasons," replied Lee. "The most important is the conflict of interest I told you about. If I call them for you, the appearance, if nothing else, is that I am involved in your defense."

His statement that Connelly and Wessel were the best wasn't a lie, not even an exaggeration. He'd known each of them personally for years and at one time or another had tried cases with both of them. The experience and knowledge he gained from just hanging around them was invaluable. He only wished he could tell them the cards were stacked on this case. *Oh well*, he thought, *they'll find out by the time the trial date rolls around.*

CHAPTER 31

Carpenter and Cardinal were arraigned the following Tuesday morning in Judge Folsom's courtroom. Although Lee had no legal obligation to attend, he felt compelled to be there, if for no other reason than to remind himself how dangerous these two could be. He needed to reinforce this fact in his own mind as graphically as possible. He would need that image to draw on later. This would probably be the worst day he had ever experienced; on par with the loss of his parents.

The case understandably garnered quite a bit of local interest. There were plenty of sensational elements: three innocent victims, not including a toddler who would grow up without knowing her mother; a fledging neo-Nazi gang; and a couple of outlaw motorcycle gangster hit men. Newsmen occupied several seats in the gallery. Lee spotted Parkland Rice among them. Parkland rose to come over, but Lee waved him off. He was not in a sociable mood.

Carpenter and Cardinal were escorted through a side door to a small holding cell with a wire screen. Each of them wore an orange jumpsuit. Each of them was shackled and cuffed. As they entered, Lee heard a slight commotion and turned around to see four young men, dressed in black, stand with their right arms held straight out in stiff Nazi salutes, modified with three fingers spread out to symbolize "W," the gang sign for the White Aryan Warriors. His client, Steve McMillan, was among the four.

Judge Folsom took the bench just before 9:00 a.m. After taking note of the number of reporters in his courtroom, he called the co-defendant case.

Both Wessel and Connelly rose and announced their presence at the podium, identified which defendant they were representing and that each was present in the courtroom, then walked over and stood in front of the holding cell. Not-guilty pleas were entered, and the statutory time for preliminary hearing and trial was waived. The felony settlement conference would be held in four weeks and the preliminary hearing in sixty days in Department Sixty-One. Trial was set ninety days out. Lee made note of the dates. There would be no bail.

In order to protect McMillan, Lee wanted his appearance and trial dates to trail the dates set by Wessel and Connolly for Carpenter and Cardinal. He would have to speak with Stokes to make sure whichever Deputy DA would be in court that day wouldn't object to his repeated requests for continuances.

Lee waited for the four skinheads to exit before standing to leave. *Why was McMillan with them?* He wondered. *Maybe he's just putting on a front to squelch any suspicion. Or maybe there's a double cross in the making.*

Tom Connelly caught up to him as he was stepping into the aisle to leave. "Hey Lee, Jim and I owe you big-time for the referral. You free to get some breakfast?"

"I wish I could, but I have an appointment I have to get to. Maybe next time, okay?" Lee walked out of the courtroom. He had a couple of hours to kill before his next meeting, but he wished the clock would just stand still. He needed time alone.

CHAPTER 32

It was quarter to twelve. Lee was early. He found a table toward the back of the little café where he and Krystal had enjoyed so many brunches together. This would probably be the last time he would see her.

Five minutes later he looked up to see Krystal bouncing through the door. As usual, she caught the eye of every male patron in the room.

"Hey babe," she said, taking a seat. "I don't have much time. We have a big client coming to talk with us about doing the graphics for a new advertising campaign. We're scheduled to meet at 12:30 and I have to prepare. This could be a huge account and I'll be in charge. Would it be okay if I just order a Diet Coke and nibble off whatever you're having?"

"I haven't ordered anything yet. I'm not very hungry," he replied.

"Are you all right?" She asked with a concerned look. "You don't sound too well. You look down. What's going on?"

Not wanting to drag it out any farther, Lee looked up and said: "Krystal, we can't see each other, at least not for a while anyway."

Krystal was visibly shocked. "What? Are you serious? What's going on?" She asked, hoping this was some kind of bad joke.

"I can't tell you right now." He said. "It's just not a good time."

"Is it something I've done or said? If it is, tell me and we can work it out. Don't I at least deserve an explanation?"

"Oh God, Krystal," he replied. "You do, but I can't tell you right now."

"Why not," she asked in a pleading voice. "Is there someone else?" Tears began welling in her eyes.

"No, it's not that. You have to believe me. There is no one else. It's just that....you wouldn't understand. I'm sorry. It's just a bad time."

"Just a bad time," she repeated. "What does that mean, don't I deserve to know?"

"I'm so sorry, Krystal. I just can't tell you right now," was his only response.

No longer trying to hide her tears, she slid her chair back and stood. "Do you know what? I was falling in love with you. Maybe it was all just a game to you, but it wasn't to me you sonofabitch!"

Lee sat in silence as Krystal walked out of the café and out of his life. Through the window he could see her hurry to her car, a look of despair on her face.

CHAPTER 33

Lee's siren alarm went off at precisely 6:00 a.m. He had hardly slept and he had another splitting headache. He'd never returned to the office after breaking Krystal's—and his own—heart yesterday. Instead, he'd driven up and down the coast, stopping periodically to sit alone on the beach and rerun the scene in the café, trying to convince himself he had done the right thing.

Checking his phone, he saw several calls and messages from Sharona, and none from Krystal. He should have gone back to the office yesterday. Sharona and Krystal were close friends and he owed her an explanation.

Knowing Sharona would already be up, Lee called her. Her greeting was all business. "Are you coming in today, Counselor?" She asked in a flat voice.

"I'll be there by seven. I have to talk to you about something."

"You're right about that. Also, your skinhead client called about four times yesterday. He said to call him as soon as I know when you'll be in. I'll set up an appointment for nine, but I'm really not in the mood to deal with someone like that today."

As Lee walked through the door, Sharona looked up and said: "we've gotta talk," then followed him into his office.

"Look," Sharona started off. "I told myself when I first introduced you to Krystal that I wasn't going to get involved, but she and I have become very good friends. She called me yesterday afternoon and said you broke up with her and you wouldn't tell her why. She was crying. Maybe you don't know it, maybe you haven't seen it, but she's in love with you. Don't you think you at least owe her an explanation?"

"I couldn't give her one, Sharona. If I did I would have had to lie to her, maybe even tell her I found someone else. I'm not going to lie to her, and if I told her the truth we would still be together and her life would be in danger. She shouldn't have to constantly be looking over her shoulder because of something I got her into. If anything were to ever happen to her because of me, I could never live with myself."

"Are you talking about that skinhead bunch?"

"Sharona, it won't be long before they find out there's an informant. It'll be in the discovery and it'll be part of the testimony at the prelim. McMillan's name won't come out at the prelim, but if their case goes to trial, which it will because it's a death penalty case, he's going to have to testify. Despite what they say, the gang's not that big, which cuts down the mathematical possibilities of who the snitch is. I'm representing a member who just got busted on a simple drug charge, but his case is going to keep getting stalled and continued because I can't resolve it until after he testifies. Without a doubt they are going to notice that his drug case is taking longer to resolve than their co-defendant triple murder. On top of that, I got off their murder case because I supposedly had a conflict, but I don't seem to have any conflict when it comes to representing one of their other members. I wouldn't be surprised if they figure it out on their own well before he testifies."

"I don't trust McMillan either." He continued. "He's a tweaker. I wouldn't be surprised if he runs. If he disappears, Cardinal and Carpenter will walk and then come looking for as much payback as they can deal out, against everyone they think betrayed them and then some. They will know that McMillan told me they did the drive-by and hired the hit men. That puts me and everyone around me at the top of the list. They've already proven they couldn't care less if innocent people go down. McMillan made that very clear at our meeting with the Supervising DA. They will have already gotten away with three murders. What's to stop them from doing it again?"

"Don't you think you should have let Krystal make the decision to stay or go?" asked Sharona.

"We both know what she would have said. I can't put her in that kind of danger."

"I think you underestimate Krystal. She's a lot tougher than you think. Maybe you don't know, but she grew up on a horse ranch with two older brothers. She had to prove to them every day that she was just as tough as they were and that there was nothing they could do that she couldn't do better."

135

"But she's not you, Sharona. Try to understand, please."

"Oh, I understand all right. I understand you just threw away the best thing that's ever happened to you."

"I know." The sadness in his voice was unmistakable.

"No, you don't. About a month ago, she turned down a promotion that would have put her into big money at that graphic art firm she's with. She turned it down because it would have meant moving to New York and she didn't want to have to say goodbye to you. Last night she told me the position's still open, and she's going to take it. She said she has to get out of here, get a new start. Our semester ends next week. They'll fly her out right after her last day. She's already packing. It's not too late for you to fix it."

"Sharona, I can't. Please understand."

"You're making a huge mistake," Sharona replied, shaking her head in frustration as she left the office.

CHAPTER 34

Steven McMillan, dressed in all black, save for the white shoelaces on his Dr. Martens boots, entered Lee's outer office nearly two hours late. Frowning at Sharona, he sauntered up to the reception desk and looking her square in the eye, said, "I'm Steve McMillan."

"Hello, Steven," Sharona replied in a dramatically cheery voice without breaking eye contact.

"Tell my attorney I'm here," he ordered.

"You're late, Steven," she replied through her teeth. "Have a seat. I'll see if he has time. Otherwise we might have to reschedule."

"I'll stand."

"Suit yourself."

Sharona stepped into Lee's office and gestured with her head toward the closed door. "Your nine o'clock just got here. Before I send him in you should know he's loaded on something. He won't sit down. His pupils dilated, and he's sweating."

Lee leaned back in his chair and looked at the ceiling and slowly shook his head. "Send him in." He sighed.

As McMillan stepped into Lee's office decked out in his neo-Nazi regalia, Lee couldn't escape the thought that, turncoat or not, this guy's associates orchestrated the deaths of three innocent people and left a young father alone to raise a baby girl. The only reason he could stomach McMillan was because he held the key to putting at least two of the shooters away forever.

"Was that your secretary at the front desk?" McMillan asked.

Lee ignored the question. He could tell immediately that Sharona was right. McMillan was high on something. "What are you on?" he asked.

"I'm not on anything. Where'd you get that, from her?" He emphasized the word "her" and gestured to the door.

"You're lying to me. You're on something. I could tell as soon as you walked in here. I don't have time for that. You lie to me again and I'll personally throw you out. Now, what is it you wanted to see me about?"

"Calm down, counselor. I want to make another deal with the DA."

"You've already made your deal. It's not going to get any better."

"What if I can get the names of the bikers who did the hit in the cemetery?"

"That might be worth something. How are you going to find that out?"

"Ron keeps an account, what the cops call a pay-and-owe ledger. That's how he keeps track of who owes him money. It's mostly for his meth business. He sells to a lot of dealers who can't always pay upfront."

"Okay, go on. I'm interested."

"Well, some of the other Warriors and I were moving his stuff out of his house; stuff we need to keep an eye on. There's a lot we don't want anybody else to see: initiation procedure, code words, membership roll, things like that."

"So, you think the hitters' names are in the ledger?"

"Not their names exactly, but their code names are."

"How do you know?"

"I saw them. We were moving a safe that the cops missed when they searched the place after he was arrested; probably because it was hidden behind a false wall in his bathroom. It was too heavy for us to get down the stairs, so we decided to open it up and empty it out and then put it all back once we got it moved."

"How did you figure out the combination?"

A smile crossed McMillan's face. "Easy," he said. "4-20-89: April twenty, eighteen eighty-nine is Der Führer's birthday."

"And the ledgers were inside, right?" asked Lee.

"There were a whole bunch of them inside. I carried out the top stack. The most recent one was on top. It goes back about a year. That's before the drive-by and the hit in the cemetery. I put the whole stack in my car. When we got to where we were going, I gave back the rest of the stack, but kept the current one for myself. When I take it back I'm going to tell them it slid under the seat while I was moving them."

"Where's everything stored now?"

"Nice try."

"How do you know the names you saw are the hitters?"

"They have to be. Their names are only in there once. They're not entered several times like the other dealers. Also, the entry is different than the others: both names are on the same line, not individual lines like all the others. After their names it says 'two p's' where he puts how much he has supplied any dealer, but there isn't a number where he puts the amount he has been paid or how much is owed. Instead, he wrote 'RIP.' It was dated two weeks after the hit at the cemetery. I checked out the dates online."

"So, what are the code names?" asked Lee.

"That's something I'm keeping to myself. That's my ace in the hole. I give that up and I've got nothing to bargain with. I'm not saying until I have a deal."

"Okay, so let me get this straight." Lee responded. "You want me to set up another meeting at which time you are going to divulge a couple of phony names that may or may not identify the killers. Of course, the cops are first going to have to decipher the possibly random code and hope the names actually are the killers. Next, they are going to have to track them down and hope by then they have enough evidence to make an arrest, right?"

"What if I can come up with the names: the real names?"

"How are you going to do that?"

"I've been thinking this over. Ron deals with an awful lot of people. Some of them he hears from every week; some of them he doesn't hear from for months. Sometimes it could be a year or more. There's no way he could remember everyone's code name. He has to have an index somewhere. I doubt it would be in the safe with the ledgers. Too many people would go down if his house got searched, so it's bound to be somewhere in his house where he can get to it easily. He does a lot of business. He wouldn't want to have to leave his house to pick up the index every time he makes a deal. I'm betting I can find it."

"I thought you said you moved everything out of his house."

"Not everything, just the stuff that we needed to move to protect the brotherhood."

"Wouldn't that include his code-name index?"

"Maybe, but I know him. If he goes down on the murders he'll take full responsibility. Without the ledgers the index means nothing. He'll take the fall, say it's all him and him alone. His allegiance is to the brotherhood."

"Where's your allegiance, Steve?" asked Lee.

"I still believe in the movement. We have to protect our race. The war has been going on longer than you know. I just can't do prison time."

"So, what is it you want? Providing you can deliver, that is."

"I want to be off probation and I want the conviction to go away. I'm going to want to own a gun when this is over and I can't do that with a felony on my record. I also want to be relocated with a different name and social security number. They already said they would put me in witness protection. The new name and social should be part of it. I also want money, a lot of it. Informants get paid all the time. They can afford to pay me."

The money would probably be the easiest part of the deal. The rest would be a complicated bureaucratic nightmare, although doable, but that was the D.A.'s problem, not Lee's. "Do you have a number in mind?" Lee asked.

"I'm working on it. I'll let you know when I get the rest of the information. Whatever it is will be non-negotiable."

Everything's negotiable, thought Lee. "Okay, I'm not going to approach the DA until you tell me you can produce the actual names. If you can't, we can maybe get you something for the code names. We'll see."

CHAPTER 35

That evening, several Warriors showed up at Steve McMillan's apartment. They said they needed to discuss strategies to get Ron and Jesse out of the mess they were in. Everyone agreed the big question was where the district attorney's evidence came from. The cops must have come up with another witness somehow. If so, they had to take him or her out, just as they had taken out the old man in the cemetery. In the meantime they would appoint a temporary president and vice president. Everyone agreed that, if it came to it, the loss of Ron and Jesse would not break them up. Staying together to defend the white race was bigger than all of them. Ron and Jesse would be seen as martyrs to the cause.

As soon as business was taken care of, one of the members pulled out a sandwich baggie containing a white crystalline substance. "Anyone?" He asked. Everyone present nodded.

As a show of solidarity and trust, no one injected himself; instead, each member prepared and injected the substance into the man next to him. Following tradition, the host was the first to be injected. Steve stuck out his arm and watched as the Warrior to his right inserted the needle and pushed the plunger.

Within seconds, his heart began pounding faster and harder and his body temperature shot up as the substance coursed through his veins: too quick, too strong; not normal. *Something's wrong;* paranoia instantly began to set in and he looked to the rest of the brothers for help.

All eyes were on him but no one was moving a muscle.

Sweating profusely, with a pain growing in the center of his chest every time his heart beat, Steve broke the silence. "Help me," he pleaded.

Not one of his brother Warriors moved. Each sat quietly, watching intently as if mesmerized by the scene playing out in front of them.

The pain in his chest was now beyond comprehension. Steve begged for someone, anyone, to call an ambulance or to help him.

No one moved.

Writhing in agony, Steve pitched forward onto the floor and, while clutching his chest, tried to push himself to the phone with his feet, but his limbs wouldn't respond.

Finally, one of the Warriors spoke up: "Steve, Steve, Steve, is there something you want to tell us?" The tone was as calm as if he were asking the time of day.

"Help me please." Steve begged, breathing heavily through clenched teeth.

"Did you rat out Jesse and Ron? Just admit it and we'll get you some help. Then you can tell us why."

"I didn't." Steve answered, his eyes shut tight and his legs now drawn up to his chest in an effort to relieve the pain.

"Yes you did." The voice was now taunting, almost singing.

"Okay, I did," came the reply. Steve was still doubled up and now nearly hyperventilating, trying to control the pain. "They were going to send me away to prison for the rest of my life," he lied, then added another lie; one that he hoped would save his life: "they already knew."

The voice came back: "Good bye, Steve. I think it's time for us to go." He said calmly.

CHAPTER 36

Lee waited impatiently in the hallway outside of Judge Folsom's courtroom. Today was McMillan's felony settlement conference and McMillan wasn't here. In less than five minutes the door would open. Sharona had left their client several messages reminding him not to be late. This was something she seldom did, but she didn't mind making an exception for McMillan, knowing how much it must irk him to constantly be ordered around by a black woman.

Judge Folsom's bailiff   opened the door at 8:45. McMillan had not yet shown up. By 9:20, McMillan still hadn't shown up. Lee got off the bench and walked into the courtroom to sign the attorney roster. Fifteen minutes later a young deputy DA walked out and called: "attorney Lee Edwards."

Lee stood and shook his hand. "Come with me," said the young man. "We need to talk in private."

In a small, private conference room, the DA said: "Senior Deputy District Attorney Stokes told me you were going to ask for a continuance and that I am not to oppose it. I'm not to ask why, even though I'm dying to find out, especially since Richard Stokes is involved." Reaching into his pocket, he continued, "Here's my card. Call me personally if you need anything. I'll be handling this case right up to the preliminary hearing and maybe all the way through."

"Glad to meet you." Lee replied.

The young DA pointed to a form on the table and said, "Go ahead and fill out that request for a continuance. Put down any day you want and any reason you feel like putting down. Like I said, I'm not going to oppose it. One thing Stokes did say, though, is that I'm to make sure your client is here. If not, I have to let him know right away."

"I don't think he's here." Lee responded. "Let me check the courtroom and hallway, and call my office to see if anyone's heard from him. I'll be right back."

No more than three minutes later, Lee was back in the conference room. "Go ahead and make your call" He said to the young DA.

Two hours later Lee walked out of the courtroom. Judge Folsom had put off calling the McMillan case as long as he could. He was even willing to give McMillan until the afternoon to show up, but only if he had contacted Lee's office. He had not. By failing to appear, McMillan picked up another felony, his bond was forfeited, and there was now an arrest warrant hanging over his head.

Those were McMillan's smallest problems, though. Unless the district attorney could track him down, Carpenter and Cardinal would be released. They would be looking for retribution. They would be looking for Steven McMillan and everybody associated with him.

Lee called his office while walking to his car. "McMillan's in the wind," he said as soon as Sharona answered. "The prelim for Cardinal and Carpenter is in two weeks. If they don't find him dead somewhere, the DA will likely be able to get Carpenter and Cardinal bound over for trial by putting one of the investigators on the stand to testify to what McMillan told them. There is no doubt Connolly and Wessel will advise their clients not to agree to have the trial pushed back any more than it already has been. That's going to limit the time the DA has to find McMillan. Without his testimony at trial, Cardinal and Carpenter will walk."

"And if he turns up dead before the prelim they walk, right?" asked Sharona.

"Wessel and Connolly will have them out before Judge Folsom's gavel hits the sound block."

CHAPTER 37

Trevor walked into his office at 8:00 a.m. on the dot. It was Monday morning and he and his son had spent a great weekend hanging out together. On Sunday they went to a car show in Escondido where Jim and Becky were showing Jim's Firebird. For Charles the most exciting part of the day was getting there. Jim and Becky invited him to ride along in the Firebird for the forty-five-minute drive south.

This weekend was one Trevor liked to call a "missing in action" weekend: one where he shut off his phone, television and computer, tuned out any news stations on the radio and did whatever he and Charles decided they wanted to do without worrying about what might be going on anywhere else on the planet. He owed weekends like this to his son. Charles would soon enough be out and on his own and the more memories they could share together, the better.

As soon as he sat down, his phone buzzed. Scott Donaldson was on the other end.

"You heard Steve McMillan is dead, right?" Donaldson asked.

"He's dead, how?" Trevor asked shocked.

"Don't know yet. Right now it looks like an overdose. He missed a hearing last week and his landlord found him dead on the floor of his apartment last Friday night. No drugs or paraphernalia found so we don't know for sure. We're waiting on the toxicology report."

"Overdose, that's a hell of a coincidence, isn't it?" said Trevor.

"Yeah, it sure is; too much of one. I'm gonna call Stokes next; see what he wants to do. Should we go see Lee Edwards, or do you want to see what the coroner comes up with first?"

"Let's call Stokes together," suggested Trevor.

"I'll be there in ten," said Donaldson.

Fifteen minutes later the two investigators had Stokes on speakerphone. He was already aware that his prime witness was dead.

"Here's how we are going to handle this: Don't talk to Edwards unless he calls you. McMillan was his client. He'll find out soon enough, if he hasn't already, and until we get the toxicology report all we know is that McMillan's dead. It could be an accidental overdose. We have a felony settlement conference in a couple of weeks. The defense attorneys won't know we lost our star witness and we don't have to tell them yet. I'll tell the deputy handling the FSC to offer two counts of second-degree murder of the two that were shot in front of the cantina and let them talk him down to voluntary manslaughter. If they don't bite, we'll just have to hope we can come up with something better than what we have right now before the preliminary hearing."

"We're working on a warrant to search McMillan's house right now," said Donaldson. "Maybe we can come up with something else."

CHAPTER 38

Lee had just walked out of the West Justice Center in Westminster, no more than 20 miles from his office, when his cell phone pinged. It was a text from Sharona, wanting to know if he was planning on coming in and, if so, when. It wasn't quite 9:30 and Monday morning traffic would still be horrible. Normally it would be less than a thirty-minute drive to the office but he gave himself an hour. He had meant to call and let her know he would be picking up discovery on a DUI case in Westminster before coming in, but it slipped his mind. He should have called. He returned her text: "I'll be there in 60."

Sharona greeted him with: "you could have at least checked in" as he stepped into the outer office.

"Sorry," was all he could muster.

"Did you see the paper this weekend?"

"No, why?" he asked.

"Steve McMillan is dead."

Lee's eyebrows shot up. "Are you serious?"

"Yeah, I am. They printed his address—just the street, no number—in the paper. I checked our intake form. It has to be him. Right now they are ruling it an accidental overdose."

"Overdose, my ass, someone in that gang figured out who snitched on Carpenter and Cardinal. I told you it wouldn't be hard to figure out." He walked into his office and dropped everything he was carrying onto his desk.

"Their felony settlement conference is in a couple of weeks." Lee continued, over his shoulder. "They won't know the DA no longer has a case and the DA is probably going to bluff all the way until the time comes to lay the cards on the table. I'm guessing he'll offer them something that'll sound almost too good to pass up. Maybe they'll take the deal."

Standing in his office doorway, Sharona said: "that isn't going to happen though, is it?"

"No, it's not, not a chance. Word will have gotten to Carpenter and Cardinal by then that the snitch is dead. That gives us until the preliminary hearing date before they are back on the streets."

Lee looked down at the carpet and then at Sharona. He didn't want to set her off again, but he had to say it. "Look, Sharona, I've gotten us into some very real danger here. You don't owe me anything. If at any time you change your mind about staying, I'll understand."

Her eyes flared. "Do I have to listen to this again?"

"No, it's just that..."

"Then quit insulting me."

"Sorry, I guess I just wanted to hear you say it again."

CHAPTER 39

Jim Wessel and Tom Connolly were riding a bench in the hallway when the bailiff announced Judge Folsom's court was open for attorneys only. As soon as they signed in, a twentysomething deputy DA called out their names. Meeting them at the podium, she introduced herself as Jennifer Ortiz and escorted them to the conference room.

The young prosecutor made a show of silently reviewing the case file, then looked up and said: "okay, here's the deal. We have your guys for three murders with special allegations including multiple murder and lying in wait. We can also tack on a gang enhancement and use of a firearm enhancement. Right now they're both looking at the death penalty. "

After taking a moment to let it sink in, she continued. "I'll settle the whole thing today if they'll plead to two counts of second-degree murder, no enhancements."

Jim Wessel was the first to speak. "That's pretty generous of you. Would you mind telling us why?"

"That's our standard offer in these types of cases." She lied. "They'll be looking at fifteen to life for each count. We'll ask the judge for consecutive sentences, and if he goes along they'll be looking at thirty to life. We get the conviction. Your guys get the chance to live long enough to see the light of day from outside a prison again and on top of that, you guys become the lawyers who turned a dead-bang death penalty case into a second degree with no enhancements. We all win."

Both attorneys had been in the game long enough to know when someone was trying to pull the wool over their eyes. "How long do we have before we give you a decision, or is this one of those 'take it right now or leave it' deals?" asked Connolly.

"No, I'll give you up to the preliminary hearing to decide, but once the hearing starts the offer is off the table forever. We will go after them full-bore and include every special circumstance and enhancement available. Your boys will end up with needles in their arms."

Wessel stood up and said: "okay, Ms. Ortiz, let's confirm the prelim date and in the meantime we'll sit down with our clients and have a come to Jesus talk with them. We'll let you know, thank you."

Judge Folsom called the Carpenter/Cardinal case first and confirmed the preliminary hearing date. As soon as the two attorneys were outside of the courtroom, Wessel turned to Connolly and said: "now that was a surprise. What do you think that was all about?"

Shrugging, Connolly replied: "I don't know, but something's going on. The only thing I can think of is that maybe the informant turned around on them."

"That's what I'm thinking," said Wessel.

Lee rang up the two attorneys on Wessel's cell phone later in the day. Wessel explained to Lee that they had conveyed the prosecution's offer to their clients and each immediately turned it down without any contemplation. Lee wrestled with the idea of telling them that the snitch had been his client and had mysteriously turned up dead. Feeling that disclosing that fact would be unethical, he kept it to himself.

As soon as he finished his conversation with Wessel and Connolly, Lee walked into the outer office and updated Sharona. Carpenter and Cardinal turning down an offer that would keep them out of the execution chamber could only mean that they knew McMillan was dead. Most likely the information was conveyed to them by one of the White Aryan Warriors during visiting hours.

He had marked the preliminary hearing date in his calendar and told Sharona that he wanted her to close the office that day, or at least until after the hearing. "I want you to come with me." He said. "I want you to get a good look at these guys. If we see them again it's going to be under an entirely different set of circumstances."

CHAPTER 40

Deputy Wilson seemed happy to see Lee walk in, even more so when he leaned Lee was only there as a spectator. He didn't know Sharona, but with her knack for instantly making friends, they were soon trading punchlines at Lee's expense. He wasn't as happy to see the seven black-clad neo-Nazis saunter in and take seats at the back of the gallery. While explaining the rules of the court to the spectators, he made it obvious to the skinheads that he was talking to them when he warned that he would take into custody anyone who gestured to, or in any way tried to communicate with, any in-custody defendant. Now and then Lee would look back to see whether they were paying any attention to him. Each time he looked he would notice one or more of them glaring back. He couldn't tell if that was because they recognized him, or possibly because he was a white man sitting with a black woman. Sharona seemed unconcerned by their stares, however, and periodically would turn and wink at one or another of them.

In the meantime, Connelly and Wessel were in chambers with Judge Mackenzie and Deputy DA Rogers, who was accompanied by Senior Deputy DA Stokes. Wessel and Connelly made it clear that their clients were not about to take any offer and that both attorneys had received anonymous calls indicating the people's witness was dead from a drug overdose. The name they were given was Steven McMillan.

"Look, Your Honor, we've read the discovery. Without Mr. McMillan's testimony, all the People have is a set of skid marks that could have come from any number of cars and a couple of spray cans with our client's fingerprints on them."

"Graffiti on the back wall," interjected David Rogers.

"Yeah, well, that's good for a vandalism charge," said Connelly. "If that's your offer, I might be able to get my guy to take it."

"Look," said Wessel. "We can go ahead with the preliminary hearing, but we're going to put an objection on the record against the presentation of any hearsay statements that will be attributed to Steven McMillan."

Judge Mackenzie looked directly at Stokes. "Your move, counselor," he said.

Stokes leaned back in his chair and looked at Rogers, then let out a deep breath. "Move to dismiss," he ordered Rogers.

"Okay, very well," said Judge Mackenzie. "Let's put it on the record."

As the judge stepped toward the bench, Deputy Wilson ordered the court to remain seated and come to order. By now, Carpenter and Cardinal had been brought into the courtroom and put into the small wire holding cell next to Wilson's desk.

Dismissing the charges against Carpenter and Cardinal would take less than three minutes. Afterwards Judge Mackenzie would order the defendants to be released forthwith.

"Okay," said Judge Mackenzie. "First order of business is People versus Carpenter and Cardinal. Counsels, please state your presence for the record." Rogers, Wessel and Connelly did so, with the latter two announcing that their clients were present in custody.

"Thank you, gentlemen, I understand the people have a motion. Is that correct Mr. Rogers?"

"Yes sir, the people move to dismiss." Rogers replied without rising from his seat.

"No objection," responded the two defense attorneys.

"So ordered," said Judge Mackenzie as he slammed his gavel down. "Defendants will be released forthwith."

As the two skinheads were escorted out of the courtroom, Carpenter turned and flashed the three-fingered gang sign to the WAW members in the gallery. As he did so, he noticed Sharona and Lee sitting in the front row and nudged Cardinal. Cardinal glared at them as Carpenter mimicked shooting them both.

Deputy Wilson looked at Lee and Sharona, hoping neither would react to Carpenter's taunting gesture. If Sharona was bothered, she sure didn't show it. She winked and smiled at Carpenter. She had just been threatened by a mass murderer who was backed up by a small army, and she appeared absolutely unmoved. In fact, she seemed to be enjoying the moment. *What made her tick?*

Lee's baleful stare, on the other hand, projected an aura of pure menace. It was obvious that his entire focus was on the two skinheads. His eyes were those of a rattlesnake—or a gunfighter—about to strike. Deputy Wilson watched in awe as Lee tuned out his surroundings and, in his mind's eye, he and his two adversaries were the only ones left on the planet. This was the same look Wilson had witnessed when Lee was mercilessly destroying his opponents in the ring. Something ice-cold lurked behind those eyes. Whatever it was, he hoped Lee could still turn it off.

The drive back from the courthouse was unusually quiet until Sharona softly spoke: "she was 24, wasn't she? I read that in the paper."

"Who was 24? Who are you talking about?" Lee responded.

"Stephanie Alarcon, the girl these scumbags murdered. The girl with the one-year-old baby" she replied, a tinge of anger in her voice.

"Yeah, she was 24." Said Lee, not sure where this was going; "why?"

"I had a sister. She was 13 when she died. That was 11 years ago. She and Stephanie Alarcon would both be the same age if they were still alive."

After several seconds, Sharona quietly said to herself: "My sister would be 24. I might have had a little niece. Nobody deserves that, nobody."

This was the first time Lee had ever heard about a sister. From the hurt and anger in Sharona's voice, he knew better than to press her. If she wanted him to know anything more, she would tell him.

Lee had his own reason to be introspective. The gesture Carpenter made as he and Cardinal were being led out of the courtroom served to remind him just how dangerous things might soon get. It also reminded him what it felt like to tell Krystal—the best thing that had ever happened to him-- goodbye. It was all because of them. The thought that these two arrogant low-lifes were not only going to go free, but openly threatened him and Sharona, was almost more than he could stand. He could feel the beginning of a headache coming on, not just an ordinary headache, but the kind he got when there was no release for his anger. He found himself actually hoping for a confrontation. If one was in the cards, it would not end well, not for these guys, not for any of them.

CHAPTER 41

Something was wrong. It just didn't feel right. It was early, earlier than usual, still dark in fact, when Sharona pulled into the office complex. As she wheeled the Expedition through the visitor parking lot and into the tenant parking below the three-story building her headlights splashed across the windshield of an aging cargo van sitting in the far corner of the lot and well out of the glare of the security lights. Nothing in particular about the van stood out, but still, it just gave her the creeps. She had learned from her tours in Afghanistan to trust her instincts, even when all logic said otherwise, go with your gut feeling. It wasn't all that unusual for transients to park in the lot after hours. They were generally harmless and just looking for a place to bed down for the night. Somehow it didn't feel that way this time. Her senses were instantly on alert.

As she inserted her card to raise the gate arm she scanned the dimly lit parking structure. Empty; no one was there and nowhere to hide; just an empty parking structure, nothing more. She pulled into her designated space and, eschewing the stairway this time, hurried to the elevator and ascended to the third floor.

Once inside the office she felt a bit more relaxed. *Maybe there was nothing sinister about the van after all. Maybe it had just triggered some long forgotten and buried memory. Maybe she was just on edge because Ronald Carpenter and Jesse Cardinal were back on the streets again.* She wanted to believe this, but her senses told her otherwise. She immediately walked to Lee's inner office and without turning on the lights, closed the door behind her. From the picture window behind Lee's desk she had an unrestricted view of the section of the parking lot where sat the van. Full daylight was still more than an hour away, but in the darkness she was able to make out its outline. Nothing stirred; nothing unusual. Still, there was something wrong. She could feel it.

She sat motionless in Lee's chair, intently watching for some sign of life. After about half an hour dawn slowly began to break. Normally this would be the signal for any transients parked in the lot to be on their way. The van didn't move. Her senses were on edge. *Something was wrong.*

There was no telling when Lee would arrive. As a security precaution since the release of Carpenter and Cardinal three weeks ago they agreed to vary their schedules as much as possible without disrupting the office operations. Today he would be coming in early. This was why she was already here: It only seemed right to be at work before the boss. She wrestled with the idea of calling Lee and warning him, *but what would she say: "watch out for the van in the parking lot?"*

As the early morning glow began to lift the darkness, Sharona saw another flash of light cross the van's windshield. At the same time she heard the distinctive growl of Lee's Porsche. A few seconds later the sound echoed, then died out. Lee was in the parking garage.

No sooner did Lee turn into the garage than the van suddenly lurched forward and with its lights out, quickly circled around the perimeter of the parking lot before coming to a stop. It was now directly below Sharona's vantage point and out of view from the parking structure.

Sharona instantly broke for the door and then her desk in the outer office. Adrenaline coursed through her veins as she retrieved the nine-millimeter pistol from the top drawer and sprinted to the stairwell. Clutching the pistol, she steadied herself with her left hand on the railing as she descended the zig-zigging stairwell two steps two at a time.

In the parking garage Lee smiled as he spotted Sharona's car. He wasn't a bit surprised that she was here first. It was just like her: always early. Lee pulled into his designated spot just past hers.

Johnny Cash was belting out the last few stanzas of *Walk the Line* over the Porsche's sound system. Lee was in no hurry this morning so he leaned back in the driver's seat and listened as his favorite Country Western singer wrapped it up. With Sharona's Expedition blocking his view he never saw the three large, black clad, intruders slip past the entry gate and the closed stairwell door before dropping to a crouch alongside of her SUV.

Before long the song ended and it was time to get going. Lee unbuckled his seat restraint and retrieved his sport coat and briefcase from the passenger seat, then opened the driver's side door.

In the stairwell Sharona was silently descending the last set of stairs. She was now forced to move painfully slow. Speed is not conducive to stealth. She couldn't risk a shootout if these men were armed. Lee's life, and hers, for that matter, depended on the element of surprise.

Next to the Expedition three figures tensed in anticipation. Each armed with a sawn-off baseball bat. Although they were there to kill the traitorous Lee Edwards, they were also there to make a statement for anyone else who might consider going against the White Arian Warriors. The penalty would be sure and brutal. Between the bats and the steel toed boots they wore, the message would be loud and clear: retribution would not come gently.

The assailants listened as Lee's car door softly clicked shut, followed by the sharp chirp of the car alarm. The two in back stared intently at their leader, waiting for the signal to spring into action.

The soft tap of Lee's shoe against the concrete floor echoed against the walls of the garage as he took his first step toward the rear of the two vehicles.

On the opposite side of the Expedition the man in front raised his right fist. As soon as Lee came into view it would drop, signaling the launch of the attack.

Two more steps echoed across the garage.

The first assailant leaned slightly forward. His club lay on the floor alongside his right knee. His hand clenched so tightly it shook, anticipating Lee's appearance. His two followers concentrated intently on the fist, each fighting the urge attack before the signal was given.

One more step.

Suddenly, Sharona in a calm, yet firm, voice ordered: "drop the weapons assholes. If any of you moves I'll kill you."

Lee stopped in his tracks. The three would-be attackers froze. The next sound was the sharp rattle of the bats landing on the concrete floor.

Lee took a cautious step back. There was no doubt that was Sharona's voice. What was going on? Another step back and Sharona came into view, her back against the wall, both arms extended and a pistol gripped in her hands, aimed at something he couldn't see.

"What's going on?" Lee called out; his voice a mixture of confusion and concern.

"I need you to walk around the front of my car and come here." Sharona replied without taking her eyes off the three men crouched alongside the vehicle.

Without relaxing her stance Sharona addressed the three captives in a voice as cold as ice: "what you punks do next; how well you follow orders, is going to have a huge impact on your life span. Put both of your hands behind your head and lock your fingers, then drop forward, face down, to the floor. Do not put your hands in front of you to break your fall and do not look back at me. If any of you do I'm going to empty my clip into all three of you." The lack of emotion in her voice confirmed she meant every word.

The three thugs immediately complied, leaving the one in front face down on the concrete and the next two facedown and overlapping the man in front of him.

"Lee, kick those clubs away. You three spread your arms, palms on the floor." Sharona ordered.

Once the clubs were well out of reach of the three prone figures Sharona stepped forward and squatted down without averting her eyes, then transferred the pistol to her left hand and, grabbed one of the bats in her right before standing up. Her voice was still eerily calm when she spoke: "I have a couple of questions to ask you punks. There are two things you need to keep in mind. First of all: your honesty will determine the condition you will be in when you leave here; Second of all: I already know the answers. I'm only asking because I want to hear them from you. Let me give you a little demonstration."

Stepping alongside the third man in line, she asked: "are you left handed?"

"No sir," he replied nervously.

"Sir? Don't call me sir! It's inappropriate!" She yelled. "You understand, punk?"

"Yes ma'am."

"Okay, let's try again. Are you left handed?"

"No ma'am."

At that Sharona lifted the club and slammed it down as hard as she could on his outstretched right hand. The man's screams instantly echoed throughout the parking structure. "You are now." she calmly stated, then: "now shut up or I'll really hurt you." She ordered, instantly quieting the man.

"Okay, now that we understand each other," she said, stiffly jabbing the second man in the ribs with the bat. "Let's start with you."

Lee noticed the middle man's hand shaking and wondered to himself if this was an interrogation method Sharona had learned during her tours in Afghanistan. She was now someone he didn't recognize.

"Who sent you here?

"White Aryan Warriors," came the nervous reply.

"Be more specific."

"Jesse Cardinal and Ronald Carpenter."

"Are you members?"

"No, they just hired us."

"To do what?"

"Kill Lee Edwards."

"Anyone else?"

"No, just Lee. We would get a bonus if we killed you too, but Lee was the target."

"How much did they pay you?"

"Five thousand each for Lee and a two-thousand-dollar bonus for you and two thousand more for anyone else with you or Lee."

While Sharona appeared calm and collected Lee could feel the anger grow within himself with each question and answer. These men were here to ambush and kill him. They didn't even know him, yet they were going to kill him. They would get a bonus if they killed Sharona. If Krystal were with him they would get another bonus for killing her, an innocent bystander whose life could be bought for two thousand dollars.

Lee's breathing quickened as the rage grew within him. His eyes narrowed and focused solely on the three men prone on the floor before him. The next thing he knew he was standing over the man lying at the front of the line. "Get up," he heard himself yell. At the same time he could barely hear Sharona shouting his name. She could have been a block away.

"I said get up!" Lee yelled again.

"Get up!" Sharona parroted. This time her voice was loud and clear.

The heavily muscled man slowly stood up. He was easily two inches taller and thirty pounds heavier than Lee. He had no doubt what would be coming next: the lawyer would throw a punch. He would be ready for it. If the woman wanted to kill them she probably would have done it by now. In his mind he envisioned a scenario where he would quickly dispose of this lawyer and the distraction would give his partners an opening to overpower her. They would earn their money, and a bonus, after all. He stood there, unflinching and sneering at Lee. *This guy is a lawyer, a business man; not a fighter. He just made the biggest mistake of his life. This is going to be easy.* Suddenly sensing a slight movement, he quickly brought his left hand up to protect his jaw.

The punch came from the other side. One cardinal rule of boxing is that you never lead with your right. Lee slightly feinted with his right, then stepped in, left foot forward, and pivoted on the ball of that foot while landing a picture-perfect left hook flush on the thug's jaw.

Another cardinal rule of the fight game is that you never stop to admire your work. With blinding speed the left hook was followed by another left hook, this one to the liver; a combination Lee had used many times to finish an opponent. Lee was now on auto-pilot. Muscle memory and reflexes took the place of conscious thought.

The opponent staggered backward, eyes wide with shock and surprise, his knees buckling, barely able to hold him up.

Lee came forward, now stalking his prey. The would-be assassin threw a wild right hand in the direction of Lee's head. The punch caught nothing but air as Lee bobbed and weaved his way in. The thug followed up with a kick aimed at Lee's crotch. With lightening quick reflexes Lee slapped the man's boot away with his right hand then dropped slightly and threw another powerful left hook to the man's body; this one landing on the rib cage, then followed by a fourth left hook that connected at same spot on the jaw as his first punch. He had yet to throw a punch with his right hand and his opponent was already out on his feet, the thug dropped both of his hands and his face took on a slack-jawed, blank expression as he began to slump to the floor. Lee wasn't done yet. Pushing off with his trailing foot he launched a powerful straight right that instantly found its target and shattered the orbital bones encompassing the eye socket on the right side of the big man's face.

The thug fell to the floor of the garage, sprawled on his back, unmoving and unconscious. If they had been in a ring the fight would be over; the referee wouldn't have bothered to count. But they weren't in a ring and this was no boxing match. There was no referee to stop the brutal assault. Lee wasn't done yet. His rage had not begun to subside. He instantly pounced on the unconscious man. Then, with one knee on the man's chest, grabbed a handful of hair in his left hand and lifted the man's head. Two punches landed just above the upper lip, shattering both front teeth and breaking his nose. The unmistakable slap of bare knuckles against skin echoed through the still empty garage as each punch landed with bone breaking power and was immediately followed by the sound of the thug's head bouncing off the concrete floor.

Three more punches followed before Sharona's voice finally pierced his adrenalin infused rage: "Lee....Lee, he's had enough! You're going to kill him!" She shouted. This time her voice came through loud and clear. Lee turned and stared at Sharona, who was still holding her pistol on the two remaining wanna-be tough guys. His eyes projected a level of rage that she wouldn't have thought possible. Then, just as suddenly as he turned it on, the anger disappeared. Lee calmly glanced at the two men lying on the floor in front of Sharona, then, with a dissociated and unconcerned expression on his face, glanced down at the man lying motionless beneath him, silently surveying the damage he has done to the man's features.

Lee stood and positioned himself alongside of Sharona. Without taking her eyes off the two potential threats lying in front of her, she jabbed the bat into the ribs of the one in back. "You, Lefty," she said. "Slowly reach up and remove your partner's wallet, then toss it to your right as far as you can. Do not move your right hand. Keep it flat on the floor, palms down. Lee, I need you to retrieve Lefty's wallet." There was no question: Sharona was still in charge.

As soon as the wallets were secured Sharona stepped forward and slammed the bat down on the wrist of the man who had given up the information, eliciting a painful wail. "Shut up. You ain't hurt." She ordered. Then, in a casual voice: "Don't want these guys to be able to hold a weapon anytime soon," she said without looking back at Lee. "You'd better grab your sparring partner's wallet too. We're going to want to know exactly who these guys are," then added: "can you believe these clowns were stupid enough to carry their wallets to what they thought would be a murder scene?"

Lee walked over to the fallen biker and rolled him on his side to retrieve the wallet. Noticing there was no movement from the lifeless form. Sharona asked: "Is he dead?"

"No," Lee calmly replied. "He's breathing. There are little blood bubbles coming out of his nose and mouth."

"You mean what's left of his nose. That could mean a punctured lung, you probably broke some ribs. When does unconscious become coma?"

"Don't know." Lee answered, walking back to his earlier position behind the other two and alongside Sharona. "Don't really care either. Anyway, I think he's coming around."

"Looks like your fearless leader is in serious shape." She said, now addressing the two men lying on the floor below her. "You'd better get him some help as soon as possible. So, here's what we're going to do: when I tell you to stand up, you slowly stand up. After that you pick up Sleeping Beauty over there and you get the hell out of here as quickly as you can. You will not take your van. Don't send anyone back here looking for it either. If you do, they are going to die. It's gonna get towed anyway. You idiots parked in a fire lane. I'm going to follow you to the street. After that it's up to you to figure out where you're going next and how you're going to get there. Don't look back at me. If you do, I will see that as an aggressive move and take appropriate action. If I ever see any of you again, even in passing, I will kill you. I will personally come after you and by the time I'm done you will be praying for death to come. You can try me if you want, but I wouldn't advise it." Then, stepping alongside the third man, she raised the club again and slammed it down on his ankle. The man immediately let out another ear-piercing cry. "Walk it off Lefty; you're a tough guy" she taunted, then in a voice that reeked of military-like authority: "now you maggots get on your feet and get the hell out of here!"

Sharona followed the three as they struggled to the street, then returned to the parking structure where she put the wallets and bats in the back of her Expedition. Once finished, Sharona turned to Lee and, ignoring his blood-stained shirt as if nothing out of the ordinary had happened, asked in a cheerful voice: "how about we go get coffee? I didn't get a chance to put a pot on this morning and I get kind of irritable when I haven't had my coffee."

"Sounds good to me." Lee responded. "I'll buy."

CHAPTER 42

t had been a month since Carpenter and Cardinal beat the system. Something had to be done. Tonight would be as good a time as any. It wasn't quite dusk yet and the dark-clothed figure was rummaging through the shed, looking to fill the list of items needed to facilitate the introduction of Jesse Cardinal to his maker. A gun would be used only as a last resort. It would be too loud, too quick and too painless. A garrote would be quiet, but the pain would only last until he lost consciousness, not nearly long enough. No, Jesse Cardinal needed to die slowly. He took part in the killing of three innocent people and left a little baby without her mother; for what? For no real reason at all. On top of that, Jesse had some information that needed sharing and he would share it, even if it took all night.

The state dropped the ball. It was time for someone to step up and take out the trash.

Of course, nothing would be accomplished without first taking Cardinal down. He was no little man and, if he were fighting for his life, he could possibly be a pretty good day's work. Sneaking into his bedroom and beaning him with a lug wrench was an option, but it could kill him. There's no way to get the necessary information from a dead man. Besides, why go through all the trouble of sneaking through someone's house when you can get him to come to you, fully incapacitated? It could be done easily enough if you planned ahead and stuck to the plan.

Not counting the gun in case everything went to hell, there were a total of seven items that were needed to get the job done. The first thing on the list was a roll of thick plastic sheeting. That was easy. There was plenty of it rolled up under the bench waiting for the next painting project. Next was the little present that would be waiting for Jesse on his doorstep. It was in the shed somewhere, in fact it used to hang on the wall. It couldn't be far.

Fortunately the shed was well organized, at least when compared to the rat trap Cardinal called home. The object turned up pretty quickly, right where it had been safely stored for the last couple of years. Preparing the damned thing would take some time, but it would all be worth it when he got a look at Jesse Cardinal's face. The final items were pretty easy: a heavy-duty lock, a couple of large tie straps, a pocketknife and, finally, a pruning saw. Jesse was really not going to like this, not at all; poor baby.

CHAPTER 43

Jesse Cardinal pulled up to his garage door and pushed the button on his remote door opener. It was well past dark and transitioning into late night. The door began to retract into the ceiling, then stopped and went back down. He pushed the remote again and the door began its journey upward, only to come to a stop, again. On the third try the door dutifully rolled fully open, but the damned light didn't go on. Of course it didn't. It hadn't worked for more than a week. About the same time, the door itself began acting up. Sometimes it would only go partially up, and then stop. Other times it would go back down on its own, and on a couple of occasions it would open without being commanded to do so. He would have disconnected the motor, but the door was heavy and he didn't want to wrestle with it every time he came home.

Still, this was one more thing he didn't need, not at all. He still hadn't finished cleaning up the mess the cops left behind when they went through his house the day he was arrested. No doubt they trashed his place just because they could, but what was he going to do, complain to the police? And what the hell did they do to the lock on his front door? Twice this week he came home to find the door wide open. Nothing was missing either time, at least not as far as he could tell, with the mess and all. When he bought the house it was already over fifty years old and in need of a complete renovation. In the five years he had owned the place he never changed any of the locks. Maybe it was time. Maybe it was time to install a deadbolt also. Now it looked like he would have to put replacing the garage door opener on the list. He didn't need this. He had more important things to do.

After pulling to a stop inside the garage, he stepped out of his vehicle. Fortunately its headlights stayed on for a few seconds after turning off the ignition. Using the light reflecting off the rear wall to navigate, Jesse pressed the controller mounted on the wall, then waited to see what response he would get. The door dutifully rolled shut and locked with a metallic snap. As he turned and stepped through the door that would take him into the pantry, the motor came to life again, lifting the door fully open. Jesse stopped and glared at the floor. Taking two deep breaths, he stared at the door, daring it to disobey as he pressed the wall-mounted button again. Without hesitation the door shut itself. Jesse waited several seconds before disappearing into the house.

Although it was only a little after ten o'clock, Jesse was exhausted. He'd been hoisting beers and playing pool at Cook's Corner, a no-frills rustic biker bar/roadhouse housed in a wooden 1880s-era building. Cook's Corner sat on Santiago Canyon Road in Trabuco Canyon on the eastern outskirts of Orange County, less than five miles from Jesse's house. Maybe the stress from being locked up for murder was still getting to him. In any event, it was time to turn in.

Just as he was starting to doze off, he heard it again: the sound of the garage door opening, followed by the unmistakable click of the door locking in place. Dragging himself out of bed, he walked through the darkened house to the garage. He wearily pressed the button with his thumb, and the door rattled closed with a snap of the lock. After about two minutes of standing in the garage, silently waiting for the door to malfunction again, he turned and headed back to his bedroom, unaware of the dark figure crouched on the opposite side of his Toyota 4Runner.

A half hour passed and the garage door motor awoke him again. Getting out of bed, he decided that this time he would run the door down, then unplug the motor; something he should have thought to do before. Tomorrow he would call someone to repair the damned thing.

Storming through the house and knowing that the object of his rage was nothing more than a machine—something he could not physically or verbally abuse—only served to raise his frustration level. The garage was pitch black. He couldn't even see the controller from where he stood in the entryway. He would have to fetch the flashlight from the kitchen drawer.

Back in the kitchen, Jesse found his Maglite and pushed the button. Nothing. He shook the flashlight as if attempting some kind of inanimate object CPR. Nothing. Throwing it back into the drawer, he realized his only other option would be to turn on his 4Runner's headlights. From that there would be enough ight bouncing off the wall for him to find his way to the garage door and pull the plug on the opener.

Walking back to the open door, he could barely make out a dim reflection of light from the kitchen and through the pantry bouncing off the side of his truck. The garage floor sat about six inches lower than the pantry floor. He had stepped into his garage countless times and didn't need to look down to do so. In the darkness he stepped down again, for the last time. This time he should have looked.

CHAPTER 44

People tend to be creatures of habit. Hit men and soldiers kill a lot of people who have a set routine. It wasn't all that hard to figure out Jesse Cardinal's routine. All I had to do was watch him leave his house, then follow him to his favorite watering hole a couple of times to know what he did and where he was when he wasn't saving the white race. One of the first things I noticed was that he had an automatic garage door opener. After that, all I had to do was drive by Cook's Corner and look for his car. If it was there, I knew the coast was clear for me to look around his house and decide what would be next for him.

Fortunately he lived in an old house. The locks were probably forty or fifty years old and best of all, there were no deadbolts. I'm no locksmith, but it's widely known that old locks are pretty easy to defeat with nothing more than a pocketknife. I would have gone in through the back door had it not been for all the poison oak. I broke in through the front door twice. The first time to get into his garage and see what type of opener he had, and the second time to program a matching remote I bought at Lowe's, loosen the opener's lightbulb, and turn on the flashlight he kept in his kitchen junk drawer and run the batteries down.

After that I didn't have to use the front door anymore. We were kind of like roommates. I could come and go as I liked and even had garage privileges. I never did bother to close and lock the front door after I broke in. There was no good reason not to other than just to creep him out. I thought about rearranging his furniture just for laughs, but the place was such a mess he probably wouldn't notice.

The newly programed remote was the most important part of my plan. With that taken care of, the rest would be easy. I could visit Jesse Cardinal anytime I felt like it.

As soon as I got his surprise prepared, I loaded everything into the back of the pickup and headed to Cook's Corner. I can't describe how good it made me feel to see his 4Runner parked in front. I just hoped he wouldn't stay all night. I had things to do in the morning and hated to be late. I only needed enough time to prepare my truck and unload a single item out of it. I had to be extremely careful while unloading the special surprise. This was going to be fun. I only hoped he would appreciate the effort I put into it.

In less than two minutes I unloaded the pickup and placed the most important item—the one that would determine whether or not I was going to have to shoot him—out of sight by the garage wall. I parked the truck up the street and around a bend and grabbed my pistol, the garage door opener and a small flashlight out of the glove compartment and hiked back down to wait in the bushes, hoping the whole time I wasn't sitting in poison oak.

It was a long wait, not unbearably long, but longer than I would have preferred. It occurred to me that he might get stopped for DUI and ruin the whole thing. That would have been just my luck.

Finally a splash of light across the bushes and the crunching of wheels on his gravel driveway announced the arrival of tonight's surprise party's guest of honor. The vehicle came to a stop and I heard the garage door begin to open. Just for the heck of it I pushed the button on my remote, instantly bringing it to a stop. Another push brought the door back down. Although I couldn't see it from where I sat, I imagined the look on his face. Inbreeds tend to be pretty easy to confuse, especially when they've been drinking. After a couple of seconds the door started up again. I made it stop again. I could have continued this wrestling match all night, but finally I let him have his way.

Still sitting outside, I waited until his living room light no longer shone on the driveway. After giving him time to settle in, I pushed the remote again. I didn't enter the garage at that time. I had to find out if he would come all the way to the door before I made any move to enter. All he did was open the door and hit the wall-mounted button, closing the door. He was swearing under his breath, obviously frustrated. I was going to have to lure him into the garage.

I pushed the control again and scampered into the garage behind his 4Runner. Just as before, he hit the switch by the door and retreated back into the house. I dragged his present to the front of the entry door and left it on the *floor. It was dark in the garage and without a flashlight, he probably wouldn't see it.*

One last push of the opener and out the door I went. If everything went as planned, no one would have to yell "surprise" when he stepped through the door. He would do it himself.

I didn't have to wait long before he lowered the garage door again. Less than half a minute later a muffled metallic snap, followed by a god-awful scream, confirmed I had caught something in my antique bear trap. I didn't have to guess what it was. I was just grateful I'd never thrown it out. You never know when you might need one.

I immediately re-opened the garage door and raced in. Jesse was flopping around on the floor, doing a pretty good version of the tuna dance and trying to scream the pain away. Without even questioning who I was or how I got there, he frantically pointed to the big, rusty thing clamped about ten inches up his left leg. Feigning concern, I immediately asked: "what happened?" Confused and probably in shock, his response was just to continue rolling back and forth while holding is leg just above the jaws of the trap and continue screaming at the top of his lungs.

Now, in your mind's eye you are probably picturing a stereotypical bear trap with huge shark-like teeth like you see in cartoons. Those traps might have existed once, but the commonly used traps have three-quarter-inch teeth spaced about three inches apart. Add to that the incredible clamping force from the jaws and you have something capable of holding a Kodiak bear, or a Nazi. I thought for sure the trap would break his leg. Somehow it didn't, but it sure looked uncomfortable.

After surveying the damage, I admonished him that he needed to be more careful if he was going to walk around the house barefooted. After all, what if he stepped on a tack or something? Those things can be painful. I also pointed out that he would probably need a tetanus shot.

I waited for him to settle down a bit and told him that my pickup was parked just around the corner. I shared with him that having a bear trap locked onto your ankle could be serious and he probably should try not to walk on it until I got back.

Once I got my truck backed into his driveway, I spread the plastic across the bed and told him to get in. He looked at me like he didn't understand and kept pointing at the trap, as if I hadn't noticed it before. It took a couple of seconds before I realized he was begging me to loosen it. I explained that each spring on a bear trap takes 250 pounds to compress and can't be done safely without special tools and he should have thought of that before stepping on it.

He kept writhing around on the ground and didn't make a single move towards my truck. He made it pretty clear that he wasn't thrilled about going for a ride with me, but I pointed out that I wasn't leaving without him and I would have no qualms about adding my weight to the trap until he changed his mind. His answer was to frantically shake his head and squirm about some more. That was unacceptable, so I rolled him over and zip-tied his wrists together and duct-taped his mouth shut after which I went inside to retrieve his cell phone, explaining that I left mine at home and might need it to make a call.

It took a while to wrestle him into the bed of the truck. He was pretty reluctant and the added weight of the trap didn't help, but I finally managed to get him loaded up. I had already put the camper shell on, but I still felt I needed to tell him not to try and sit up while we were underway. In doing, so I warned him that if he sat up I would dump him on the road and leave him there. Of course, that was a lie. I would have never dumped him alongside of the road. That would have been littering, not a good image for a trash collector.

About twelve miles out on the Ortega Highway a forest ranger's station sits on a seldom-used dirt road that goes deep into Cleveland National Forest. The drive from Jesse Cardinal's house is about a half hour, then maybe another ten or fifteen minutes to the end of the dirt road.

When we got there I dragged him out of the pickup bed and about fifteen feet into the bushes to a large oak tree. As soon as we stopped, Jesse started twisting and writhing again and screaming through the duct tape. He was pretty upset and acted like he thought I intended to hang him. It makes sense that he would think that: there's no shortage of oak trees in the area.

I assured him I didn't have a rope with me, so hanging was out. His relief only lasted until I explained what I did have in mind. Truth be told, I showed him. I dragged him to the tree until his legs were straddling it, then wrapped the trap's chain tightly around his right ankle and secured it with the padlock. He tried to resist, but he didn't have a lot of energy left, what with all the blood loss and all.

Once I had his legs secured, I cut the zip ties binding his wrists, just in case he had to scratch his nose or something. It was the decent thing to do. Have you ever had an itch on your nose you couldn't scratch? There were a lot of insects out there. What if one of them were to land on his nose or something? Not being able to scratch your nose can be torture. I wouldn't wish that on anybody. After freeing his hands I told him I would let him pull the duct tape off of his own mouth, since I wasn't sure how fast I should do it.

Next came the ultimatum: if he coughed up the names and contact numbers of the two bikers he and his boss hired to kill Manuel Trejo, I would leave him with a way to get loose. If he didn't give me the names, or if he lied to me, I would leave him chained to the tree and let the mountain lions and coyotes have him. Almost immediately he spit out two names: "Big Bob" and "Trout." Then, as if reading my mind, he said to look in his phone's contact information and their numbers and addresses would be there. He even added that they could usually be found at Cook's Corner, or at a small biker/cowboy bar in Silverado called the Gold Rush. To say he was anxious to hand over the information would be an understatement, which proves something I've said all along: pain is a good motivator and extreme pain is an extremely good motivator.

Satisfied that I'd probably gotten all I needed from him, I kept my promise not to leave him without a way to get loose. I went to the truck and came back with the pruning saw and an old McDonald's bag that I found under the seat. I handed him the saw and told him he might be able to cut the tree down with it before the local wildlife smelled blood and came calling, but I doubted it. Then I told him he had a couple of other options. The best option was probably for him to take the saw and cut his leg off, or if he were a real man, gnaw it off. At that I reached into the McDonalds bag and tossed him a couple of unopened ketchup and salt and pepper packets.

It was time for me to leave. He had options to consider.

CHAPTER 45

Jesse Cardinal was on the verge of panic as he screamed at the pickup rumbling away into the night. As truck followed a bend in the dirt road its taillights disappeared. He was now in total darkness and all alone. For the first time since becoming a member of the White Aryan Warriors he was completely powerless. *What just happened? Where were the Warriors? They were always supposed to have each other's backs.*

The throbbing pain in his lower leg was nearly unbearable and he could no longer feel his foot. *How long can a limb go without circulation before you lose it?* His ankles were bound together so tightly that he had to lean way over to his side and strain to barely make out the shape of the trap. All he was sure about was the pain. He had no idea how badly his leg was mangled. All he had on were the underwear he wore to bed. He was freezing cold and the blood he lost made the chill worse. He was exhausted, but afraid to fall asleep. He might never wake up. Instead, he screamed and screamed again. His fear was heightened by the sound of something moving in the dark through the bushes nearby.

He picked up the pruning saw and started to run its teeth back and forth into the bark of the oak tree. After an eternity of sawing he was dripping with sweat and had barely cut into the tree's outer skin. The saw was woefully inadequate. It would never cut through, even if he worked it for a hundred years, but he didn't have a hundred years. Unless he could get free his life expectancy would be measured in hours, not years. Another sound: something was moving through the bushes again. Was it closer this time? What was it? Knowing no one was coming to rescue him, and knowing he was almost out of time, he sat in the darkness, shivering with cold and fear until finally, he closed his eyes and tightly clenched his jaw before setting the saw's teeth into the skin just below his left knee.

CHAPTER 46

Scott Donaldson had been in his office all morning; filling out paperwork on a simple bar fight that turned into a homicide when one of the participants pulled a knife, when he got the call. Hikers had found a body in San Juan Capistrano. Sheriff's deputies were on the scene and one of them would meet him at the Ranger station to guide him in. As morbid as it sounded, Donaldson much preferred looking at bodies than writing about them.

Upon arrival, one of the deputies walked him to the body, explaining that a couple of hikers had driven their Jeep to the end of the dirt road. As soon as they got out of their Jeep they smelled a strong odor of rotting flesh and spotted something just off the road. When they realized what they were looking at they ran back to the Jeep and hightailed it back up to the ranger station to report what they found, then called 911 and waited for the emergency vehicles. The chance of getting useable tire marks was pretty slim. The road was narrow and rocky and the hikers had driven their Jeep over it coming and going.

The first thing that stood out was the large, rusted steel trap clenched over the body's lower leg. Someone wanted this guy to hurt big time and die an excruciating death. The fact that his legs were chained together with a lock meant this wasn't a body dump. The victim was still alive when he was brought there. Whoever he was died at the scene. Did the killer watch the spectacle; maybe even eat a meal while he enjoyed the show? There were a couple of ketchup and salt and pepper packets lying next to the body. Whoever left them there took the bag and meal wrappers with them.

Identification would be difficult likely requiring dental records or DNA. Not only was the body bloated and decomposing, but the critters had been at it. Most of the face was missing and nearly the entire left leg was chewed down to the bone. At this point the only thing he had to go on was the victim's bald head and what appeared to be remnants of a huge swastika tattooed on his chest. A large dark spot around the lower leg indicated he lost a huge amount of blood before he died.

Something else drew Donaldson's attention. The victim was holding what appeared to be a pruning saw in his right hand. Saw marks were visible on the tree where he had tried in vain to cut it down. There was no way he brought the saw with him, which meant the killer left it, probably wanting to give him some kind of false hope that he could free himself. Surveying the scene a bit more, Donaldson spotted a significant wound on the victim's left leg, just below the knee. Animals had ripped away much of the skin, exposing a large section of the tibia, and Donaldson could make out a clean cut nearly all the way through. John Doe had tried to saw his own leg off.

Stepping back, Donaldson realized he might have seen John Doe before. He had seen that tattoo, or one identical to it, when he rousted Jesse Cardinal out of bed a couple of months ago.

It was well past noon by the time Donaldson was finished with his preliminary investigation and headed back to the office. He was hungry and was looking for somewhere to buy a quick bite on his way in. Deciding he would stop at the first fast food place he spotted, he headed north on Interstate 5. He had just merged into traffic when his cell phone chimed over the car's hands-free device. The only reason he took the call instead of letting it go to voicemail was because it was from Trevor Wilkins.

"What's up?" asked Donaldson.

"Thought you would want to know I got a call from Parkland Rice this morning."

"Let me guess," said Donaldson. "It's something about Jesse Cardinal."

"It looks like it probably is. How'd you know?"

"Was it another poem?' asked Donaldson.

"It was, and it was written in Morse code again. I just finished deciphering it, but how'd you know it was about Jesse Cardinal?"

"Read it to me, then I'll tell you."

175

"Okay, here goes: dot dot, dash dot dash, dot dash, dot dot dash."

"Very funny," said Donaldson. "Now, can we do it in English?"

"Sure," Wilkins replied:

"I caught a Cardinal in a trap

He committed a Cardinal sin

And because he didn't take the RAP

I had to do him in

Love, The Trash Collector"

"Well, at least the poetry's getting better. And it's almost certainly about our boy, all right. A couple of hikers found a body alongside a dirt road off of Highway 74 this morning. It'd been there for a few days with the bugs and animals using it for a buffet. There wasn't much left of the face, but it had a shaved head and a swastika tattoo on its chest, same as Cardinal."

"Were you able to tell how he died?"

"I'm not sure yet, but you won't believe what I saw. I'm about to grab a burger and head in. I'll tell you more about it when I get there."

"How sure are you that it's Cardinal?   "

"Ninety-nine percent. I sent a couple of deputies over to his house to do a welfare check. How'd things get so upside down that we're doing welfare checks on murderers?"

"I know, I don't get it either," said Trevor, then added, "Hey, on your way in can you swing by McDonalds and pick me up a burger and fries? Get a couple of extra packs of ketchup and salt and pepper too."

Forty-five minutes later Trevor was consuming the cold hamburger and fries and warm Coke that Donaldson brought him.

"So there's no doubt the Ward and Cardinal murders--if it does turn out to be Cardinal—are related. The only people who know about the Morse code messages are the killer and us, so the message Parkland Rice got has to be legit," he said.

"Actually, you missed one," replied Donaldson.

"Who?"

"Parkland Rice knows too, and as long as he gets the letters first he has a scoop on all the other newspapers. How do we know for sure he isn't producing the letters himself? That way he has a ready excuse for his fingerprints being on them."

"Except for one thing," said Trevor.

"What's that?"

"The first Trash Collector murder, Morse code and all, was several years ago in San Luis Obispo and the note was tacked to the victim's door, it wasn't sent to any newspaper."

"Yeah, but he wasn't even running a newspaper to send the note to back then. He was a freelance photographer with his own schedule. These things go deeper than just publicity. You can tell that by who the victims are and how they are killed. I'm not ruling him out yet."

"I'm not either, but while we're at it, what about Lee Edwards? He has been involved in some way, shape, or form with both Orange County murder victims. He got Ward's case dismissed, so maybe he didn't feel he had done society a service and decided to make things right. We know his involvement in the Carpenter and Cardinal case. On top of that, I don't know if you saw it, but I did: when Carpenter and Cardinal were being escorted out of the courtroom, Carpenter pointed to Lee Edwards and his office manager and mimicked shooting them. Maybe Edwards decided the best way to protect himself and the girl working for him would be a preemptive strike."

"That's a good point," replied Donaldson. "As nice a guy as he seems, I could see him doing something like that. After our first meeting with him I looked up some of his fights on YouTube, just to see if he was really as good as I keep hearing."

"So, was he?" asked Trevor.

"Not just good, but brutal," Donaldson responded. "There's something lurking beneath that nice-guy façade. When the bell rang it was like someone flipped a switch. In a couple of his fights, I swear, if the referee hadn't pushed him away he would have been just fine with killing the other guy. That picture in his office of him nonchalantly stepping over his unconscious opponent, no compassion whatsoever, pretty much sums up what I saw. I'm no psychologist, but I don't think that's an instinct that just goes away. We certainly can't rule him out."

"Let's go pay a visit to Mr. Edwards, and see how he reacts when we tell him it looks like he won't have to worry about Jesse Cardinal," said Trevor as he wadded up what was left of his hamburger and tossed it into the trashcan.

Donaldson didn't mention his third suspect.

Sharona was just finishing up typing a court appearance reminder to a client when Trevor and Donaldson walked into the reception area.

"Uh oh, two of you, must be serious," said Sharona, looking up from her desk.

"Hi, Sharona," said Trevor. "Is Mr. Edwards available for a few minutes?"

"Well, we don't have anyone who goes by 'Mr. Edwards' around here, but we have a Lee Edwards, let me check and see how busy he is," replied Sharona, punching the intercom button. "Sheriff's Investigators Wilkins and Donaldson are out here; do you have time to talk with them?" she asked.

"I've got a few minutes. Go ahead and send them in."

Not bothering to rise, Lee looked up at the two investigators as they entered his office. "Investigator Wilkins, Investigator Donaldson, what can I do for you?"

"We just wanted to let you know," said Trevor. "We're pretty sure Jesse Cardinal is dead."

"Is that so?" said Lee, rocking back in his chair. "What do you mean: 'pretty sure'?"

"Let's just say it's unofficial at this point. We're waiting for confirmation," said Donaldson.

"Can you tell me how he died, or is that also 'unofficial at this point'?" Lee asked, making air quotes with his fingers.

"Truth is, we don't know yet," said Donaldson. "All we know is that it happened a few days ago, probably before the weekend."

"Can't say I'm sorry to hear about it, in fact, I can think of a lot of people who won't be sorry to hear about it. There are at least two families I can think of off the top of my head who probably won't shed a tear."

"How about you, Lee?" asked Donaldson. "I saw the gesture Carpenter made at you and Sharona in court the day he and Cardinal got released. That was an obvious threat. How'd you feel about that?"

"What are you getting at?" Lee asked, looking Donaldson straight in the eye. "If you're here because you think I killed Jesse Cardinal, bring a warrant. In the meantime, this conversation is over. There's the door. Close it from the other side."

As the two investigators rose and turned to leave, Lee added: "by the way, if you find out who the real killer is, send that person my way. I'm offering free representation. Jesse Cardinal needed killing."

Stopping in his tracks, Donaldson turned back to Lee. "'Needed killing,' isn't that the exact same thing you said to us when Joshua Ward was murdered?" he asked.

"Goodbye, gentlemen," Lee responded.

The two investigators were barely out of the office before Sharona stepped through Lee's door.

"What was all that about?" she asked. "They looked a lot happier coming in than they did leaving."

"They came to tell me Jesse Cardinal is dead. They wouldn't say how or when, just that he's dead."

"Okay, so what did you say to hurt their feelings?"

"I kicked them out because they think I did it."

"Do they really?" Sharona asked, surprise evident in her voice. "You mean I've been working for a vigilante and didn't even know it? I'm going to order some new business cards."

"Sharona," he said, looking up from his desk, "how is it that you can always make me laugh?"

"You ain't gonna be laughing next time we negotiate my salary, white boy," she responded, then added: "by the way, Ricky and I are going to the fights next week at the Del Mar Race Track down by San Diego. There's a carnival going on, too. Why don't you come with us? It'll be fun."

Sharona could see a hint of sadness in Lee's eyes as he said: "no, I appreciate the offer, but I've got some stuff going on." He was lying and she knew it. "Thank you anyway, maybe next time."

After a pause, Sharona softly asked: "you really miss her, don't you?"

"Just a little, I guess," he replied, now avoiding eye contact.

"Yeah, I guess so," she said, and turned and quietly left the room.

CHAPTER 47

Another quiet night, thought Donaldson as he sat in his unmarked vehicle half a block down the street from Ronald Carpenter's house. It had been nearly three weeks since Cardinal's murder and since then Donaldson had been infrequently surveilling Carpenter's home on the off chance something might turn up. The reference to a mortal sin left in the note was too obvious to miss. It had to be referencing the drive-by shooting on Fourth Street and the murder of Manuel Trejo at the cemetery. With Cardinal gone, it only made sense that Carpenter would be next.

Surveillance was always an exercise in boredom, even more so if you were carrying it out on your own. Donaldson was doing this one off the clock, even though he wasn't exactly sure why. After all, he was spending time he could be at home with his family instead of trying to stop someone from killing a killer who never asked for protection. It was more than just the cop in him that put him watching Carpenter's house. *We don't live in the Wild West anymore. There is no room for vigilantism. Murder is wrong anyway you cut it, no matter who the victim is. The Trash Collector is a murderer and has to be stopped before innocents start dying.* This one-man surveillance couldn't go on forever, though. He'd give it another couple of nights, then back off and wait for the other shoe to drop.

It wasn't quite 10:00 when he noticed a dark Chevy El Camino cruise by slowly. He had seen that same pickup, or maybe one exactly like it, pass by in the same direction less than fifteen minutes earlier.

Donaldson moved his car onto Carpenter's street, facing the direction the pickup was headed. The car would look empty to anybody driving up on it from the rear, and the streetlight reflecting onto the windshield would prevent anyone from seeing inside from the front. After another ten minutes the truck appeared again, cruising slowly up the street.

Donaldson crouched down, barely glancing over the dashboard. This time he was able to get a look at the pickup's license plate. If no one made a move on Carpenter tonight, he would run the number at the station tomorrow. He could call it in, but that might raise more questions than he was prepared to answer. He hadn't told anybody he was surveilling Carpenter's house, not even his own partner. Donaldson didn't need word of his clandestine activities getting out.

CHAPTER 48

Unbeknownst to Donaldson, he had already been spotted by the very person he had a growing suspicion might be The Trash Collector. The driver of the El Camino chuckled and drove on, contemplating whether to take another lap just for laughs. Donaldson could sit there and watch Carpenter's house from now till doomsday. Nothing was going to happen. Donaldson should have realized from the start that the house would never be a good option; too many houses too close together on a narrow street. Besides, Ronald Carpenter was a big guy. It would be too much work to wrestle him around in close quarters, not to mention all the noise it would generate. No, Ronald Carpenter would surely be taken care of away from prying neighbors and hero cops.

CHAPTER 49

Like the others before him, Carpenter's exit into oblivion would require special preparation. A large army field jacket and green watch cap, along with a pair of military issue leather gloves without liners and a pair of handcuffs were purchased for cash at two different surplus stores in San Diego County. A pair of used work boots two sizes too large, and an assortment of old clothes, were found at a Salvation Army store. A large can of beef stew and a cheap can opener were purchased at a 7-11 just down the same street. Finally, a homeless man agreed to take $100 for his old, nearly unusable shopping cart and even threw in the two-foot length of one-inch galvanized pipe he used for personal protection. Duct tape and a filet knife were already in the truck. As always, the supplies included a nine-millimeter pistol for backup in case things didn't go as planned. A .22 caliber revolver was added to the arsenal just for persuasive purposes. All that was left to do was to find a suitably filthy parking lot or dirt field and drive the pickup over the clothes a few times to give them that "lived-in" look, then wait for Saturday night. Like they say, nothing good ever happens after midnight. Of course, that depended on how one defines "good."

CHAPTER 50

Two a.m., Sunday morning is closing time at The Gold Rush. As the last patron in the bar, Ronald Carpenter had to be politely herded out. Tonight was a particularly raucous night and it was going to take a lot of work to clean up before the staff could go home. Carpenter had consumed more than his share of alcohol; so much, in fact, that the bartender made his usual suggestion that he sleep it off for a while in his car before getting on the road. He was a big tipper and no one from the bar would bother him if they saw his car in the parking lot when they left.

"See ya later, Ron." The bartender called out as Carpenter made his way out the door.

No he wouldn't.

CHAPTER 51

Remember what I said about how setting a pattern could get you killed? Wouldn't you think you might start looking over your shoulder after your best friend was found dead, chained to a tree and wearing a bear trap for an ankle ornament? Wouldn't it be wise to vary your pattern even just a little bit? Evidently that theory escaped Ronald Carpenter. In less than three weeks I was able to pretty much predict what was on his agenda for any given day.

Most important was how he spent his Saturday nights. Every other Saturday, he and his fellow morons held some kind of meeting at one or another of their houses. The meetings tended to get a bit loud by ten, and by midnight they usually broke up. His other Saturday nights were spent at either Cook's Corner or the Gold Rush. It wasn't lost on me that those were the same bars Jesse Cardinal told me the two biker hit men also hung out. Carpenter liked to close the bar down and was generally the last to leave. It was obvious he had a serious drinking problem. I had a sure-fire way of curing him of it.

Of the two bars, the Gold Rush was best suited to my plan. Not only was it smaller and catered to fewer customers than Cook's Corner, it fronted a large, unlit and unfenced dirt-over-neglected-asphalt parking lot. In order to prevent door dings caused by other patrons who were as toasted as he was, Carpenter always parked his 442 as far away from any other cars as possible. Tonight he should have parked closer to the front door. It might have saved more than his paint job.

It was after midnight when I scouted out the Gold Rush's parking lot. There were four or five cars sitting at the front and a white Oldsmobile 442 parked all alone at the far end. If Carpenter stayed true to his pattern, he wouldn't be coming out for another couple of hours. That gave me plenty of time to park, put on my surplus jacket and gloves, load up the shopping cart and open my can of beef stew.

I parked my truck in front of a vacant lot about two blocks away, then remembered I needed   to fill my one-gallon gas can. I didn't want to fill it at any local gas stations, and siphoning it out of someone's car was out of the question. That would be stealing and I have a particular dislike for thieves.

I ended up driving about fifteen miles before I found a gas station where I could fill my gas can without drawing much scrutiny from the attendant. I grabbed a baseball cap and pulled it down as far as I could and tried to avoid any security cameras, then went inside and paid cash for twenty dollars' worth of gas. I could have just as easily paid with my card at the pump, but that would have left a trail. I could have just bought enough to fill my can, but I didn't want the attendant questioning why I was only buying one gallon at this hour. I didn't think he would believe me if I told him I was mowing my lawn in the middle of the night and the damned thing ran out of gas. A story like that would surely be one he might remember if by chance the law came around to ask questions.

I set the can on the ground between my pickup and the gas pumps, out of sight from the attendant, and filled it first, then put the rest in the truck. The round trip to and from the gas station took about forty-five minutes. I still had plenty of time to put my plan into action, starting with opening the can of beef stew.

Wearing my dirty field jacket, boots and watch cap I could pass for a homeless person even in broad daylight. Add a squeaky shopping cart loaded with old clothes, in a nearly deserted parking lot at two in the morning, and you have someone most people won't even look at twice, unless of course there is a reason to look.

So there I sat on the curb about thirty feet from Carpenter's pride and joy, watching the remaining barflies stumble out of the Gold Rush while patiently waiting for my guy to appear. He was parked facing away from the tavern. His car was a beautifully restored classic and he was cautious of anybody dinging his door. However, he had taken up two spaces. I really hate people who take up two spaces. What the hell gives them the right? The way I see it, taking up two parking spaces is on par with parking in a handicapped zone. If nothing else, that alone would be justification for what I was going to do to Carpenter and his damned car. I doubt any jury would convict me. On the bright side, after tonight what's left of him would probably fit comfortably in a shoebox and he would never again take up two parking spaces.

I had been sitting on the curb for about twenty minutes before I saw Carpenter stagger into the parking lot. As soon as he was about halfway across the lot I got up and started pushing my cart past the rear of his car. As soon as he saw me, he yelled at me to get the hell away. I stopped and looked at him then dutifully pulled my cart backward and into the first parking space that didn't have part of his car in it.

He staggered passed me, slurring something incomprehensible. From the smell of his breath it was obvious his tank was full. If I had just thought to strike a match I probably could have immolated him then and there. Instead, I took another step back and waited patiently for him to pass, as would any other lesser being when in the presence of the President of the White Aryan Warriors.

When he finally made it to his car door he fumbled with his keys for a couple of seconds while periodically glancing over his shoulder at me. I could have easily taken him then and there, but I had a plan and opted to stick to it.

Things happened pretty fast. As soon as he found his way into his car I walked my shopping cart firmly into its left rear quarter panel. The door immediately burst open and he hopped out, intent on hurting someone. By then I was bent over his trunk, concealing the can with my head and shoulders and making my most convincing retching sound as I poured the beef stew all over his trunk and down the side. Have you ever noticed how much beef stew looks like vomit?

By now he was about to explode. Not only had some street denizen hit his precious car with a shopping cart, almost certainly scratching the paint, but this lowlife was following it up by puking all over it. Somebody was going to clean it up right now and then pay; with blood. Carpenter stormed towards me.

Before he got a good look at the side of his car, I traded my can of beef stew for the galvanized pipe. It's funny how fast even a drunk can move when he's boiling hot. It was no more than just a fraction of a second before he stepped within range and reached out with his left arm to grab my coat. His right arm was already cocked back, ready to punch my lights out. He should have made a better assessment of the situation. He really didn't have a battle plan. He had a goal, but no real plan, and he woefully underestimated his enemy.

My left shoulder was still toward him when he grabbed my unbuttoned and unzipped jacket. As soon as his hand touched my shoulder I spun to my left

187

o face him and swung the pipe full-force down on his right collarbone. I swear I heard something snap when I made contact. Then, using the momentum I just created, I dropped into a squat and swung for the fences, hitting him square on the left shin with the pipe. He let out a high-pitched scream that somehow didn't bring the staff out of the bar—maybe they had the jukebox on—and dropped to the ground, where, dazed and confused, he kind of half sat up to look at me. Not being one to pass up an opportunity, I thrust the pipe straight out as if I were a sword fighter and jabbed him square in the middle of the forehead with the threaded end. By this point, all he wanted was to survive, the hell with the car. I'm pretty sure it would have been okay with him if I'd puked all over it again.

After I landed what I now like to call my "patented galvanized pipe punch," he lay on his back and covered his eyes with his left arm and began pleading with me that he'd had enough. It was in no way lost on me that his victims never had the chance to plead for mercy. I pulled his arm off his eyes to survey the damage and to duct tape his mouth shut.

There was no doubt his collarbone was broken, but because he had on long pants, I couldn't get a look at his shin. The slowly expanding wet spot on the crotch of his pants told me he wasn't quite the warrior he professed to be. However, not wanting to embarrass him, I didn't mention it. Instead, I poked at his damaged shin and let him know the pain he was feeling was nothing compared to what I could bring on him if he didn't do exactly as I instructed. Then, just to convince him that I was serious, I rapped him again right where I'd nailed him the first time and asked him if he understood. He frantically nodded, his eyes wide open and his breath quickening through his nose almost to the point of hyperventilating as he tried to scream through the duct tape. With that I just said: "good" and rapped him again on the same spot for no good reason other than I just felt like it. The coolest thing I saw, though, was the perfect ring the end of the pipe left in the middle of his forehead from my patented galvanized pipe punch.

When I finished admiring my artwork I pulled the nine-millimeter out of my jacket and told him to get in the passenger seat. With his mouth duct-taped, he did a pretty good impression of a mime as he tried to get me to understand that he couldn't get up. If I'd had time I would have told him to mime the "man in the invisible box." That one always cracks me up.

As soon as I stuck the pistol on his forehead—right in the middle of the ring—he found a way to load up and slide over. As soon as we were both in the car, I told him to stick his left arm out so I could handcuff him to the steering wheel. He didn't seem very motivated to follow my instructions so I pulled out the little .22 caliber single action revolver and put it against his kneecap, then cocked the hammer back and pulled the trigger. Even though it was only a .22 the noise inside the car was almost deafening. I realized right then I should have brought earplugs. Fortunately all the doors and windows were rolled up and closed so the sound was pretty much restricted to the inside of the car. It must have hurt like hell because he tried again to scream through the duct tape before dutifully sticking out his left hand to be cuffed; like I always say: "pain is a good motivator and extreme pain is an extremely good motivator."

In a somewhat sincere attempt to make things better between us, I asked him if he wanted something for the pain. He nodded his head up and down furiously, probably thinking I was going to give him a shot of morphine or some other opioid. I explained that I couldn't do that because I'm not a doctor and I could get in a whole peck of trouble for administering medicine without a license. However, I did have something to relieve the pain. At that point I got out of the car and went back to my shopping cart and came back with a handful of clothes and my gas can.

I scattered the clothes all over the interior of the car, then right before I opened the gas can I realized I had forgotten to bring matches. He didn't want to tell me if he had any matches on him and I had only loaded one bullet in the .22, thinking that would be all I'd need. I started my search by looking through the glove compartment and lo and behold, I found a cheap plastic lighter, sitting there pretty as you please.

As soon as I found the lighter I pulled the filet knife out of one of the pockets in my field jacket and tossed it on the dashboard and told him he might want to use it to commit hara-kiri before the flames got to him. I explained that the proper method was to insert it into the abdomen and slowly move it from left to right, although I'm not sure he would be able to accomplish that with a broken collarbone and all. On the other hand he might just be able to do it. Fire can be a great motivator also. Just ask any witch who's been burned at the stake.

I splashed about half the can of gasoline over the clothes that I scattered throughout the interior, then rolled the driver's side window halfway down for ventilation and stepped out of the car, then poured the rest of the gas over the exterior. I leaned back through the window to say goodbye and flicked the lighter and lit one of the rags, then took a quick glance of the abject fear on his face and tossed the burning rag in and trotted away. If I left any footprints behind they would be looking for someone with a foot two shoe sizes bigger than mine.

I didn't bother taking the shopping cart with me. It's not like it could be traced and I didn't expect I could get my hundred bucks back from the guy I bought it from, even though I could prove it had a defective wheel when he sold it to me. Looking back, I probably should have taken it out for a test push around the parking lot before plunking my money down.

CHAPTER 52

The car's interior was filled with the odor of fumes rising from the gasoline-soaked rags. Ignition was spectacular and accompanied by a huge "WHOMP" and an explosive flash of light that briefly lit up the parking lot as if from the Devil's own flashbulb.

Inside the car, Ronald Carpenter struggled mightily against the cuffs holding his left wrist to the steering wheel. Nothing budged. Behind him, where most of the gasoline-soaked rags were scattered, he felt the heat grow in intensity as the cotton seat covers ignited and the flames started their relentless climb upward. The back of his neck and head turned red with first-degree burns then turned a darker red and began to blister as the burns evolved into second degree and to third as his now-blackened skin began to peel away.

With all his resolve, and crying out from the pain radiating from his shattered collarbone, he tore the duct tape from his mouth, then, desperate for oxygen, he inhaled as deeply as he could. With the pain increasing by the millisecond as the heat mercilessly roasted him where he sat tethered inside his four-wheeled crematorium, he stretched his wounded arm toward the filet knife on the dashboard. It was out of reach. Gasping for air, he whipped his head back and forth, hoping against hope to find some means of escape. Each gasp brought more superheated black smoke past his throat and nasal passages and searing his lungs. Ronald Carpenter's final act was a vain attempt to cry out through his charred vocal cords.

By the time the fire department extinguished the flames, the formerly showroom clean muscle car was reduced to an unrecognizable remnant of itself.

nside, burned beyond recognition and still handcuffed to the melted steering wheel, lay the smoldering remains of Ronald Carpenter.

CHAPTER 53

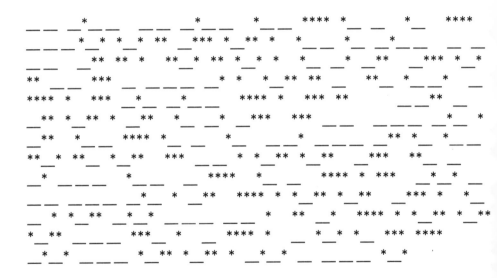

Donaldson stood over Trevor's desk as the latest message to arrive at Parkland Rice's office was decoded and read back to him. This time the salutation included Donaldson:

My, my, what a horrible way to die;

Fire and brimstone lit up the sky

He sizzled and smoked, what a godawful smell;

But now that he's cooked, he'll be welcome in hell.

Love, The Trash Collector.

"Tell you the truth, I'm not sure which side public opinion will be on when we catch whoever's doing this," said Trevor, shaking his head and looking away from his notes. "Actually, I guess I do know. So far all this 'Trash Collector' has done is what the state should have done, but couldn't. There's going to be a lot of public sympathy."

"Yeah, but there could be other, not so deserving, victims or future victims out there," Donaldson replied.

"I'm not so sure." Trevor responded. "Look at the modus. These aren't just run-of the mill murders. Each of these guys was killed in some creative and spectacular manner. Every one of them was known to the public through media coverage. The Trash Collector is out there doing what the public knows we weren't able to do and making examples out of these guys at the same time. I'd bet my paycheck against there being any innocent victims."

"So, what do you think; are the notes about embarrassing the department? Is it someone who has a grudge against us because they feel we didn't go far enough when they needed us and they want to rub our noses in it?

"Well, I think we can rule out it being aimed at the Department. Don't forget this actually started a few years back when I was with the San Luis Obispo Sheriff's Department. Now whoever it is has turned up again in my back yard. Either it's personal with me or The Trash Collector just wanted to be sure we knew the murder up there was committed by the same person as the ones down here.

I don't know. It certainly has all the earmarks of someone wanting to make us look bad, and it does seem personal with the taunting messages. On the other hand, every one of them did something they should have been executed for. Maybe it's just exactly what it looks like on the surface: some vigilante who is only interested in dispensing their definition of justice to deserving individuals."

"Then why the coded messages? That seems to be pretty personal."

"The only possible reason is that the Trash Collector wants to be sure we know who's behind each of the murders. This wouldn't be the first serial killer who left messages, even Jack the Ripper supposedly left little items with his victims and look at the Zodiac killer; look at all the coded messages he left.

After all, why go to these lengths to kill a string of bad people and not get full credit?"

"Even if that is the case," replied Donaldson, "How do we know this psychopath isn't going to decide someday there are other crimes that should be executable offenses?"

"I guess we don't know," said Trevor, "but to our knowledge it hasn't happened yet. Also, let's not assume we have a psychopath on our hands. I know the method of execution may suggest that, but maybe that's a red herring. Maybe this person wants us to believe we have a psychopath in our midst. I don't think there is any doubt we are dealing with a very smart individual here. And I think we can agree that everyone we know of that The Trash Collector has killed—with the possible exception of Reggie Santana-- should be sitting on death row right now. These guys may not have died the way the justice system would have put them down, but there are plenty of people out there who feel lethal injection is way too easy and that The Trash Collector has the right idea. Does that make them psychopaths also? I say instead of concentrating on looking for a psychopath we look at the thread that ties the murders together: Reginald Santana ruined the lives of an undetermined number of underage girls; we know Joshua Ward killed Cooper Jansen and probably at least four other young boys; Carpenter and Cardinal murdered Stephanie Alarcon and left a little baby without her mother. None of the killers got what they deserved, at least until the Trash Collector came to visit. Maybe we have a parent out there whose child was murdered or maybe abused in some way and the perp got away with it."

"Well, we also have the fact that Ward, Carpenter and Cardinal were all represented by Lee Edwards," said Donaldson.

"Yeah, but how does Santana fit in? Edwards didn't represent him. In fact, he wasn't even an attorney then," replied Trevor.

"So where do we go from here."

"My guess is we're going to find out pretty soon whether or not The Trash Collector knows who killed Manuel Trejo," replied Trevor. "Pretty ironic isn't it? Somewhere out there are two murderers who should be hoping that we catch them and lock them safely away forever before they have to face judgment day at the hands of someone else we are trying to catch. If I were these two bikers I'd opt for the long prison sentence and eventually the needle instead of the express train to hell that The Trash Collector will surely send them on."

"We don't even know whether our perp knows who they are, though", observed Donaldson.

You're right, we don't know," said Trevor. "Like I said, we'll probably find out pretty soon."

Donaldson never mentioned the third and most obvious thread.

CHAPTER 54

Just over two months after Ronald Carpenter was roasted alive, an American tourist stepped into a small, nondescript doctor's office in Tijuana, Mexico, just over the border from San Diego. After a brief conversation and a cash exchange of $200, the tourist was given a prescription, and then filled it at the pharmacy three doors down for another $50. Everything else: the super glue, the duct tape, two more pairs of handcuffs, and four quarters could easily be found back in the States. Easter was just around the corner. The time to deal with Big Bob and Trout was almost here.

      True to his last words, Jesse Cardinal's cell phone included contact info for Trout and Big Bob; street addresses, phone numbers, and all. Once that was confirmed, tracking and surveillance revealed all that was needed to know about the two. The nicknames couldn't have been more fitting. Big Bob stood at least six foot four and went probably over 250 pounds. Trout was maybe six foot, and thin, with a narrow face, sharp nose and wide-set eyes that appeared to bug far enough out of his head that his nickname could just as easily have been "Chameleon." Both men sported black, greasy, shoulder-length hair and were covered with prison tattoos. While neither appeared to belong to any particular club, they did dress the part. Their black leather vests, dirty blue jeans and motorcycle boots left no doubt they were bikers, albeit lone wolves. Both men lived in the city of Stanton, no more than a ten-minute drive from what had been Ronald Carpenter's house in Fountain Valley. They came to Silverado at least once a week to visit the Gold Rush and Cook's Corner. Carpenter and Cardinal had been one of their sources of product and Silverado was a great place to hook up with customers who shared their interest in better living through chemistry.

The beauty of Cook's Corner and the Gold Rush is that neither fit the stereotype of a biker bar. Riders of all makes and models mingle amicably, whether riding a full-dress Harley or a street racer, each accepts the others' devotion to two-wheeled travel. When the seasons turn cool, patrons are just as likely to show up in the family sedan or SUV as on two wheels, though for the most part they continue to dress the part. Seasonal parties tend to alternate between the saloons.

The Gold Rush puts on one of the premier parties of the year: the annual "Good Friday Day of Fasting and Penance Parking Lot Party," which is anything but a day of penance and fasting. The party starts at six a.m. and goes on until closing time twenty hours later. Pigs, hamburgers and hot dogs are barbequed in three temporary pits and alcohol is served throughout the entire affair. The crowds can number from as few as fifty to over two hundred, depending on the hour and there is always a live band setting the mood. The bar's owner often jokes that he loses money all year and is then resurrected "just like Jesus" after he tallies up the proceeds on Easter Sunday.

Big Bob and Trout showed up for the Good Friday bash just after sunset. There was still plenty of room in the parking lot and they parked Big Bob's Ford Escape just far enough from the festivities to make it easy to return to the vehicle for any purpose. Other vehicles were steadily streaming in and out and The Trash Collector's pickup didn't draw anyone's attention.

Three hours of steady drinking and partying took a heavy toll on the two men's sobriety. Going into the fourth hour each was staggering and slurring apologies when they inadvertently bumped into someone. One person in particular was extremely understanding and seemed not to be offended at all, and in fact bought each of them another bourbon and water. After a couple more drinks one of the three noticed they hadn't properly met. Big Bob introduced himself as Robert Lawson. The other was named Daniel Targo, but explained that everyone just called him Trout. Both claimed to be out-of-work plumbers. Their newfound friend claimed to be a trash collector.

Pretty soon the new friend mentioned how much the drinks cost and asked if they wanted to go grab a bottle of Jim Beam that was "kept under the front seat for just these types of occasions." Each of them grabbed a fresh red plastic cup and headed into the parking lot.

They wouldn't be back.

CHAPTER 55

So here I was, leading two murderers through the same parking lot where I literally roasted Ronald Carpenter. In fact when we passed the space where Carpenter met his fate I swore I could still smell the odor of his simmering fat. That was a bit unsettling to say the least, until I realized the breeze had shifted and the smell was actually coming from one of the barbeque pits. By the time we got to my truck, I had almost forgotten about it. There were more pressing things to worry about than whether the parking lot was haunted.

At my truck we dropped the tailgate and they sat down while I went up front to retrieve the bottle. Looking back, I probably could have gotten away with buying cheaper whisky. At this point they were both too toasted to notice.

I took their cups with me, telling them I didn't think we should be sitting with a bottle in plain view while the bar was trying to make a profit selling liquor in the same parking lot. It just seemed like bad form. Neither of them even suggested we sit in the cab. As soon as I was out of sight I poured some of the ground-up contents from the pill bottle sitting in my door compartment into each of their cups and filled them the rest of the way with the bourbon.

Now, I'm no pharmacist, and I've never claimed to be one. All I know is that Ambien is supposed to put someone out pretty quickly, and I've read that you shouldn't mix it with alcohol or bad things could happen. I've heard the same thing about Seroquel, so I wasn't sure if it was a good idea to grind up and mix three capsules of each and dump them in their drinks, but I figured what the heck. After all, I wasn't going to be the one abusing prescription drugs.

It didn't take long before Big Bob flopped down on his back into the bed of my truck.

"Uh oh," slurred Trout. "There goes Big Bob; happens all the time. For as big as he is you'd think he'd be able to hold his liquor better. I'm gonna need help lugging his big ass back to his car when we leave."

I told him not to worry about a thing. He could depend on me.

It took a bit longer for Trout. He finished his drink and two more before he too went belly-up. This was great. They were about to go on the adventure of their lives. Unfortunately for them, they wouldn't be coming back to tell anyone about it.

Both of them were lying so still that I thought for a minute that they might be dead already. That would have been extremely disappointing. Once I determined they were still alive I pulled the tailgate up, handcuffed each of them behind their backs, and closed the back of the camper shell. I didn't bother to tape their mouths shut; they would be out for hours and no one would hear them anyway. I needed to blindfold them if my plan was going to work. I could have just used the duct tape, but I always wondered what it would be like to Super Glue someone's eyes shut; maybe they could tell me when they woke up. Once I glued their eyelids together, I super glued the four quarters I had brought along over their closed eyelids. I didn't think it was particularly necessary, but you can't be too careful. Maybe if they managed to get their eyes pried open they could use the money to buy a map so they could figure out where they were.

Borrego Springs is a tiny unincorporated desert community located in San Diego County, about a hundred- and thirty-mile drive from the Gold Rush. With its miles and miles of dirt roads and washes it is an ideal place to commune with nature. It's not uncommon for a nature lover to go days on end without seeing another human being.

The drive out there took a little more than three hours; not bad considering that I realized along the way that I needed a pair of scissors. I stopped at an all-night convenience store/gas station outside of Oceanside and picked out what looked to be a well-made pair. About fifteen miles down the road I pulled over and parked at a rest stop and cut all the clothes off both of my passengers and threw them in a dumpster. They wouldn't need them anymore. I kept the scissors, though. After all, I paid for them.

Old, deserted dirt roads aren't all that easy to find in the dark and more than once I turned off the highway onto one that looked promising only to find it went back less than a mile or had a house at the end. I needed something that would take us back at least ten miles with no structures at the end. It took quite a while to find what I was looking for.

About fifteen miles into the desert, I pulled over. The road seemed endless. It followed a string of electrical transmission towers and could have gone another twenty miles or more as far as I knew, but this was as far as we needed to go. It was covered with deep, fine dust. Obviously it was rarely used.

When I opened the back I was pleased to see signs of life in each of them. Big Bob spoke up first, and had a bunch of questions. He wanted to know where they were, why he couldn't open his eyes, why he was handcuffed, and on and on like a little kid. I told him he passed out and I decided we should to take a ride to the desert. When he asked again why he couldn't open his eyes I told him it was because I super-glued them shut. When he asked why, I told him because sewing would have taken too long. Finally, tired of answering their silly questions, I told them they would find out soon enough why they were handcuffed and not to even bother asking why they were naked.

I asked if the name Manuel Trejo brought anything to mind. After a long pause, Trout claimed it didn't ring a bell and asked who he was. To say it wasn't a very convincing act would be an understatement, but I played along and told them that in that case I guessed I would have to set them free. They both seemed relatively pleased to hear that. I guess they thought it also meant I was going to take them back to their car. That wasn't going to happen. I let them know that and then told them both to scoot out.

Once they got out of the truck I stood them side by side and told them I would let them loose, but they were going to have to find their own way back. Big Bob wanted to know how I expected them to do that when they couldn't see and had no idea where they were. I told them that was their problem, not mine, but I would draw them a map if they thought it might help. Otherwise, they would just have to do the best they could. Besides, it was springtime; perfect weather for an early morning walk.

After listening to them whine, beg, and grumble for a bit, I marched them about fifty yards off the road, and then walked Big Bob a couple of hundred feet further and told him he could start looking for Trout anytime he wanted.

If you've never witnessed two naked outlaw bikers playing a desperate, grown up version of "Marco, Polo" during the wee hours of the morning, you have no idea what you've missed. If I'd known how entertaining it was going to be, I would have sold tickets. Big Bob walked directly into a cactus and then a *ucca tree, shredding the skin from his right shoulder to his knee. Right after that Trout stepped straight down on a huge cactus leaf. There were also plenty of sharp rocks and desert plants growing here and there. After about twenty minutes I'd had enough. My sides were aching and I wanted to get back home. I needed to get some sleep and I had a poem to write. They were both grown men. They shouldn't need to have someone watch them play.*

CHAPTER 56

After nearly an hour Big Bob and Trout closed to within twenty feet of each other. Each man was already in excruciating pain and limping badly from encounters with cactus and other bushes, and walking on the shale and sharp rocks littering the desert floor. It took another twenty minutes before they were standing side by side without a clue which way they were facing or what to do next.

Once together they started walking in a randomly chosen direction with Big Bob in the lead and talking constantly so that Trout would have an idea where he was. This arrangement didn't last long, however, because Trout couldn't keep up with a cactus leaf stuck to the bottom of his foot. After more discussion they decided to let Trout lead at whatever pace he could manage. This decision probably saved Big Bob's life; at least temporarily.

Their painfully slow progress included several rest stops and countless encounters with various species of desert flora. The temperature began to rise in steady, almost imperceptible increments. The warmth gave new hope to each man as they blindly envisioned daylight and the possibility of rescue. By now they had each gone nearly a full day without water, and were close to dehydration thanks to the previous night's heavy drinking. Because neither of them was sure he could get back up if they sat down, both men stood through each rest stop. Eventually the temperature rose to what would be considered comfortable if they had been in a position to enjoy it. It was also the time when the desert's reptilian members of the animal kingdom emerged to warm themselves.

As Trout shuffled and hopped as lightly as possible, attempting to avoid driving the cactus needles any further into his foot, he brushed his calf against what he could only guess was one of the spiny bushes he had seen so often when driving through the desert. At the same time, he felt something snap against his already damaged foot, then another snap as he quickly pulled back. It wasn't until he heard the distinctive rattle that he realized what had happened. "Rattlesnake!" He screamed to Big Bob, who was walking no more than three feet behind him. "Oh God, it bit me!"

Both men froze in their tracks. In the still morning air the snake's warning seemed to grow in intensity, and then slowly died out.

"Is he gone?" Bob asked, his voice dripping with panic.

"I don't know." Trout replied, trembling with fear. "What do I do?"

"Stand still until we know he's gone," replied Bob.

"I'm snake-bit. I'm going to die." Trout whispered.

"Stay calm, don't move," said Bob. "We gotta make sure he's…" Bob's voice cut off as a chill raced down his spine and his heart began to hammer within his chest. Something was sliding across his bare foot.

"Make sure he's what?" asked Trout.

"Shhh," came the reply.

"What's going on? Tell me!" Trout demanded; his voice now much higher.

"He's on my foot," whispered Bob, sounding as if he might cry at any moment.

After what seemed like hours, Bob could feel the cool, ribbed surface of the snake's rattle glide across his instep. The snake was huge and there were obviously several rattles. Bob stayed frozen in place for several minutes. The snake was on the move, maybe they were safe.

"He's gone, keep moving." He said in a much calmer voice.

"What am I going to do?" He bit me. What am I going to do?" cried Trout.

"We have to keep moving. Sometimes they don't inject their poison. Maybe you just got a dry bite."

"But he hit me twice. What if he injected me both times?"

"All we can do is keep moving." Bob said. What he didn't say was that he had already made plans to split up. Even without the snake bite, the cactus stuck to Trout's foot prevented him from going more than a couple of steps without stopping to rest and recoup. On top of that, each man was getting

204

weaker and thirstier by the minute. Dehydration would set in before long. They needed to keep moving to have any chance of making it out alive.

The immediate pain from the snake's bite was effectively masked by the intense pain radiating from the bottom of Trout's foot, where the cactus needles continued to dig deeper into his flesh. Before long he began to notice a tingling sensation radiating up his leg. He could feel himself sweating and was beginning to feel nauseous. "I have to stop again, that snake got me good." He slurred.

"I'm going to have to go on without you," announced Bob. "It's the only way to get help." He was sure it was already too late for Trout.

"Don't leave me, I can't see, I don't know what's happening." Trout pleaded.

"It's the only way," said Bob.

"No, it isn't," whimpered Trout. "Maybe somebody will come."

"No one's going to come," said Bob. "It's the only way."

"Please!"

"I have to go." Bob started to shuffle slowly away.

"Please, don't leave me out here. I don't want to die alone, please!" Cried Trout.

With the loss of vision came a heightened sense of hearing. Half an hour later, Bob could still hear Trout's desperate pleas. In that time he had unknowingly covered less than 200 feet in a wide circular path.

Trout tried his best to follow Bob and continued to call his name, begging him to wait. However, Bob had quit responding to his pleas. Trout had no idea where his partner was.

As near paralyzing fear turned to outright panic as the rattler's venom circulated through Trout's body at an increasing rate. He was slowly dying.

The venom marched on, destroying skin tissue and blood cells, resulting in internal hemorrhaging where it coursed through his veins. His face became numb and he could no longer feel his limbs. His breathing became labored as nausea set in and he began to vomit uncontrollably.

The venom marched on.

Eventually, his blood pressure dropped and he became light-headed and disoriented. He could go no further. He slowly spiraled to the desert floor. He wasn't dead yet. His suffering would increase for several hours before merciful death came.

Unaware that Trout was in the final stages of dying, Big Bob assumed he had finally decided to sit down and rest and let Big Bob seek help. By then each of them had gone more than twelve hours without any kind of liquids. The dehydrating effects of the alcohol they consumed the night before had taken its toll. On top of that, they were constantly on the move. Big Bob had a headache. He chalked it up to the stress of hearing Trout plead with him to stay. It never occurred to him that his body was trying to tell him he was becoming seriously dehydrated. If he didn't get water soon, he would die.

By mid-afternoon, Big Bob's headache was nearly unbearable. His mouth had gone dry hours earlier and he was no longer sweating. Although it was spring with temperatures no higher than the low 80s, the sun constantly beat down on him and without enough water in his system to keep him cool, his core temperature began to rise. Before long, his blood pressure started to drop. He became increasingly disoriented and began talking and mumbling incoherently. The bottoms of his feet were shredded by shale and other sharp rocks littering the desert floor. Although his legs were torn and ragged from numerous encounters with various cacti and large rocks, the pain no longer registered.

Before the sun set, Big Bob succumbed to nature's relentless attack on his body and dropped on his knees into a prickly pear cactus, then fell unconscious before the pain could fully register. Like Trout, he would not die a mercifully quick death. Instead, he would awaken several times, unable to move and in intense pain. He would survive the night while his internal organs systematically shut down, further incapacitating him. By noon the next day he would take his last breath, his body slowly baking in the desert sun.

CHAPTER 57

Following Easter Sunday, Parkland Rice took a ten-day vacation to camp and surf outside of Ensenada, Mexico. As expected, he was met with a stack of mail sitting on his desk when he returned. Among the letters was a normal looking business-sized envelope postmarked the day after Easter Sunday from San Diego. Inside was the all-too-familiar looking letter with its printed salutation greeting Parkland and Investigators Wilkins and Donaldson. Like before, the body of the letter was handwritten in Morse code. He reached for the phone and called Lee Edwards. Sharona picked up on the second ring.

Parkland explained he needed to see Lee, "today if possible."

"I'll see if I can fit you in." Sharona responded.

"It's really important that I see him as soon as possible," said Parkland.

"Well, you know the going rate for an unscheduled audience with the Courtroom King, right?"

"I think I know, but tell me again." He replied.

"Simple: if it's important, you get us four seats to the fights at the Hangar. If it's really important you get us four ringside seats for the fights at the Hangar. Is it still really important?"

"It is."

"Good, you're in luck. The only openings we have left are for really important consultations. We're booked solid on run-of-the-mill important consultations."

Taking the bait, Parkland asked: "just out of curiosity, how long are the important consultations booked up till?"

"Until they become 'really important' of course," came Sharona's deadpanned reply.

"That figures."

"I'll let you know ahead of time when we'll need the tickets."

"You got it. Thanks, Sharona."

"Be here at two. I can get you in," she replied.

At 1:55 Parkland walked into Lee's outer office. Sharona looked up and smiled. He had obviously learned that being early was the best way to stay on Sharona's good side.

"What can I do for you?" Lee asked, shaking Parkland's hand. The meeting took about twenty minutes, and Parkland walked out of Lee's office armed with all the legal advice he would need before calling the two sheriff's investigators.

Within an hour Trevor and Donaldson presented themselves at the *Orange County Times* offices. Parkland was seated behind his desk, looking down at the letter when they entered. "There it is, boys." He said. "Has there been another murder I haven't heard about?"

"We haven't heard either," said Trevor, "at least not another one that fits the M.O. of the Trash Collector."

"So, what's it say?" asked Parkland.

"You don't need to know," said Donaldson.

"Whether or not I need to know is irrelevant, Inspector," replied Parkland. "That letter was addressed to me as well as to the two of you. According to my attorney, that means it's as much mine as it is yours and I have as much right to know what it says as you do. I've abided by my agreement to withhold mentioning these letters in my paper. You either tell me what it says or I start publishing articles about the mysterious coded letters that began turning up on my desk right after each the sensational Orange County murders. Of course, that will be after I get a court order to gain access to the rest of them. After all, it is my mail. I've kept my word and refrained from disclosing anything about them. The least you can do is let me know what they say."

Trevor looked from Donaldson to Parkland. "Okay," he said, "you've been fair and kept your word to us, and you're right, it is your mail as much as it is mine. How about we do this? We copy the letter and put it in an evidence bag, and I decipher it right here, and in return you promise to keep it out of your paper?"

"After that, you tell me what the other ones said," responded Parkland.

Trevor nodded. "You've got a deal. Where's your copy machine?"

Five minutes later Trevor was back with a copy of the coded message:

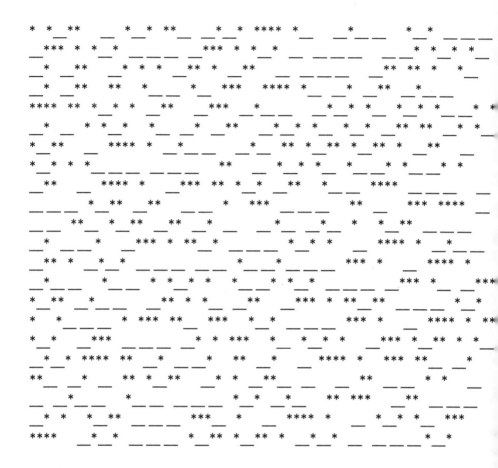

It took Trevor nearly fifteen minutes to decipher the code. Trevor then glanced up at Donaldson. "It looks like we may have another murder on our hands. Actually, it could be a double murder this time."

"What's it say?" asked Parkland.

El Trucha y Roberto Grande

Needed to die and I was handy

Hired by Carpenter and Cardinal they killed Trejo

I trapped the bird who told me so

It won't be long before they decompose

They were probably dead before Jesus rose

Their bones are bleaching in the sun

Until next time my work is done

Love, The Trash Collector

"What the hell does that mean?" asked Donaldson.

"The first line is Spanish," said Parkland. "El Trucha is the Trout, 'y' means 'and,' and Roberto Grande would be 'Big Robert,' maybe 'Big Bob.' Whoever sent the message claims these guys are the ones who killed Manuel Trejo, the guy who was shot gunned at his nephew's funeral."

"Okay, we know who Carpenter and Cardinal are, what's all the talk about a bird?" asked Parkland.

"That's easy," said Trevor. "A Cardinal is a bird. Jesse Cardinal was found with his leg locked in a bear trap, hence the line 'I trapped the bird.' He must have forced Cardinal to give up this 'Trout' guy and 'Big Roberto' or 'Big Bob.'"

"Can't say I disapprove of the interrogation techniques," said Donaldson. "They seem to be pretty effective."

Trevor continued: "my guess is 'bleaching in the sun' means the bodies weren't buried. 'It shouldn't take long before they decompose' might mean they were left out in the elements; maybe in some area that gets a lot of sun."

"You mean like sunny Southern California?" asked Donaldson. "That's not real helpful. What about this stuff about Jesus?"

"We just had Easter," said Trevor. "It probably means they were killed sometime before then."

"Then why does it say: 'they were probably dead' by then, wouldn't their killer know when they died?" asked Parkland.

"Maybe they were left somewhere to die. Maybe they were wounded and left somewhere where they would likely be dead before anyone would find them."

After a long moment of silence, Donaldson took a closer look at the envelope in the plastic evidence bag. "This was mailed more than a week ago. Why did you wait until today to call us about it?" he asked Parkland.

"Because I didn't see it until today, I took a vacation and just got back. It was on my desk mixed in with that stack of mail," replied Parkland, gesturing to the pile of opened and unopened envelopes on his desk.

"Where'd you go?" asked Donaldson.

"Down to Mexico; Ensenada, if that's important to you."

"Where'd you stay?"

"I camped out in my truck."

"You passed right through San Diego, didn't you?"

"Yeah, why?"

"Oh, no real reason, except it just seems pretty coincidental that you were in or near the same city on the same day this was mailed," said Donaldson

"What are you trying to say?" asked Parkland, a tinge of anger in his voice.

"Nothing," said Donaldson. "We'll see you later."

"Yeah," Parkland replied as the two investigators left his office; "and make sure I get those other messages today. Otherwise you can look for your names on the front page of the *Times.*"

Trevor and Donaldson hardly spoke a word as they drove back to the sheriff's office. As they parked, Trevor broke the silence: "let's go to my office, we need to talk."

In his office, Trevor shut the door and sat behind his desk, facing Donaldson. "Look," he said. "Next time you decide to start interrogating a suspect, let me know ahead of time. There's no reason we couldn't have gone back to see him after getting on the same page."

"Yeah, well it just came to me when I looked at the postmark."

"Then you should have kept it to yourself. He's not going anywhere. You know better than that."

Donaldson's only response was to quietly stare at Trevor.

"Here." Trevor handed over the plastic evidence bag containing the envelope and coded message. "How about you take this to the lab while I copy my notes on the earlier messages?"

"You're not really going to give those to him, are you?"

"You bet I am; I have no doubt he was right about them being as much his as ours. Now that you've gone and torqued our relationship with the only guy who can keep a lid on them, I'm not about to challenge him to follow through on his threat to put the whole story on the front page of his paper."

Donaldson shook his head and left with the evidence bag. "See ya tomorrow." He said without turning around. *If Trevor is upset now, just wait until tomorrow.*

As soon as Trevor finished copying the decoded messages, he faxed them to Parkland Rice. It was time to go home. He could start going over the clues left in the latest message tomorrow, after he calmed down. Things would be better then.

Trevor was almost all the way home when his cell phone chimed with a message from Undersheriff Mason's secretary. He and Donaldson were to meet in Mason's office at eight a.m. *Now what?* He thought. *Did Donaldson go running to Mason and tell him I hurt his feelings. Is he going to want me to apologize?*

CHAPTER 58

Julius Mason, tall and fit with close-cut steel-gray hair, was in his thirtieth year with the sheriff's department. Like most deputies, he started his career as a jailer and worked his way up the ladder until landing at his current assignment, where he would likely retire. He was known as a "sheriff's sheriff" who would go to the ends of the earth to stand up for one of his men, as long as that man had not done anything to bring even the slightest speck of tarnish to the badge.

Mason's secretary greeted Trevor as he approached her desk: "go ahead on in," she said with practiced cordiality. "Investigator Donaldson's already here."

"Investigator Wilkins, take a seat." Mason said as Trevor closed the door behind himself. "Would you like something to drink: water, coffee, tea?"

"No thank you," said Trevor, glaring at Donaldson.

"Okay," said Undersheriff Mason, looking directly at Trevor. "This is the part I hate the most. You have the right to remain silent." After reciting the entire Miranda warning, he asked if Trevor wished to have an attorney present. Trevor did not. Mason asked if he wanted to make a statement, and reminded him that he could invoke his Miranda rights at any time.

"I know my rights, am I under arrest?" Trevor asked, his voice a mixture of anger and confusion.

"No, at least not yet," replied the undersheriff.

"So, am I free to go?"

"Not yet, we'll call this a detention at this point."

"Then what do you want to know?"

"First you should know this is being recorded." Mason responded. "Let's start with when you were working in San Luis Obispo. You know who Reginald Santana is, or was, right?"

"Yeah, I was on that case."

"It was never solved, was it?"

"Not while I was there."

"There was a poem written in code on Santana's door, wasn't there?"

"Yes, there was."

"Do you know Morse code, Investigator Wilkins?"

"Yeah, I do, along with thousands, if not millions of other people."

"Okay, so the next time one of these Morse code messages comes up is when Joshua Ward was killed, several years after you left San Luis Obispo and came to work with us, right?"

"That's right," responded Trevor.

"Do you have any explanation for that?'" asked Mason.

"Nope, maybe you should ask whoever sent it."

"It was also addressed to you, right?"

"Yes, it was."

"Didn't you investigate that case?"

"Yes, I did."

"And he was killed—or at least his body was discovered—at San Clemente State Park's beach. That's what, about two miles from your house?"

"Yeah, I guess that's about right."

"You also investigated Ronald Carpenter and Jesse Cardinal before they were killed, right?"

"Right again."

"Do you remember where you were when Jesse Cardinal was killed?"

"I wasn't aware we even knew the exact date and time. If it happened at night I might have either been home or maybe fishing off the San Clemente pier."

"You do that often?"

"Every chance I get," said Trevor. "It's a great way to unwind; just sit back and relax and hope you don't get a bite."

"Did you have your cell phone with you?"

"Nope, I told you I go there to unwind, not to talk on the phone."

"How about your son, would he have been with you?"

"Probably not; he's at that age when hanging out with Dad isn't as cool as it was a few years ago. Most likely he would have been over at our neighbors.' the Kovacs, making a pest out of himself, bugging Jim with questions about flying or muscle cars, or pestering Becky to convince me to get him a kitten."

"Mind if we talk to your son?"

"You're damned right I mind. Leave him alone." Trevor responded, anger rising in his voice.

"How about your neighbors: the Kovacs?"

"You can try, but I doubt you'll be able to catch Jim when he isn't busy. He's an airline pilot. As for Becky, go ahead and try, but I'm gonna want you to film it, particularly when she tells you to go to hell."

"Why would she do that?"

"Just for sport; she's a lawyer. She can tell you to go to hell in ways that you won't even know you've been insulted until you look up what she said."

"How about when Ronald Carpenter was killed, do you know where you were that night?

"I don't really recall. I don't keep a log of where I am on my days off.

"Maybe home, maybe fishing?"

"Maybe, maybe somewhere else. How about you, do you know where you were?"

"You own a 1970 Chevy El Camino, right?"

"Yeah, I do, at least for now. It's an SS 396 in case you're interested."

"I've never seen you drive it to work; didn't even know you had a pickup," said Donaldson. "Is there some reason you've been keeping it under wraps?"

"You bet there is," said Trevor. "I bought it for my son. It's going to be a surprise birthday present when he turns seventeen. He deserves it. He's a good kid. I rented a garage to keep it in while Jim Kovac and I restore it. I didn't know there was some kind of department rule that I had to report my vehicle purchases to the department. And, by the way Donaldson, that's the last question you get to ask me or this conversation is over and the two of you can take it up with my lawyer."

"It's going to be a surprise," repeated Undersheriff Mason. "So, does that mean you never take it out of your rented garage?"

"No, it doesn't," replied Trevor. "I take it out periodically to circulate the fluids and keep the battery charged. A car needs to be driven now and then."

"Any reason your pickup was spotted driving past Carpenter's house three times in one evening shortly before he turned up dead?"

"I told you, I was driving it to circulate the fluids and keep the battery charged. Why three times past Carpenter's house? Probably the same reason Donaldson here was sitting down the street when I went by," Trevor responded, turning to look directly at Donaldson. "You didn't even know I spotted you, did you? You're horrible at surveillance. Maybe you need some retraining. The last time I drove by I almost stopped to take a picture, but I didn't have my cell phone with me."

"How about the latest message: 'El Trucha y Roberto Grande?'" Mason asked, trying to regain control of the meeting. "You know anything about that?"

"Yeah, I know whoever wrote it apparently knows Morse code and maybe a little Spanish. Unless I'm missing something, we don't even have a body—or bodies, plural—yet. Until then, we don't even have a murder. I don't recall any law against sending a note written in Morse code to a newspaper."

"How about the fact all the notes have been addressed to both you and Parkland Rice?" asked Donaldson.

Quickly turning to glare at Donaldson as if ready to spring from his chair, Trevor growled: "Guess you're conveniently forgetting the last one was also addressed to you, Donaldson. And you don't listen too well, do you? You've already used up your quota of questions. Julius, tell your pet squirrel here to keep his trap shut. I've got nothing to hide, but I'm not going to sit here and be questioned by this clown."

In response Donaldson aggressively surged toward Trevor, each hand on the armrests of his chair. "Did you just call me a clown?" He challenged.

Looking Donaldson straight in the eye, Trevor responded: "at least your hearing's okay."

"Okay, take it easy, both of you," ordered Mason, then, looking at Trevor: "do you have anything to add?"

"Not unless you have any more questions."

"All right, Investigator Wilkins," said Mason, "I'm placing you on paid leave until we get this figured out one way or the other. In the meantime, I need you to turn in your badge and gun. Off the record, you have a stellar record, and I hope it turns out you didn't have anything to do with this. If not, you'll be reinstated and I will personally hand you back your badge and gun and apologize to you."

Trevor stood and pulled his badge and holder from his wallet and slammed it on the undersheriff's desk next to his service pistol. He shot a withering look at Donaldson and hissed: "keep your distance, clown," before walking out the door. He needed to call a criminal defense attorney before the investigation got any deeper. He probably should have done that long ago.

CHAPTER 59

Lee was on a misdemeanor assault trial and wouldn't be able to see Trevor for at least three days. That was fine; no one would be coming to arrest him that soon. There was a lot of investigation to be completed before there would be enough evidence to file charges against him, if ever. Three days would be plenty of time to decide what, and how much, he wanted to reveal to Lee. By the third day he had decided to tell the whole story, and he wanted Sharona to hear it. He trusted her at least as much as he trusted Lee, maybe more.

Friday morning at 8:00, Trevor was early for his appointment. By 8:15, Lee was finished with everything he had to do before seeing him. Unsure whether this visit would be as contentious as the last one, Lee stayed seated as Trevor walked in. "Where's your partner?" He asked.

"I don't have one." Trevor responded. "In fact, right now I'm not even a cop."

"Really, so what brings you here?"

"I need a criminal defense attorney, or at least I may need one before long."

"For yourself?"

"Yeah, for myself, but before we go on, would it be okay if Sharona were present while we go over this?"

"You understand that if she listens in with your consent, there will be no attorney-client privilege, and she can be called to testify against you."

Trevor nodded. "I understand." He said.

"Okay," replied Lee, reaching for the intercom. Once Sharona was seated and briefed, he turned to Trevor. "Okay," he said, "start wherever you like."

"First of all, I guess I should tell you that I'm being investigated for four murders, maybe six. I'm on paid leave while the investigation goes on. I didn't commit any of them. In fact, you have been considered a possible suspect yourself," he said, looking directly at Lee.

Lee slowly shook his head. "I kind of gathered that the last time you were here." He said. "You said maybe as many as six murders, who else?"

"Joshua Ward, Ronald Carpenter, Jesse Cardinal, Reginald Santana, and maybe two more who were probably connected to Manuel Trejo's murder but we haven't found yet."

"I'm not familiar with Reginald Santana, who's he?"

"He was a parolee who was killed in San Luis Obispo a few years ago when I worked up there. I investigated the case. It was never solved."

"So, how am I a suspect on that one? I've never even heard of Reginald Santana until just now."

"According to the archives of the local newspaper, you were up there competing in a surf contest on or about the date the murder occurred. In fact, there's a picture in the paper of you posing with your third-place trophy."

Lee was incredulous: "are you kidding me?" He asked. "Let me get this straight: I once came in third out of five surfers in the novice division of a surf contest. In fact, that's the only surfing trophy I've ever won. And that somehow ties me to a murder? This is ridiculous. Tell me you're pulling my leg."

"Look, you know as well as I do that all it means is that you were in San Luis Obispo when the murder was committed. For that matter, so was Parkland Rice. He took the photograph of you that was in the paper. Either of you could physically have killed Reginald Santana and neither of you can conclusively be ruled out, at least not yet. Now, eight years later, you are both down here and there are similar murders happening again."

"The same applies to you," said Lee.

"You're right. They could probably build a case against me with what they already have, maybe one strong enough to get an indictment. The difference is, I didn't do it, but I know who did."

"You say you didn't do it," observed Lee.

"Okay, fair enough," Trevor replied. "I'm saying I didn't do it."

"How do you know they're even connected?" asked Lee.

"Oh, they're connected. There's no doubt. The murderer goes by the name: "The Trash Collector" and there is some key evidence that conclusively points to the same person. We've been withholding it from the start. What we don't have is an arrest. I have no doubt I know who it is. That's why I may need a lawyer."

"I'm lost here," said Lee. "You're being investigated for as many as six murders. You say you didn't do it, but you know who did, so you may need a lawyer. It seems to me like you could save yourself a lot of trouble and expense if you just give the information over to the sheriff's department and cleared your name."

"It's not that easy. I investigated the Reginald Santana murder in San Luis Obispo. It was very well executed, the only evidence that was left at the scene was what the murderer wanted us to find, except for one thing: A man walking his dog on the evening we believe the murder was committed saw an unfamiliar car parked in front of Santana's house. He happened to be part of Neighborhood Watch, so he wrote down the license plate number, along with a few other numbers and minor complaints like sprinklers running into the street. He put the paper in his pocket and pretty much forgot about it. On his walk he stopped and visited with some friends and neighbors and when he came back, the car was gone. He was in his late seventies with nothing better to do, but his memory wasn't what it had been when he was younger.

"Santana's body wasn't discovered for a couple of days when he didn't show up for work. There are a lot of people living on that street and they get their share of visitors, meaning it's not that uncommon to see unfamiliar cars. The neighbor didn't remember exactly which house he saw the strange car parked in front of, or for that matter, which street it was on, but decided a couple of days after the discovery of the body to call us.

"I met him at his house and he gave me the note. Unfortunately the slacks he was wearing that night had been washed along with the paper he wrote the license numbers on. The paper wasn't completely destroyed, so I ended up with one or two complete plate numbers and a couple of partials. I ran the numbers I had and systematically filled in numbers on the partials. After chasing down the names and addresses attached to the plate numbers, one number stood out: it belonged to an Army National Guard soldier. Camp San Luis Obispo has for years been one of the places where reservists and National Guardsmen go for their two-week annual training. As it turned out my person of interest was training there at the time Santana was murdered."

"So what happened? Why didn't you just go out and make the arrest?"

"I didn't have enough to prove anything. Parking on the street isn't illegal and the soldier might have been visiting friends."

"Did you talk to the soldier?"

"I should have, it was my sworn duty, but I didn't because Reginald Santana was an evil person who had taken advantage of who knows how many runaway teenage girls and ruined or maybe ended their lives. No one will ever know how many deaths he was responsible for. He deserved to die in the most brutal way possible. I buried the information, and took an oath to myself to protect the killer's identity as best I could. It was a choice that to this day I don't regret. In fact, I'm still doing it. I thought it was over back then with a single homicide. We didn't have another incident until Joshua Ward was killed down here in Orange County. I made the choice to protect the perp then, and right or wrong, I stand by that choice until the wrong person gets hurt or killed, but I don't think that is going to happen. The individual we are dealing with is too smart for that to happen.

"If they dig deep enough they'll find out what I did. It won't lead them to the Trash Collector, but it'll be obvious I withheld, or buried important information. If that happens, I'll need an attorney. We all know what happens to cops in prison."

"Do you want to tell me who you think it is?" asked Lee. "We can ask Sharona to leave the room to protect attorney-client privilege, if you'd like."

Trevor grimaced and laid his hand on his chin while resting his elbow on the armrest of the chair, apparently lost in thought. He drummed his fingers against the other armrest as he pondered his options and glancing at Sharona as if contemplating her trustworthiness.

Finally, he looked up at Lee and said: "no, I don't think I'd better. Would you be interested in representing me if it gets to that?"

"You bet," said Lee. "I agree: these guys needed killing. Let's hope it doesn't come to that."

Trevor got up and left without another word. Once he was gone, Lee broke the silence. "He sure had a tough time trying to decide whether to identify the killer. Did you notice how he was drumming his fingers? What do you think? Do you think it could be him? You think maybe he was contemplating whether to come clean?"

"He wasn't drumming his fingers. He was tapping out Morse code," said Sharona.

"I didn't know you knew Morse code."

Sharona looked him in the eye, then winked. As she stood to leave, she smiled and calmly replied: "There's a lot you don't know about me."

She was two steps from the door when Lee stopped her in her tracks with four simple words: "he's right, you know."

Sharona turned and asked: "what do you mean?"

"That message he tapped out. He's right. One of us three is The Trash Collector."

Visibly shocked, Sharona blurted out: "you mean you know Morse code too?"

This time it was Lee's turn to wink. "There's a lot you don't know about me, either."

EPILOGUE

A little over three months had passed since Parkland Rice received the letter about Robert Lawson, aka: "Big Bob," and Daniel Targo, aka "Trout." The bodies remained yet to be found and there had been no messages since. No charges had yet been filed against Trevor Wilkins and he remained on paid administrative leave. He kept in constant contact with the union and was anxious to file a grievance to get his job back, but as the representative pointed out, he was still drawing full pay and benefits and his retirement continued to accrue. In other words, he hadn't been terminated and was technically still a full-time sheriff's investigator.

Sharona constantly bugged Lee to go out on the town with her and Ricky. Lee quietly refused each time, claiming he would be busy that evening. Finally, she dramatically increased the pressure. Her persistence paid off when she conspired with Parkland Rice to get them ringside seats and very aggressively insisted that he go to the fights at the Hangar with them to watch Malcom McAllister destroy another opponent. As hard as Lee tried to resist, Sharona just wouldn't take "no" for an answer this time. Following what was once their tradition, they met at Vitaly Café at five.

The three of them were sipping their coffee and discussing the upcoming fight card when a young man holding a rolled-up poster tapped Lee on the shoulder from behind.

"Excuse me," he said. "Are you Leroy Edwards, the former light-heavyweight contender?"

"I guess I am. What can I do for you?" Lee responded.

"My whole family used to watch you on TV. Mind if I ask why you never got a title shot?"

"Guess I wasn't good enough," Lee replied.

"That's not true. You were badass, no one wanted to give you a shot. No one wanted to fight you."

"Thank you for that," said Lee, "even if it's not true."

"My sister said she met you once. She said you were the nicest guy in the world outside of the ring. She said you always had time to talk with anybody who approached you. I guess she was right."

"Tell your sister I appreciate that."

"Look, I don't want to take up any more of your time, but I have this poster of you I bought in a sports memorabilia store. I knew you were a lawyer with an office in Newport and I was hoping I could stop by and ask you to sign it. When I saw you sitting here I got it out of my car. Would you mind signing it for me?"

"Not a problem," said Lee. "I hope you brought a pen or Sharpie."

"I did," said the young man, producing a sharpie out of his jacket pocket.

"So, who do I make it out to?"

"Could you make it out to my sister? Her name is Krystal."

"Krystal?" Lee repeated, obviously taken by surprise. "I once knew a girl named Krystal."

"Did she spell it with a 'K'?" came a voice from behind. It was a voice Lee had longed to hear again, a voice he would have given anything to hear just one more time.

Lee's head jerked slightly as if shocked by an electrical current. He spun on his heels and found himself looking once again into the most stunning ice-blue eyes he had ever seen.

"I should punch you. Sharona told me all about why you broke up with me," said Krystal. "Don't you think I should have been included in the decision? I would have stood by you. I'm a big girl. I'm fully capable of thinking for myself."

"Go ahead, I deserve it," said Lee, putting both hands behind his back while raising his head and tightly closing his eyes as if anticipating actually being punched.

"You deserve more than that, but I don't want to ruin your image by getting flattened by a girl," replied Krystal, trying to suppress a smile.

"So, how do you like New York?"

"It's great; they gave me a beautiful office overlooking the New York skyline. The company gave me a secretary, a cappuccino machine, you name it. Every office even has its own personal Alexa. All you have to do is tell it what song to play and it comes on."

"So, what brings you back here?" Lee asked. From her vantage point at the table, Sharona could clearly see the fingers on both of his hands crossed behind his back. "How long are you here for?"

"I went into the vice president's office and told him I left something in California that I wouldn't ever find in New York and he would have to transfer me."

"Really, just like that?"

"He told me they needed me in New York. He said I would have to stay."

"So, how long are you here for?"

"I'll be here as long as I want to be. I got my transfer."

"How did you swing that?"

"That was easy. I just said, 'Alexa, play "Take this Job and Shove it,"'" and walked out of his office. I was packing my things when he came in and told me they found a place for me back here in California."

Lee was shocked. "That's my girl," he said proudly.

Krystal smiled. "Not yet, but we can work on it."

######

ACKNOWLEDGMENTS

This book; my first adventure into the world of literary authorship, would never have been completed if not for the following people:

My wife, Janice, who constantly suppressed her laughter when I told her I was writing a novel and who actually encouraged me when she realized I was serious.

My daughter, Lyndsey, who never doubted my seriousness about wanting to fulfill my goal of writing a novel and who came to my rescue and helped me format this book when she realized my computer skills really do qualify me for handicap parking.

My son. Reece, who never doubted I would successfully complete this book and who's encouragement gave me the confidence

Sharon Teget, an author and editor extraordinaire who patiently reviewed the first couple of drafts I regurgitated from my keyboard, including the one I tossed before starting over again from scratch. Without your input and encouragement, I would likely have abandoned ship long ago. Through you I have gained a whole new perspective on what it takes to write a novel. Thank You.

Jim Wessel, my very good friend who constantly encouraged me to continue on with this project to the point of making me believe I may have some semblance of writing skills.

Becky Kovac, another very good friend whose encouragement I can't thank you enough for.

These are the primary suspects. I'm sure I have missed a few and I apologize for that.

If you liked the book, thank them.

If you didn't like it, blame me.

- Tom Connelly and Jim Wessel: are actual Southern California attorneys. It was no exaggeration when my character (Lee Edwards) referred to them as "the best." I have tried cases with both of them and can unequivocally say that, if I needed an attorney, these two would be the first I would call.
- Jim Kovac: Is just as depicted in the book. He is a retired Air Force Colonel and current pilot for United Airlines. He actually does own the Camaro and Firebird described in the book. Thank you for your service, Jim, and thank you for allowing me to put you in my novel.
- Becky Kovac: My law school study partner and long-time very good friend. Thanks in no small part, and much to the chagrin of the California State Bar Assn., Becky was instrumental in my successful completion of law school and passing the bar exam. Thank you. Becky for allowing me to put you in my novel. I figured it would be the only way I could get you and Jim to read it.
- Malcolm McAllister is a real person and former National Golden Gloves champion.

DISCLAIMER

Although most of the locations depicted in this book are real, this book is a work of absolute fiction. Other than the individuals specifically cited in the Acknowledgments, everyone depicted and/or named therein are purely fictional. Any resemblance to any of the fictional characters is purely coincidental.

ABOUT THE AUTHOR

Chester Bennett is Journeyman Lineman, attorney and former professional boxer living in San Clemente, California.

23476352R00131

Made in the USA
San Bernardino, CA
25 January 2019